Everyone has that one secret... that one skeleton in their closet... which will never see the light of day. No psychiatrist, priest, spouse, or best friend will ever hear this secret, yet the urge to share this information can be found in most people's natural psyche... People want to share their experience with others... They want to tell someone their deep, dark secret. Although this secret rides on the subconscious - scratching at the surface to be revealed, it's most often too embarrassing, or horrifying, or scandalous...

What better way to get that secret off the mind, and out of the closet than to tell someone who is a complete stranger? Someone who will not judge what has been said, and what has been done? This method is safe, anonymous, and there is no accountability or judgment - and if there is, the keeper of the secret can simply walk away.

Meet fourteen individuals who have decided to clean at least one skeleton out of their closet by confiding in a complete stranger whom they meet at a local coffee shop. Unassuming and safe with no judgments passed, learn about these secrets first hand, as if you were a fly on the wall listening in during their confession.

Everyone has a secret.
What's yours?

Corner
Confessions

Everyone has a secret.
What's yours?

Kiersten Hall

'Corner Confessions was a good read; definitely kept me interested and wanting more!'
S.S. – Austin, MN

'I wish I had thought of such a fun job – listening to so many interesting stories. But the next best thing was reading the stories in Corner Confessions. It was hard to put the book down, and I am waiting with baited breath to read the second book in this series!'
N.B. – Owatonna, MN

'Corner Confessions is my second book by K.Hall & I'm loving it! The characters have real depth and real world issues we can <u>ALL</u> relate to. I can't think of a better way to enjoy a relaxing afternoon.'
D.B. – Delavan, MN

'Corner Confessions had me hanging on the edge of my seat wondering "What will they say next?" This book is full of emotions!'
D.S. – Sparta, WI

Corner Confessions

ISBN: 978-0-692-78291-0 Paperback
ASIN: B01MSNW5RD Kindle
www.cornerconfessions.com
khallbooks@gmail.com

Cover photo, design, and editing by
Chelsea Farr ~ chelsea.m.farr@gmail.com

For my
younger self
who used
to turn
all of
her books
into
screenplays
throughout
primary school

www.idovideostories.com
www.cornerconfessions.com
www.khallbooks.com

Corner
Confessions

Everyone has a secret.
What's yours?

Sandy
Grab a cup of
tea + Enjoy! :)

Kiersten Hall

Meet...

Tom & Steph

"I could see that," Steph said, nodding her head into her next sip of coffee. She then spotted a woman who walked into the shop wearing an outfit suitable for working in an office environment, and asked, "How about that one? What do you think her story is?"

"Oh, I wager she's a mom of three pre-teens whose schedules run her ragged when she isn't workin'. And…." Tom said as he leaned back in his chair to observe one more point. "By the look of it, she doesn't have a ring, which means she's working nearly 24/7 and is losin' her mind."

"How do you get all that out of someone standing in line to buy your overpriced coffee?" Steph asked as she went in for another sip.

"Ah, you want to know my secrets, do ya'?" Tom said as wisely as he could while he mixed the sugary sediment off the bottom of his coffee cup. "Well, I saw her get out of that minivan 'cross the lot and it has sports decals in each corner of the back window with a third decal in the middle. There's your three kids guess. And I already told ya' she doesn't have a ring, so from experience, she works a lot and is losin' her mind."

"From *your* experience?" Steph asked with a smile.

"When were you a single mom with three kids?"

"I got my experience from helpin' out one of my little sisters with her three children when she worked countless hours to provide for them because her deadbeat husband was drunker than a skunk, day in and day out. Fortunately, he's no longer in the picture. But, technically, I counted her as a single mom."

"Oh. I'm sorry. I didn't know," Steph responded quietly while looking into her coffee cup.

"Well, how would you know unless I bothered to tell ya'?" Tom said, reaching across the small table and jokingly slapping Steph's upper arm. Settling back in his chair with his hand on his stomach, he said, "Don't let it bother ya', cuz' it sure as hell doesn't bother me! My lil' sister, Janie, is doing much better these days – she went out and found herself an upgrade the second time 'round! I just made sure, while I was doing the dad-thing, I didn't pull that kinda shit. I was there for my kids, and I was sober." Tom took another drink of his coffee and wrinkled his nose realizing he had put too much sugar into this cup. "How 'bout your dad? Was he a good dad?"

"The first two, not so much," Steph answered while looking at Tom's surprised face. "The third one was a vast improvement, but by then, I was out of the house so, it didn't matter a whole lot."

"I didn't see that answer comin'," Tom said, leaning back into the table and starting to smile. "By the looks of you, I was guessin' you came from the 'Leave It To Beaver' household."

"Well, like you..." Steph said hesitantly, "I guess I didn't want to repeat the cycle. I don't want three husbands. I don't want to marry losers. I don't want to be involved in the bullshit I grew up with, and I certainly don't want to make any future kids I get around to having live through that crap."

"You're not married now, are ya'?" Tom asked with

concern in his voice.

"You make that sound like a bad thing... or a good thing? I can't tell," Steph answered back with a smile. "But no, I'm not married. I was engaged once, but he got cold feet when we started going on appointments to plan the wedding. Deposits were being required to hold the date, and out the door he ran."

"It looks like it's my turn to say I'm sorry for askin'," Tom said quietly as he looked squarely at Steph.

"No worries. I'm happy he ran off before money was put down and the dotted line was signed," Steph said. Then with a smile, she waggled her fingers in front of Tom's face and said, "Plus, as you can clearly see, I don't have a wedding ring so I must not be married!"

"Do ya' need more coffee?" Tom offered while he began to stand up. "I need to get a new cup, altogether. I put way too much sugar into this one."

"Yeah, I'll take another. Thanks," Steph answered, handing him her cup.

While Tom was up getting more coffee for the both of them, Steph glanced around the shop looking at the different people who were there. People on their computers, two people standing in line for their toasted bakery items to go with their custom coffees, three people in the back corner chatting near the gas fireplace, holding their oversized mugs with both hands. One dad and two bouncy kids had just left the shop and were busy getting into their car.

Behind the counter, Tom was helping the new hire find something in the cupboards. There was one older guy standing next to the toaster waiting for the correct toasting cycle to end. There was a younger woman busy mixing a mocha cooler for someone at the drive-thru window. Steph looked at Tom while he was busy filling their two cups, thinking back to how she had first met him and what had led to their weekly coffee ritual, every Tuesday morning around nine thirty, after the breakfast rush.

Three years ago, almost to the day, Steph had first met Tom when she stopped into the shop to sell him some advertising for a locally circulated travel magazine nearby hotels gave out free to their guests. He sat down with Steph and throughout her presentation, would continually steer her off track by asking other questions. It was good Steph didn't have any other appointments that morning because she sat in the coffee shop for two hours, jaw-wagging with him. She'd give him this much, he certainly was a good conversationalist.

After a few weeks of return visits and Tom steering the conversations off track, he did, *finally*, buy an ad from Steph. A small one, but he still bought an ad. He promised her a bigger ad purchase on the next printing if she made sure to stop for coffee and conversation, every so often as a part of good customer service. Steph agreed and initially signed herself up for every other Tuesday morning. Now, almost three years later and a permanent full color, full page run every printing, she was in the shop every Tuesday morning and almost every Thursday afternoon if her schedule allowed, although Tom wasn't always there in the afternoons. They generally talked about the news of the day, what happened in his shop when she wasn't there, Steph's experiences from being out on the road with sales and the people she met along the way, his dogs and all of their antics, her inability to have any pets due to her hectic schedule, that kind of thing; your basic, general banter between two old friends sharing some coffee and soaking up some extra time.

Truth be told, she initially viewed Tom as one more sales conquest for her travel magazine. After a while though, she came around to seeing him as more of a friend she enjoyed spending time with over their visits of coffee - the nectar of the gods, as far as she was concerned. His role in her life wasn't so much a father figure or an older-brother of sorts - although he had no problem sharing his opinion and advice anytime he believed she needed guidance, whether welcomed or not - she simply viewed Tom as a friend.

Tom, on the other hand, saw a little bit of his three daughters in Steph. His two oldest daughters were already in their late thirties and had established families of their own. His oldest daughter, Beth, lived in Alaska. Given their location, Tom rarely got to see her and her family except over Skype and through all of their pictures on FaceBook. His other daughter, Trisha, lived about thirty minutes down the road. Although she was definitely closer, she seemed to be continually busy being a 'hockey mom', a 'baseball mom', a 'football mom' – it really depended on the season. Tom's youngest daughter, Annie, was in her late twenties… she was the surprise child after the vasectomy. A little over a year ago, she and her college sweetheart tied the knot. Now they spend every family gathering - on either side - dodging questions about the pitter patter of little feet. Between running the restaurant, and his daughter's locales and schedules, their family was relegated to seeing each other in person on major holidays, and only if they were lucky. So, to have Steph stop in for a visit every Tuesday morning, Tom was more than happy to supply the coffee and participate in the conversation. Steph had the independent wild streak of curiosity Beth had when she was growing up. She possessed the traits of caring for others and being a hard-worker, which Trisha had displayed. And lastly, she was only a year older than Annie. So, when he and Steph visited on Tuesday mornings, he got to feel like he was still a part of his daughters' lives, somewhat.

Tom got back to the table with Steph's cup and a new cup for himself. Steph caught a whiff of hazelnut as he set the mugs down. "Trying out a new flavor? Something other than *sugar cane?*" she asked with a smile.

"Yeah, that last cup didn't work very well," he confessed while sitting back down. "It's all trial and error in the quest for the perfect coffee."

"I'm happy to know I have already completed that quest with my one sugar packet and my one cream with a rich Columbian Roast," she proclaimed, confidently while adding the precise ingredients to her cup. Smiling, she added, "I sleep better knowing this secret, and can now dedicate my life to more menial pursuits."

"What were ya' thinkin' about while I was getting our refills?" Tom inquired. "You looked like you were deep in thought."

"Oh, I was just glancing around realizing all of the people in here, including you and me, all have stories no one would ever suspect by just looking at them," Steph mused as she scanned the restaurant from side to side. "I find that fascinating."

"Sort of like the sayin', *don't judge a book by its cover.*"

"Yeah, but deeper than that," Steph said, leaning back into the table and resting her arm on the table top. "No one should judge anyone by their looks, though I know everyone does. But what I'm talking about goes deeper than that; everyone has at least one story. A story not too many people know about, or maybe no one knows about."

"Oh, you mean a deep, dark, family secret..." Tom

lyrically replied in a hushed, undercover tone.

"It could be, but it doesn't have to be dark, or even have the family involved. But it's definitely deep," Steph replied between sips of coffee. "Actually, I don't even know if *deep* is necessarily the right adjective; it's just something someone has done or still does... or has experienced... or is currently experiencing... and you would never know it just by glancing at them or even looking at them... or better yet, wouldn't know even if you were interacting with them. The only way you would know is if they straight out told you."

"Who would ever tell ya' something like that? What you're talking about?"

"It's in people's nature to talk about things, and I bet it feels safer to tell a complete stranger about something happening in your life rather than someone close," Steph answered, straightening her posture in the chair. "Think about it, you go to the hair stylist and sing like a canary, don't you?"

"I don't go to the hair stylist... I have no hair!" Tom interjected, patting the top of his bald head.

"You know what I mean... When people take a cab, some people can't shut up until they get to their destination. Or bartenders! I bet they hear everything and then some! It's like the subconscious clears itself out when the opportunity of a listening but non-judging ear shows up. No accountability to a stranger!"

"Ah, I get what you're talkin' about. Sort of like 'Dear Libby' or 'Dear Ann' – those advice columns in the paper where everyone remains anonymous," Tom acknowledged then looked down at his cup again and mused, "This cup of coffee is *much* better."

"What would you think of me interviewing a person or two a week, for a month, in your coffee shop?" Steph asked eagerly. "You know, just for fun!"

"You have a weird sense of *fun*. What would you even do with the info? What would be the point?" Tom asked with a quizzical look on his face.

"Self-satisfaction... Confirming my belief in this hypothesis..." Steph said a little louder, her arms in the air as if she were holding an inflating balloon above her head; this imaginary balloon representing her growing and expanding ideas. "To learn new information about people, and where they have been and what they have done... That kind of thing... What do you think?"

"I don't see why not. It should bring in more business with you sittin' there talkin' their ear off like you talk mine off every Tuesday," Tom said with a smile.

Who talks whose ear off every Tuesday?"

"Well, I may start," Tom conceded with a wink, "But you definitely carry the conversation. I mean, I'm just goin' about my Tuesday mornin' and you come boppin' in here and I say 'hi' and the next thing I know, nearly *two hours* have flown by and the lunch crowd starts comin' in!!! Thinkin' about it, *you* are the reason I get nothin' done on Tuesdays!"

With a wink back, Steph rebutted with, "Let's just keep in mind whose idea this all was in the first place."

"So, what you are proposin' is to sit in here, every so often, and pick someone's brain for an hour or so?" Tom asked, folding a sugar packet wrapper, repeatedly.

"Yep."

"But why? I don't get it."

"Something for me to do... and it'll confirm my theory... If you think about it, it might give some the opportunity to air out their subconscious," Steph said with certainty. "Look at it this way, I am providing a free public service!"

"Do people need this service?" Tom asked while folding another empty sugar packet from the table. "I guess I just don't understand why you would do this, and who would want to talk to you?"

"Well, that makes me feel all fuzzy and happy,"

Steph said as she slapped the top of the table with her hand, starting to get somewhat frustrated with Tom's line of questioning.

"No, you know what I mean. Do people need this kind of *service*? Do people need to talk to other people about their deep secrets?"

"I don't know, but we could certainly find out," Steph said, dunking her spoon in and out of the coffee mug. "I could give it a whirl, and if it works? Great. Likewise, if it doesn't work? Great. Nothing lost except a bit of my time."

"Why don't you go home an' watch TV if you have all this extra time?" Tom asked, subconsciously folding the two sugar packets together.

"I don't own a TV. So, I have to go outside of my house and interact with other people not watching their televisions."

"Well, that explains a lot, too," Tom laughed. "I'm learnin' all sorts of things about you today, aren't I?"

"That's my point, exactly! People interacting with other people; this would give me the opportunity to learn from other people. Maybe they would learn something from me? I don't know what, but maybe..." Steph pointed out, excitedly.

"Ya' get too carried away with these ideas!" Tom said as he started gathering up the garbage off the table and pushing it into his coffee cup. "You can chat with people in here as long as you'd like with as many people as ya' like, I just don't see who would be willin' to share their deep secrets with you or any other stranger, for that matter. And if anyone does, what in the world are ya' gonna do with the information collected? Or why would you even spend your time doin' this? I'm sure you could think of other ways to constructively use your time."

"Thank you for the permission to use your coffee shop and the confirmation of my craziness!" Steph said with a cheerful voice as she got up from the table and started gathering her backpack and coat. "This'll be good. I'll put together a sign-up sheet and place it over there by the napkins and straws... I'm thinking two a week for a month, to see how it goes. Plus, this should prove my point about people's natural urge to talk about things not normally spoken about in everyday conversation. Who knows? I may even make some more friends, or not? You never know unless you try, right?"

"You're an odd duck," Tom stated, walking away with the dirty dishes and garbage. "Ya' can talk with whomever you wish, whenever you wish, but I am still holding you to our nine-thirty chats on Tuesday mornings. That's my time slot in your hectic calendar!"

"Definitely!" Steph said with a smile, and heading toward the door. At the door, she turned around and pointed to the back corner of the coffee shop, "I could hold the appointments in the back corner, over there... I'd be out of the way of the rest of the customers."

"You're a weird one!" Tom called out to Steph.

"Thank you!" Steph exclaimed while waving goodbye to everyone behind the counter, using her back to push the door open and step outside.

While walking to her car, Steph's mind started racing: Who would put their name down as her first appointment? What if no one signed up? That would look ridiculous... But at least she would have tried! What would she put down as a disclaimer? She certainly didn't want to know anything illegal – that would be a bad position to be in... She would have to make a sign including a disclaimer in bold letters along with the fact that she wasn't a certified therapist of any kind – just an anonymous stranger... How would she make the sign? She should make it look good... Design it and then print it at the office supply store – that would look better than her printer at home which never seemed to work properly... Should she go with the word 'appointment'? Or maybe the word 'secret' would be better? Or should she pick another word? Within a few seconds, she had the perfect word: 'Confessions'! Oh, that word would be a perfect fit with being in the back corner of the restaurant; sitting in the corner confessing! But what if Tom was right about people not wanting to share any of their secrets? But then again, Steph knew the stylist who cut her hair every eight weeks knew a lot more about her and what she thought than the people she saw every day, including any of her family members; which made sense since she didn't see her family members all that much, anyway. But that was beside the point. As Steph neared her car, she made her final determination that her idea was going to be helpful to people; she had a feeling a handful of people would be willing to talk to her. Not in the sense of a therapist, or anything - just a listening ear for people who wanted or needed to clear their conscious, if it needed to be cleared.

Rob

"So! Today's the first day of hearin' people's deep, dark secrets, huh?" Tom asked, sitting down at Steph's table. "Are you ready to hear the weirder side of people's lives?"

"I'm as ready as I'll ever be, I suppose," Steph answered, shoving her daily crossword puzzle to the side of the table.

"You have quite a number of people already signed up, I see," Tom said with a bit of surprise in his voice. "Last I looked, five out of eight time slots had already been taken!"

"Yep... I didn't realize so many local people had so many secrets."

"What are you gonna do with those secrets?"

"In one ear and out the other, as far as I'm concerned..."

"What if someone tells ya' somethin' illegal?" Tom asked, tapping his fingers on the table.

"Besides printing the disclaimer in bold on the sign-up sheet, I will verbally state my illegality disclaimer to each person I sit down with."

"What are you gonna say to 'em?"

Clearing her throat and sitting up straight in her

chair, Steph repeated what she had been memorizing for the past two weeks while people signed up to meet with her, "Before we get started, I will tell you my disclaimer: I'm a law-abiding citizen who'd rather not hear about anything illegal done by you or anyone you know because I don't want to be put into the position of knowing something that should be reported."

"Do you think people will follow your rule?" Tom pressed.

"I would imagine so," Steph answered confidently. "Any person in their right mind - if they've done something illegal - would not confess, especially to someone they don't know, and risk being caught."

"Would they? If someone is doin' somethin' illegal, I would already see them as not being in the right frame of mind."

"True. But they might also lie about all or some of what they tell me," Steph countered.

"Will you be able to tell if they're lyin'?"

"I would imagine," Steph laughed lightly. "I'm pretty good at reading people, and lord knows I've observed plenty of people try to lie to me over the course of my sales career."

"You get a lot of people who lie to you in your line of work?"

"Oh yeah..." Steph confirmed with a flippant wave of her hand.

"Like what?"

Counting off on her fingers, Steph started listing examples of lies she had heard over the years: "I'm asking for a friend... That's a classic one. Or, I'm not interested, but they are unable to give me a reason why or won't give me a reason why. You know... the stupid stuff people come up with to avoid opening themselves up to possibly purchasing something. These are usually the people who know they have no self-control to walk away from a possible sale after they have heard all the facts... the impulsive shoppers are the ones who usually use the tactic of going cold turkey rather than learning about something new which may benefit them. They know if they hear all the facts, their brains switch to the 'buy mode' instantly, rather than 'consideration mode.' So, they lie. It's stupid and transparent to me, but they think they're being convincing. I see it as funny... It doesn't help my bottom line at all, but still pretty funny."

"Was I lyin' to you when we first met?" Tom asked with a coy smile.

"No. You considered the route of advertising I had to offer, and you purchased an ad... It's paid off for you, right?"

"If it hadn't, I wouldn't have continued buyin' bigger ads."

"Exactly. And would you consider yourself an impulsive buyer?"

"No. I weigh the pros and cons of each of my purchases."

"Right... Well, there are some people who don't do that, or are incapable of doing that. So, they shut others down immediately to protect themselves from spending money and just end up coming off as rude," Steph confirmed. "Put it this way - if you were one of those rude people, I sure wouldn't be sitting here right now, and I sure wouldn't have been having coffee with you over all these years. I do my best to not hang out with rude people."

Acknowledging Steph's compliment, Tom simply answered, "Thank you."

"You're welcome. Now, I will get back down off my soapbox," Steph joked, rapping a fist on the table.

"So, who's your first person up?" Tom asked, changing the subject.

"Rob."

"Is that his real name? Sure sounds generic to me."

"I don't know. I guess," Steph surmised. "I only asked for first names. It was up to them if they were going to divulge their real names. Honestly, I don't know... I didn't really consider that."

"I wonder what Rob is gonna tell you?" Tom asked, smiling and crooking a brow, curiosity in his voice.

"I don't know, could be anything, really."

"I wonder what *all* of them are gonna tell you?" Tom asked, his imagination starting to run a little wild. "By the way, if that sign-up sheet fills up, are you going to add more appointment times?"

"If you're okay with it," Steph nodded. "I mean, if it's going well, why not?"

"Yeah, that's fine. You're doin' this on Wednesday mornings at ten, and Thursday afternoons at four, right?"

"Yep... I'm hitting the morning crowd on one day and the afternoon crowd another day. I'm being accessible, as much as possible, to hear people's woes," Steph confirmed, again with a nod of her head.

"Now, they know you're not a psychologist or anything, too, right?"

"Yep. I put that on the sign-up sheet in big block letters."

"I would suggest including that in your verbal disclaimer too; of all the years I have been in business, I have found individuals to be intelligent, but the population as a whole, not so much. I would include that in your initial speech; would hate to see someone try to start shit with you just because you're tryin' to help people."

"Oh, I know. There are trolls everywhere; people who just like to stir up trouble."

"As long as you protect yourself..." Tom kindly warned Steph, wagging his finger at her.

Steph looked at her wristwatch, stood up, and looked toward the door, "Hey! It's almost ten o'clock and Rob is due here any moment. I am going to quick run to the bathroom. If he arrives while I'm in the biffy, please show him where I'm sitting back here."

"How will I know what he looks like?" Tom asked while standing up.

"I would imagine he'll tell you he's looking for the person who is listening to secrets and ask you where she is sitting?" Steph said with a smile. "And if all else fails, if someone walks in here looking for someone, as well as looking guilty about something, then that would probably be Rob."

"Will do," Tom agreed, weaving his way back to the front counter through the tables and chairs. "Good luck, too. Are you sharin' the secrets afterwards?"

"No. That's my promise to these people."

Tom stopped walking and turned to her, "But you don't owe 'em anything."

"Ethically, I do. So, no, I'm not telling any secrets. Good try on your part, though!" Steph smirked, again turning toward the restroom.

Tom snapped his fingers in defeat and continued on his way back up to the front of the coffee shop.

Steph came out of the bathroom just as she saw Tom directing an older man over to the corner table where she had set up camp. As Rob made his way to the back corner, Steph walked past her table to greet him midway. "Hi! You must be Rob," she said, offering a handshake.

"Yes, I am. And you must be Stephanie?" Rob replied, moving his full coffee cup from his right hand to his left so he could shake her hand. "Yep, but you can call me Steph," she answered, accompanying Rob back to the table in the corner. "Here, have a seat."

Rob set his coffee mug on the table, pulled out the chair, sat down, and waited for Steph to get settled before he began speaking. "How do you want to do this?"

"Well, first I'm going to tell you my disclaimer, and then you can tell me what you need to tell me."

"Okay."

"Okay, then," Steph began, sitting up a little straighter. "My disclaimer is I'm a law-abiding citizen who would rather not hear about anything illegal done by you or anyone you know because I don't want to be put into the position of knowing something that should be reported. I am also not a licensed psychiatrist so, anything I say should be considered as just two people sitting in a corner, chatting over coffee."

"Got it."

"What would you like to tell me?"

Rob took a big breath, closed his eyes, and before he could lose his nerve and change his mind, blurted out, "I have been wearing women's underwear for about the last decade and I like it." When he opened his eyes, he stared at Steph for some type of answer, verbal or otherwise.

Without thinking, Steph asked, "That's it?"

Rob sat there for a moment, still locked with Steph's gaze. "Well, don't you think that's odd? I think it's odd and I'm the one wearing the panties."

"Well, when you put it that way, it's actually funny... The way you said it, I mean," Steph admitted with a giggle.

"So, you don't think that's odd?" Rob asked with surprise.

"Actually, no... I'm sorry... Did you want me to find that odd?"

"Well..." Rob's voice trailed off perplexed.

"I suppose from a traditional viewpoint, it could be considered as odd. But honestly, I don't find it that odd," Steph clarified, leaning in and resting both her forearms on the table top.

"You don't?"

"No. For me, at least, I am more interested in the person rather than what type of material they choose to wear against their butt."

"When you put it that way, I guess it doesn't really matter, does it?" Rob said, smiling with relief.

"No. For example, are you decent person to everyone you meet, including your family?"

"Yes."

Steph continued to ask questions, wanting to drive her point home. "When you go to bed at night, can you face your reflection in the mirror, eye-to-eye, and tell yourself you did a good job that day? You did your very best by the people who crossed your path on that particular day?"

"Always..."

"Then you're just fine," Steph stated, dispensing her non-licensed therapist wisdom.

"But while I'm looking in the mirror, I'm also seeing myself standing there in women's underwear, and I think I look nice," Rob pointed out.

"It's good to have a healthy amount of self-confidence," Steph said with a reassuring tone, then added, "If it helps at all, I will only shop for jeans and socks in the men's department mainly because of cost and comfort, but also because women's jeans are cut according to how designers *think* women are structured, which is not my body type. I fit better in men's jeans."

"Do those jeans and socks turn you on?"

"Well, no... But I do think I look pretty good in them and maybe my other half, if I had another half, would feel the same way?"

"Well, wearing women's underwear turns me on."

"How? Is it the material?"

"Partially the material; I like how soft and silky it is, or if I go lacy. The feel against the skin is different than the straight cotton of the tighty-whities."

"Yeah, I can see that. Although I will tell you, cotton is a lot nicer to wear on hot summer afternoons or while working out than something with polyester. Cotton breathes... You don't sweat as much," Steph shared with another laugh. "I'm speaking from personal experience over here!"

"But I will admit I am not fond of thongs! I will wear them occasionally, but they make my crack sore and they tend to bunch up a certain part of my anatomy, and then it gets really uncomfortable."

"Fortunately, I don't have that anatomical issue, but yes, they can make your crack sore. I agree with that statement. Here's a tip though," Steph continued, leaning back in her chair, "If you go with a solid material thong rather than a lace thong, your butt will be a bit more comfortable. I have found that when the lace bunches up, it becomes scratchy and that's what rubs the skin raw. Well, that, and any sweat."

"I can't believe I'm having this conversation with someone!" Rob confessed, blushing deeply.

"Me neither," Steph admitted, eyebrows arching.

"I'm not talking about here and now with you, but overall, with anyone... I've been keeping this a secret for nearly ten years!"

"How did you start? Or why did you start?"

Rob took a moment to re-situate himself in his chair before beginning his story. "When I was a little boy, I remember seeing my Mom's unmentionables hanging on the clothesline in the backyard. At that point in time, they were just items made out of warm, soft material hanging out in the sunshine and I would play in between the clotheslines, wrapping myself up in the sheets or running my hands past the silkier items...
That went well until my Mom caught me and gave my butt a smack with her hand. Then into my teenage years and beyond, when the Sears catalogues would come out, I would always manage to find my way to the

underwear section after I looked through the tool and the sporting goods sections..."

"I remember the Sears catalogues!" Steph interjected, clapping her hands together. "Talk about a blast from the past!"

"So," Rob continued, "Nearly ten years ago, I was dating a woman who wore the sexiest underwear and I told her how much I liked them. I would sit there and literally talk about how lovely it would be to wear those soft and silky items against my skin rather than the cotton I was subjected to wear because of what society dictated. After listening to me enough times and realizing I wasn't teasing, she had me put on a pair of her underwear, and I've never looked back!" With a wave of both his hands through the air as if he were presenting a new idea, Rob declared with a bigger smile, "Oh! They were so soft and smooth and silky. No more cotton for me!"

"Well, it sounds like you have sold yourself on the idea. Are you still with the lady who got you started on this?"

"No," Rob started to say, then took a sip of his cooled coffee. "Her job moved her out of the area, and I stuck around here since my kids live nearby and I'm established. However, I've started seeing another woman and she doesn't know about my panty fetish yet. Do you think I should tell her or start wearing men's underwear again?"

"Well, you could play it one of two ways..." Steph held out her right hand, palm up, offering her first opinion, "One, you could come straight out and tell her you like wearing lacy, pretty unmentionables. Or..." Steph continued, showing her left hand palm-up, "Two, you could wear men's underwear and then somehow get her to lend you a pair of her underwear and for 'fun', have you wear them, that way she thinks it's her doing rather than having you confess, straight up. That would work, I bet. What do you think?"

"I could try that second option. She's not as wild as the first lady from ten years ago."

"Maybe she *is* wild, and you just don't *know it* yet?" Steph suggested, hope in her voice.

"Eh, she could..."

Steph put her hand up and interrupted Rob when she noticed Tom walking toward them with a fresh pot of coffee, "Hold on, Tom is coming over. Do you want anything other than more coffee?"

"I could definitely take a warm up, but I'm good otherwise," Rob shook his head. "Thanks."

"Sure, okay..." Steph said, looking up at Tom when he reached the table.

"Sorry to interrupt, but do you two want more coffee? Or anything else?" Tom asked, trying not to sound too nosey.

"We'll both have some more coffee," Steph said, both her and Rob holding out their mugs.

"Here you go..." Tom said, topping off Rob's coffee and then turned to warm up Steph's coffee, too. "And okay... You two are good back here, then?"

"Doing good... Thanks, Tom."

Tom turned around and maneuvered his way back to the front counter through the tables and chairs.

Steph dropped her gaze back down to Rob's face and asked, "Where were we again?"

"I don't know if she's as wild as the first one, but maybe?"

"You might get lucky two times in a row!" Steph suggested with a reassuring smile.

"The other thing about wearing women's underwear, too, is that it's taboo. That taboo is a turn-on for me."

"Ah..."

"I mean, while I'm fully dressed, I have a little secret no one knows about," Tom said, taking a cautious sip of his coffee. "God forbid I get into a car accident, though! I guess the paramedics would discover my secret!"

"Pretend you're out cold... I'm sure they've seen stuff far worse than a guy wearing women's underwear."

"Are you sure?" Rob asked, still taking little sips of his coffee.

"You could always *say* you lost a bet," Steph suggested. "And then joke about holding up your end of the bet on the *one day* you wind up having an accident."

"What if I'm unconscious?" Rob asked.

"Then hope you never meet the people who pulled you out of the car. Or if you do, wait until they bring it up – don't bring it up otherwise – and tell them about the bet you lost."

"I suppose..."

"One other question for you... You also said you get turned on because it's taboo?"

"Yeah, as I was saying, it's my own little secret - what I'm wearing, plus it feels good," Rob shared, leaning in a little closer and starting to blush. "Sometimes it feels so good, well... sometimes I can't stand up!"

"Why can't you..." Steph began to ask, until her mouth caught up to her head. "Oh! Never mind. I get it."

"Yeah, I'm kind of addicted to all of that, too."

Steph sipped at her coffee, "Well, I can think of worse things to be addicted to!"

"Yeah, but I can only imagine what people would think."

"Unless you want to run around telling everyone what you're wearing and why, then you should have nothing to worry about anytime soon," Steph pointed out in a motherly tone. "As for the lady you are currently seeing, she might just be into what you have going on, or she won't care about it. And who knows? If she's upset about it, then she might not be the right one for you. My grandmother always used to say, 'Men are like buses; give it ten minutes and another one will be by.' I would imagine that rule could also apply to women."

"Maybe in your case, but for me, it takes a bit longer than ten minutes for another woman to wander by and pay any attention to me," Rob countered, looking a little forlorn.

"Then maybe this woman is into your taboo and into you and then it will all work out, right?"

"I hope so. I'm just nervous about spilling this secret to anyone. Other than this, I am a perfectly normal guy."

Steph started in with a variation of a speech she had heard many times from her own mom, "*Normal* is a relative term. What is *normal*, really? Plus, do you really want to be like everyone else? Every other guy that you know of is wearing cotton undies while you're rocking the lace and satin! Do you really want to *be normal* and wear cotton briefs like *every... other... person...* you consider to be... *normal?*"

"I see your point, and no, I don't want to be like everyone else."

"Then it sounds like you have solved your dilemma!" Steph declared, leaning back in her chair with the satisfied smile of a job well done.

"It would seem that I have," Rob decided. He took a thoughtful sip of his coffee before continuing, "Thank you, by the way, for listening to me and for not finding me odd."

"The only way I would see any of this as being odd would be if you were to run around wearing the panties on your head!" Steph said with another smile. "Then I would wonder about you! I think a lot of people would find you odd and wonder about you!"

Rather unexpectedly, Rob asked Steph, "So, is there anything I can help you with?"

"Like what?"

"Well, you listened to my problem and gave me some friendly words of advice... Do you have anything you want to talk about?"

Steph took a moment to consider, then shook her head, "No, not really. But thank you for asking."

"Everyone has deep, dark secrets... Are you sure?" Rob probed.

"Well, I already told you I buy my jeans from the men's department because I have a cylindrical body. That's about as crazy as I can think of for a deep secret, although it's not really that deep."

"So, nothing then?"

Again, Steph took a moment to think, looking up in the air before answering with a small laugh, "Not really... Today was meant for you to clear your mind. For me, by the time I realize I might have a secret, I am well on my way to forgetting about it since that's what my flea-sized memory is so good at doing... Forgetting things."

"Then it sounds like you're a good person to share secrets with, since you're so forgetful!" Rob pointed out.

"Just don't give me any car keys to lose," Steph cautioned with a laugh, "And we should all be good."

"I only ask because my mom ground it into each one of her kids, the following rule: If someone gives you something, you always follow suit with giving something back."

"That's a good idea!"

"You've put my fears to rest on this particular issue and I was just wondering if there was anything I could help you with, in return?" Rob offered one last time.

Steph really couldn't come up with anything. "No. Not really. But thank you, I appreciate the gesture."

"Alright, then, thank you for the lovely visit. I actually have to get going. Today is my day to volunteer for the local Meals on Wheels chapter; I have lunches to get out today. People are depending on me!" Rob said while he stood up and stepped to the side of his chair, scooting it under the table.

Without missing a beat, Steph offered up one more reassuring thought, "And I bet none of them will *even think* about *what you are wearing under your pants*! They're more interested in *you as the person* who is delivering their lunch and spending a few moments visiting with them."

"Good point!" Rob acknowledged, extending his hand for another handshake.

"Have a good day then, and drive safe!" Steph returned the gesture.

"You too, Steph... Nice meeting you..."

"Nice meeting you, too, Rob."

A few minutes after Rob left, Tom wandered over as Steph was gathering her things to leave the coffee shop, too.

"So, how'd your first confession go?" Tom asked as he approached the table.

"It went well," Steph said with a smile, "Were you being genuinely helpful with that coffee refill schtick? Or did I detect some nosiness?"

"I was *not... being... nosey*!!!" Tom answered, feigning shock at such a preposterous idea.

Her suspicions confirmed, Steph shook with suppressed mirth, "Uh huh... I *thought* so..."

"I was merely being hospitable to a patron of the coffee shop," Tom said, trying to wiggle his way out of the accusation.

"Is this a new policy for you?"

"What do you mean?" Tom asked.

"Wandering around the coffee shop with a pot of coffee offering warm-ups for people?" Steph teased Tom.

"Well, I wanted to make sure your appointment felt as though he had good service here."

"Yes, Rob was happy and he had a good time… And I think he even liked the coffee. So, *all is good!*" Steph gave a thumbs up.

Trying to sneak in the question he'd had on his mind for the last half hour since Rob first arrived, Tom blurted out, "So, what did he have to say?"

"Who?" Steph asked, playing dumb.

"Rob!" Tom nearly shouted, bursting at the seams with curiousity.

Pushing her chair in, Steph reiterated with a hearty laugh, "I told you, I'm not telling! Good grief! I had no idea you were this nosey!!!"

"I'm not nosey! I'm curious!" Tom quipped.

"Curious… Nosey… Tomayto… Tomahto…" Steph sang, shoving her arms through the straps of her backpack.

Tom spun around, "Oh! You're killin' me!!!" he sputtered before walking back up to the front counter.

Steph followed Tom up to the front and reminded him of the deal they made about how he sold the coffee and the bakery items, while she sat in the back corner offering a listening ear to those who wanted to come in and unclutter their minds.

"One down and many more to go," Steph said setting her coffee mug down on the counter.

"We're still on for next Tuesday at nine-thirty?" Tom asked, rounding the side of the counter.

"Yep, same time, same place, different day," Steph said, heading for the door.

Laughing, Tom hollered after her, "You're a buzz kill!"

As Steph was walking out the door, she waved to Tom behind her, "And you're nosey!"

Patti

Steph was busy watching people pull into the parking lot, get out of their cars, and go on about their lives through the plate glass window next to her confessional table in the back corner. Sitting in the magnified warmth of window-tinted light, she was making bets with herself on who would be her next appointment, and what secret they might share, when she caught movement out of the corner of her left eye.

"I bet you didn't know the mayor is having an affair, did you?"

"What?" Steph asked as she turned and faced the woman walking toward her with a cane, and a purse in her other hand.

"The mayor... I bet you didn't know he was having an affair, did you?" she repeated herself, pulling out the chair across from Steph and sitting down.

"Truth be told, I don't even think I know who the mayor of this town is," Steph revealed with a shrug of her shoulders.

The woman sitting across from Steph furled her brow and slapped her left hand down on the table, "How can you not know who the mayor is? *She's* an absolute bitch!"

"Wait. I thought you just said the mayor was a 'he'," Steph said skeptically, wondering if she had simply misheard.

"You're right, I did," the woman said smiling while she placed her handbag on top of the table.

Perplexed, Steph asked this strange stranger across from her, "So, is the mayor a he or a she?"

"Both."

"What?"

Stretching her left arm across the table for a handshake with her palm down, this woman introduced herself with a smile, "Hi, my name is Patti and I'm the town liar."

With a confused look and fumbling with her arms to figure out which one to use for the return handshake - unusual as it was, Steph asked, "Don't you mean *crier*? And I don't want to seem rude, here, but are you my four o'clock appointment today?"

"It depends on who you are and if you'd like me to be," quipped Patti.

"My name is Steph and..."

"Nice to meet you Steph," Patti said, pulling her arm back to her side of the table, then picking up the coffee pot and shaking it to gauge how much coffee was left.

Steph motioned toward the coffee pot and said, "There's still quite a bit left in there," and then continued with the pleasantries of, "Nice to meet you, too... I'm sorry, I just forgot your name."

"My name is Penny."

Steph sat there for a moment, quickly replaying the last two minutes of conversation in her head while looking at this person sitting in front of her and then slowly asked, "Was it Patti? Or, was it Penny?"

"Either one works for me," as she smiled and poured coffee into the clean mug sitting next to the pot.

Steph leaned back in her chair smiling with the realization she was being toyed with, but she didn't fully understand why. Although she tried to suppress her instinct to go into the smooth-talking, fast-paced, shark she could easily become when people started talking circles around her – typically when trying to dissuade her from continuing on with her sales spiel - she couldn't help herself and decided to play along. "Well then... nice to meet you Patti-Penny."

Patti-Penny paused for a moment after she poured her coffee and smiled at Steph. Upon quickly deciding she could have a stimulating conversation with a possible worthy opponent, she began, "So, what brings you to this fine coffee shop to discuss life with people?"

"Probably the same thing that brought you here to chat with me on this fine day," Steph replied with confidence that she knew she was on the verge of a very interesting afternoon conversation.

"What do you do for a living?"

"Advertising sales, and you?"

"I'm in sales, too."

"Really? What area?" Steph asked, looking directly at Patti-Penny.

"Self-confidence," Patti-Penny answered quickly, looking directly at Steph.

"How so?"

"I build people up; I make them feel good about themselves," Patti-Penny answered with a glowing smile while mixing three packets of artificial sugar into her coffee.

"So, you're a success coach?"

"You could say that, but...." Patty-Penny smiled while she continued to stir her coffee with her perfectly manicured hand, never breaking her gaze with Steph.

"But what?"

"I always win," Patti-Penny answered instantly without blinking and still smiling, all the while still mixing her coffee.

"Always?"

"Always," Patti-Penny assured Steph, finally blinking and keeping her eyes shut for an exaggerated amount of time before opening them again. She pulled the spoon from her coffee and set it down on her napkin.

Without pausing for Patti-Penny's odd behavior, Steph said, "You sound fairly confident."

"I am."

"What do you win?" Steph asked.

"My payment..."

"What's your payment?"

"It's whatever I choose it to be," Patti-Penny said with a smile in a singsong voice while she fanned her hands out in front of her.

"And what is it you typically choose for a payment?"

Patti-Penny put her hands back in her lap and leaned forward, "Typically money; isn't that what you choose for your payment, too?"

"Yes, but I wouldn't exactly say I *win* it."

"Win it... earn it... same thing."

"Is it?"

"Boy! Aren't we full of questions today?" Patti-Penny said leaning back in her chair with a satisfied smile.

Steph left Patti-Penny's question unanswered, and routed the odd conversation into a new direction, "Who do you work for?"

"Me. And you?"

"Primarily myself as a self-employed subcontractor, but at the moment, I sell ads for a travel publication."

"Exciting! Do you get to travel a lot?" Patti-Penny asked before she took a sip of her hot coffee.

"Not really. I basically stay in my sales territory... How about you?"

"Mmmmm hmmmm, my business takes me everywhere. The better I do on my current job, the further I go for the next job."

"Further, how?" Steph asked.

"Either in distance or extravagance, or both..."

"Give me an example of extravagance."

"Monaco versus this small, backwoods town of less than fifteen thousand people," Patti-Penny answered, pursing her lips with widened eyes and a tilt of her head.

"That's a good example of extravagance."

Steph's appointment continued to keep her gaze locked on Steph with a Cheshire Cat smile, so Steph continued to ask questions to keep the oddly stimulating conversation going. "Are you familiar with my disclaimer of not being interested in hearing anything illegal?"

"Yes."

"Are you going to tell me anything illegal?"

"Wasn't planning on it...."

"You wouldn't be lying, would you?"

"If I lie, you won't know," Patti-Penny continued to answer quickly to keep the fast-paced conversation going.

"Are you lying now?"

"If you have to ask, how would you know if I was lying or not, right now?"

"Point taken," Steph conceded as she took the opportunity to breathe after that round of questioning.

"Now it's my turn to ask questions," Patti-Penny said with glee while sitting up a bit straighter in her chair.

"It is?"

"Yes. Why are you doing this?"

"A mere experiment, on my part," Steph said re-adjusting her position in the chair.

"Please explain further," Patti-Penny requested, lifting the mug of coffee back up to her lips with both hands.

"Over the years, and with as many people as I have spoken to, I know a lot of them have skeletons in their closet they would like to get rid of, but some secrets will never see the light of day, ever."

"Mmmm hmmmm, keep going," Patti-Penny interrupted between her sips of coffee.

"We all have something that makes us tick; several *somethings*, as a matter of fact. But some of those things are too.... " Steph paused as she thought of the perfect combination of words to describe what she wanted to say, "Too personal... embarrassing... horrifying... whatever... to tell a shrink, or a priest, or their best friend, or their spouse."

"True," Patti-Penny interjected again.

"But sometimes people will open up to a stranger who won't hold them accountable, and even if this stranger winds up judging them to any degree, the person who told the secret can simply walk away and the judgment from this stranger won't count; it won't make one bit of difference in their world."

Without saying anything, Patti-Penny was nodding her head in agreement with Steph. Continuing on, Steph finished with her train of thought, "That's what this all has become; I'm merely the stranger who will listen and converse if the person wishes me to do so. I have seen and heard so much in life, I know whether or not I judge won't make a difference in their lives. I also know whatever is told to me throughout these appointments will, most likely, not make one iota of difference in my life, either... or at least not directly."

"Wow! That's quite the answer. Thank you..."

"You're welcome. So, what's your secret?" Steph immediately asked in order to take control of the conversation again.

Picking up on what Steph just did, Patti-Penny smiled and asked, "Me?"

"Yes... you." Steph confirmed with a smile, refilling her coffee mug and preparing another cup of perfection.

"Hmmmm, you want to hear a secret, do you?"

"Do you have a secret or confession to tell?" Steph prodded.

"Oh, let me think of one..." Patti-Penny played along, crossing her arms in front of her while tapping her chin with her right index finger and looking up to the left. "I have many, if I set my mind to it."

"Okay...." Steph said, testing the secret recipe for her coffee.

"Oh! Here's one!" Patty-Penny said while leaning into the table to confess. "I once dated the Prince of Denmark for about a week..."

"And this is a deep, dark secret of yours?"

"Yes, because I can't believe I almost fell into that trap!"

"How was it a trap?"

"Marriage! It's a trap!"

"For some, yes," Steph agreed hesitantly.

"Well, I'm one of those!" Patti-Penny exclaimed as she held up her right arm as if to be counted in a poll.

"It's good you figured that out before you walked down that aisle, then," Steph continued to agree with her but then asked, "So, if you don't mind me asking, how did you meet the Prince of Denmark?"

"I was driving through on the way to my next job, and stopped in for a beer at a dive bar out there, and there he was in all of his glory, sitting at the end of the bar."

"Was he in a disguise?"

"No, why would he be?" Patti-Penny asked, reaching for the coffee pot.

"I can't see the Prince of Denmark sitting in a dive bar having a beer," Steph offered up as a logical reason.

"Well, he was there - flirting with every female that walked by. The bartender pointed out he was known as the Prince of Denmark for his remarkable talents with the ladies," Patti-Penny said, rolling her eyes while she poured more coffee into her mug.

"What do you mean, *known* as the Prince of Denmark? He either is or he isn't. It's a birthright title."

"I'm sure he was a cute kid, but most guys don't have that title at birth."

"Guys who are *princes* do, and how is it you only dated for a week?" Steph asked, even more curious now.

"I didn't really have a timetable to adhere to so I played it out to see where it would go," Patti-Penny answered, sprinkling another three packets of artificial sugar into her fresh cup of coffee. "But a week into it, he started tossing ideas around about marriage and my red flags started flying at full mast!"

"*A week?*"

"Yeah, I found out from the bartender that he had five kids from two former girlfriends who took off on him and the children. Now he was looking for a wife to keep in the house to permanently babysit his kids. I wanted no part of that!"

"I don't blame you, but I still can't get over the Prince of Denmark sitting in the bar part... What did his house look like?"

"I never did see his house, thank gawd! But the bartender told me it was a rundown shit shack, why do you ask?"

Steph skipped answering Patti-Penny and questioned her again, "And how is it he had five kids with two different women?"

"These things happen..." Patti-Penny answered before she took a drink of her freshened-up mug of coffee.

"The Prince of Denmark, huh?"

"Yeah," Patti-Penny answered as she set her mug back down on the table.

"Can you tell me what route you took to Denmark? You know, how'd you get there?"

"I was travelling from Augusta out to Charleston..."

"South Carolina?"

"Yes..."

Steph interrupted, "Is this *Denmark* a town in South Carolina?"

"Yes."

"Oh! I thought you were talking about the country of Denmark!" Steph said rather loudly, leaning back and putting both of her hands on top of her head in exasperation.

"No, no... The town of Denmark in South Carolina." Patti-Penny confirmed.

"Why didn't you specify this fact earlier in the conversation?"

"Because it's fun to watch the confusion on people's faces," Patti-Penny confessed.

"So, why did you divulge the information then?" Steph asked.

"I had allowed you to figure it out by the info I told you; I could've withheld the info from you, or told you something else to continue the confusion."

"But *why* would you do that?" Steph asked, leaning in toward the table again.

Bored with that round of conversation and questions, Patti-Penny took that moment to take back the control of the conversation with an off the wall answer to Steph's last question by asking, "Do what?"

"Create confusion with people... I thought you said you create self-confidence."

"No, I don't create self-confidence, I build it up."

"Isn't that the same thing?" Steph asked for clarification.

"No, not really..."

"It seems like it's the same thing to me," Steph said.

"No... *creating self-confidence* is making something new – something that was never there before. *Building up self-confidence* is making something already there, bigger than what it originally was," Patti-Penny explained.

Growing more baffled, Steph asked, "And you make

money off of this?"

"Yes."

"I don't understand how?"

"I build up self-confidence by selling grandiose. Once established, I verbalize my intent in a number of indirect ways until I get what I want and then I disappear," Patti-Penny said, bringing her hands up while shrugging her shoulders.

"So, what was it you wanted from this Prince of Denmark?"

"Ah, you're catching on..." Patti-Penny revealed while continuing to grin at Steph. "This Prince of Denmark put on a good show; a well-dressed man with an expensive sports car... talked big... could've been a player if he hadn't knocked up two women and been left with the residuals of his past actions. The one big mistake he made was to allow his self to get caught up in the game."

"The game?"

"Yes, the game. I was playing him to get to any money he had – I should have done my homework... My intuition told me to do my homework, but I ignored it and almost got sucked into the game... *his* game! He was playing me to find a babysitter for his five brats at home so he could get on with his life without the responsibilities."

"Playing..." Steph said out loud while she quickly thought about what she had been told so far. As soon as it clicked, she snapped her fingers and pointed at her appointment, "You're a con artist, aren't you?"

"Con artist, player, grifter, hustler, swindler, deceiver, scammer, pretender, imposter..."

"Charlatan," Steph chimed in.

"Exactly!" Patti-Penny exclaimed, clapping her hands together in the pure joy of Steph realizing what she was talking about.

"Okay so, how would the Prince of Denmark story

work for you?"

With a careless wave of her hand and a continued smile, Patti-Penny started in with the description of how she would have played that con, "Oh, that one is a small job... I would create a friendship with you and divulge certain information as a friend. After a while, I would suggest we go to Denmark for fun with all the grandiose stories I would've told you. Once your self-confidence had been built up, and you had faith in me as a *true friend*, I would insist that I could arrange the travel plans, too, since I was very familiar with the lay of the land and could get a good deal on the airfare! I would even sell you on it by telling you we would be staying with some friends of mine out there to save on hotel expenses but... I would still need the money from you to book the airfare. Once I got your money – no checks please – I would disappear and there you would be sitting, wondering where I went?"

"Have you done this before?" Steph asked.

With a twinkle in her eye, Patti-Penny asked, "It's a good theory, isn't it?"

"But have you already done this?"

"I told you I would abide by your disclaimer and not tell you anything illegal."

"But that sounds very illegal."

"I gave you that as an example – didn't say I had already done it. It's a good working theory, though," Patti-Penny mused, placing her elbow on the table and resting her chin in her hand.

Steph realized she wasn't going to get a straight answer out of her appointment, "Okay then...."

"What else?" Patti-Penny asked immediately, sensing she was losing Steph's interest.

"What about the *mayor*?" Steph asked.

"What *about* the mayor?" Patti-Penny asked.

"You said he was a she and she was a he, the mayor was both... what's the deal on that?"

"It would be a helluva story to tell the local newspapers, wouldn't it?" Patti-Penny suggested as she shook the coffee pot again to check the level of the liquid inside. "If you knew something, or had some blackmail evidence, or if it was celebrity-gossip you could sell to those grocery store tabloids... It'd be pretty fun, huh?"

"Have you done that?"

"No."

"Then why did you say it?"

"It was a good way to break the ice," Patti-Penny smiled, pouring the last of the coffee into her mug.

"It was definitely an interesting conversation starter, that's for sure."

"It worked. That's all we need to take from that unless you work with a tabloid, and you'll give me money for a farfetched story..."

"No money," Steph said, holding up her hands.

"Then no story to tell over here," answered Patti-Penny.

"What about your name?" Steph asked, watching her guest mix only two packets of artificial sugar into her coffee this time around.

"What about it?" Patti-Penny asked, looking back up at Steph.

"What's your real name?"

"Priscilla."

Steph paused, and with a small chuckle, she looked down and shook her head in disbelief. Exasperated, she leaned back in her chair for a moment, and after deciding on her next question, Steph leaned back into the table, "*Earlier*, you told me it was Patti... then Penny. Now it's *Priscilla*?"

"Yep..."

Realizing she simply needed to *go with the flow* with this unknown person sitting across from her, Steph changed the direction of the conversation again. "Do you live in town, here?"

"No," the now-Priscilla answered before she took a sip of her coffee.

"Then how'd you hear about this experiment?"

"What experiment?"

Steph pointed to the table and then to the rest of coffee shop as she said, "This... people coming in to talk with me, sharing secrets, etcetera."

"Oh, yeah... Every so often I stop in for coffee; I have a house here in town," the now-Priscilla answered with a true twinkle in her eye from all the fun she was having with this afternoon conversation.

Steph exhaled and couldn't keep from smiling. After a few seconds of staring at her mystery appointment incredulously, Steph answered, "But you *just said* you don't live in town."

"Correct, I don't *live* in town, but I do have a house here."

"So, you live here then," Steph restated for clarification purposes.

"No, I have a house here which stores my belongings; I live elsewhere all over the world – wherever my travels take me. *Residing* in this town is not the same as *living* in this town."

"Ah, gotcha," Steph said, snapping her fingers and pointing at her guest again while she fell back in her chair, once more.

"Do you?"

As Steph dropped her hands down to her sides and hung them toward the floor, she confessed, "Probably not."

The now-Priscilla sat back and continued to smile at Steph who was at a loss for words. After a moment of silence, the now-Priscilla asked, "Is there anything else you'd like to know?"

"Well, it doesn't really matter what I ask..."

"Why not? This is fun!"

"Fun for you? Yeah. But for me? Not so sure..."

To ensure the continuation of the conversation, the now-Priscilla asked, "Would you like to hear about how I got involved in all of this?"

"Sure, why not?" Steph answered with exasperation and sat up straight.

"Ah... Okay. I'll tell you the truth," the now-Priscilla leaned back with an air of superiority and a look of satisfaction from the stimulating conversation thus far. With an exhale, she continued, "Let's see... Well... way back when, at the age of fifteen, I was a well-endowed teenager, and my uncle was a bookie in Jersey. I was hanging out with him one day while my Mom was out running errands, and he noticed how every time one of his guys came in for a talk, none of them could keep a coherent sentence going when I was within eyesight. He said it was even funnier to listen to them when I would bend over, either facing them or facing away... "

"But that's disgusting!"

"But that's the truth of life. Men really only think with their dicks – that's what makes them *such* easy marks!"

"But you were only fifteen years old!"

The now-Priscilla leaned forward and looked Steph square in the eye and stated, "Yes. I was a fifteen year old who learned *very... early... on...* not to get involved, while making a lot of money in the process."

"How did you make money at this?"

The now-Priscilla sat up, straight again, in her chair and continued. "My uncle would have his boys go play dice or the shell game out on the corners, or in the bars he frequented. I would go with them, but separately, to make it appear like we didn't know each other. When the gaming started and the bets were placed, I would walk by and stop to pick something up, or look in on the game and adjust my undergarments through my blouse – you know, move things around. The guys would usually forget what they were doing, look up, then lose the bet since they looked away for a brief moment to catch a glimpse of whatever may have not been very well-secured by my brassiere, on that particular day...”

“Well, that would explain the shell game, but how about the dice?”

“They were good at short-changing people, especially when those people looked away and had their attention spans interrupted by yours truly,” the now-Priscilla said while pointing to her own self.

“Where did these guys learn the techniques?”

“My uncle taught his kids and some of the neighborhood kids how to do these tricks, just for fun; some of the kids got really good at it and had a knack for it, so they went semi-pro and started making money.”

“What do you mean semi-pro?” Steph asked, crossing her forearms on the table and leaning in.

“They didn’t do it full time. They had their day jobs to keep the ruse of an honest living. But on the side, they made sure ends met by doing these jobs.”

“So... how’d you make money with all of this?”

“Although my cousins and these other kids were good at what they did, I played the crucial role in sidetracking the mark’s attention so, I got my third of the pot.”

“Why did you only get a third of the pot?”

“I got a third, my cousin got a third, and my uncle got a third; us kids did the work and my uncle made sure we were safe out there and didn’t get into any trouble, or got us out of trouble if something happened. You know, paid off the right people to keep things quiet.”

“Did you run into trouble often?”

“Sometimes yes and sometimes no... Sometimes other cons would pick up on what was going on, or they would watch us work and then try to shake us down later. My uncle was very well-respected in the community, and once outsiders knew who they were screwing with, they'd usually disappear."

"Disappear as in... *on their own*? Or disappear as in... *Jimmy Hoffa*?" Steph asked.

"I only concerned myself with whether or not they disappeared. I didn't care how the job got done."

"Ah, I guess not," Steph surmised, waving her right hand.

"Remember, don't get yourself involved. Work the gig and then get out," the now-Priscilla reminded Steph before she finished off the last of her coffee.

"So who were your targets? I would imagine people in the community were clued in on the scam, right?"

"We'd get a lot of tourists who would come in to gamble, or come out for their summer vacations... Those were the ones we'd hit up because they would see the games in the movies, and think it would be fun to participate on vacation. You know, *a little fantasy lived away from real life...* all fun and games until their money disappeared. If they were smart, they would walk away. If they weren't that smart, then they would disappear with a little help from the family."

"Uh huh..." Steph said, realizing she might be sitting across the table from a relative of a mob family.

The now-Priscilla continued, "In my late teens, my parents were eager to marry me off and turn me into a good, god-fearing Catholic wife fraught with children scattered throughout the house. But I'd already gotten hooked with what I'd been doing on the side for the past three years, under the table with my uncle and my cousins... I certainly wasn't about to give that up!"

While Steph held her coffee mug - contemplating finishing the last of her cold coffee - she asked, "How did you get yourself out of your parent's plans?"

"I simply told them I was accepted to a college out on the west coast on a couple of scholarships so they wouldn't have to pay... They bought the story, and I left."

"Did you ever see them again?"

"Oh, yeah, I've been back. But I never came in asking for money, and I always had a story. Then I would go away… it was all clean. No emotional or financial baggage, and no responsibility to them."

"Caring parents, huh?" Steph asked, sarcastically.

"Well, that's how it was back then. With a son, he went off to college, then came back to take over the family business. With a daughter, you got her married off as quickly as you could, so she was someone else's problem."

"Nice…" Steph said, placing her coffee mug back down onto the table.

"I didn't want to live my life as someone else's problem, so I went off on my own… With my uncle's tutelage and help from some of his buddies, I honed my skills and have been travelling the world ever since."

"And that's it?" Steph asked.

"That's it… can't complain."

"I guess not."

The now-Priscilla picked her spoon off the table, and dropped it into her coffee mug causing a muffled clink. "So, do you have any more questions for me?"

"I guess not, although this was really never an interview," Steph stated, straightening up in the chair again.

"You sure asked a lot of questions for something that wasn't an interview!"

"Yeah, I guess I did," Steph said, trying to process all of this off-centered information in her head.

"Well, if we're done here, then I should get going. I have much to do before I set off, out into the world again."

"Where are you off to next?"

"Haven't decided yet… I guess wherever the wind blows me!"

Steph stood up, extended her hand toward Priscilla and said, "Thank you for coming in and sharing your stories with me, Priscilla. I enjoyed hearing about your past, and your life's adventures..."

Priscilla got up and met Steph's hand with hers to complete the formal handshake. With a wink of her eye, she added, "You're welcome Steph. Thank you for your time, and you may call me Pauline."

Steph stopped the handshake and asked, "Seriously? What is your name?"

Priscilla-Pauline smiled and whispered, "Can you keep a secret?"

"Yeah..."

"So can I!" And with that final answer, Patti-Penny-Priscilla-Pauline let go of Steph's hand, picked up her handbag and cane, turned around, and promptly walked toward the door, and out of the coffee shop.

After what seemed like a few minutes, Steph finally sat down and just stared straight ahead, replaying the entire appointment over in her mind. Tom, noticing Steph sitting by herself, excitedly ran over.

"Hey!" Tom said, snapping his fingers in front of Steph's face. "Yoohoo! Is anyone home? Bueller?"

Startled by all of the noise in front of her, Steph jumped; her eyes darted up toward Tom. "Yeah, I'm here."

Tom sat down in the chair recently occupied by Patti-Penny-Priscilla-Pauline, "I got back to the shop here 'bout twenty minutes ago and realized who you were talkin' to!"

With her face twisted in confusion, Steph asked, "Who was I talking to?"

"Didn't she introduce herself?" Tom asked eagerly.

"Oh, yeah... She introduced herself *four... different... times!*"

"What do ya' mean she introduced herself four

different times?

"She gave me four different names throughout the entire time we were talking," Steph answered.

"Didn't she tell ya' who she was?" Tom asked again, but this time his excitement was replaced with confusion.

"Well..." Steph began as she started to count off on her fingers. "First it was Patti... then Penny... then Priscilla... then Pauline... When I finally asked her, straight up what her real name was, she told me she could keep a secret. Then she left."

"That was Devorah Smithson!"

"Who?"

"Devorah Smithson! She's a Pulitzer Prize Author & New York Times Bestseller a couple o' times over!" Tom announced with a big smile while he slapped his leg with his hand.

"What?"

Tom, beginning to get confused as well, sat straight up in his chair and asked, "What part of this are ya' gettin' lost on? And who are all of these other people ya' just listed off?"

"She said those were her names, none of which sounds like Devorah..." Steph answered, continuing to stare out the window.

"No, they don't, but that was definitely her!"

"But why would she tell me such off the wall things? And with all of the different names?"

"What did she tell ya'?" Tom asked, leaning in a bit closer with the hope of catching Steph off-guard and finally getting to hear about some of the topics being discussed.

"Huh?" Steph asked absently.

"What'd she tell ya'?"

Turning her head to look at Tom again, Steph playfully scolded him with, "Oh, I can't tell you! You know that!"

Tom sat up straight and dropped his forearms onto the table in front of him. "Well, *how* am I supposed to *help you* if I don't know what you're talkin' about then?"

"I don't need any help... I'm just confused by the last hour of conversation."

"Can you tell me *anything*?"

"Do you know where she lives?"

"Yeah, she's got that big house up on the hillside overlooking town," Tom answered while pointing out the window with his left hand. "But I'm pretty sure she has other houses, too..."

"Where?"

"Why?"

"Just tell me where," Steph answered quickly.

"Ah, I don't know.... Sometimes there's talk of her spendin' a lot of her time out in Europe."

"Where in Europe?" Steph asked, leaning in toward the table again.

"I don't know... One of those small countries in the middle... Switzerland, Belgium, Austria... Somewhere, in there... Why?"

Steph's eyes lit up and she eagerly asked, "Denmark?"

"Could be, I don't know. Why?"

"Just trying to make sense of everything she told me, if that's even possible."

"Well, if it's that confusing, maybe the point is to *not* figure it out; for it to *remain* a mystery?" Tom suggested with a tilt of his head.

"*Is* she a mystery writer?"

"I believe she writes primarily fiction, but not much to do with mystery."

"Well, she can certainly spin a good story," Steph said with a large exhale as she dropped her forearms onto the table, too.

"Was it that unbelievable? Or... believable?"

"I thought so," Steph confessed, "Or both. I'm not

really sure right now..."

"Well, I've always heard writers tend to write about what they know," Tom said in an effort to snap Steph back out of the inner thought process she was beginning to slide into again.

"Then she either knows a lot, or has certainly led an interesting life!" Steph responded, shoving her spoon and napkin into her coffee mug.

Tom leaned back in his chair and asked with a hint of defeat, "And I bet you aren't gonna tell me about any of it, are you?"

Steph smiled at Tom and then asked, "Can you keep a secret?"

Tom breathlessly answered, "Yes!"

"So can I!" Steph admitted then put her hand up to her closed mouth, turned an invisible key, and tossed it over her shoulder.

Mike

"Back in for another one today, huh?" Tom asked, when Steph entered the coffee shop.

"I think this is becoming my second job. I should have taken up psychiatry!" Steph answered in an exasperating tone as she sat down at the counter. "I had no idea there were so many tortured souls among us!"

"What are all these tortured souls tellin' ya', so far?" Tom asked casually, in an attempt to get something out of Steph.

Catching on to what Tom was going for once again, Steph smiled and said, "Nope. Not going to say... I told you, I'm not going to divulge any secrets. But that was a good try!"

"If you take on all these secrets and you don't tell anyone else, then you might get all clogged up with bad stuff and explode! You should really tell someone... That would be the healthy thing to do, and you should start with me... I'm a very good listener."

"Nope. But I will take a caramel roll today, please," Steph said, pointing to the bakery display.

"Alright, have it your way," Tom warned Steph, shaking his head while he took a roll out of the display and placed it in front of her. "But when your head suddenly explodes from all this negativity and bad stuff, don't come cryin' to me!"

"I won't be going anywhere if my head explodes."

"You know what I mean," Tom said hotly, giving her a fork and a napkin.

"Yes, I do, and don't worry about me. I'm thinking I should really write a book about all of this but keep out real names, of course. Maybe tweak the timelines and situations a bit... I could use it for journaling purposes to get my personal feelings out onto paper so it doesn't all sit inside my brain and fester."

"That would certainly be an interesting book... I would *finally* be able to learn what you've been hearin' about in that corner this entire time!" Tom said, lightly slapping the countertop.

"I would have to get it out to the masses a few years after the fact, too, so things don't sound too familiar. Plus, it would probably take me that long to write anyway... I still have another job I have to do to pay my bills," Steph answered before she took a bite of the caramel roll.

"Well, it looks like you're in demand. Your sign-up sheet is full now," Tom said, leaning on the top of the bakery display. "Have you given anymore thought about extending your experiment, and offering another month's worth of appointments?"

"Yeah, sure... Again, if you're okay with that idea, I'm game..." Steph agreed, using her fork to slice off another bite of her roll. "I will also start having something at the table, back there, and list it on the sign-up sheet to denote who I am in case someone comes in and all of you are busy up here helping customers... I forgot to do that with the first month of appointments, actually."

"Good idea," Tom agreed, reaching down to the coffee bean-filled flower pot near the register and plucking out

a pen with a big, white plastic daisy taped to it.
Handing the pen to Steph, Tom said, "Here, use this so
people know who you are..."

Steph took the pen from Tom and said, "Yeah, this
would work. I'll make a note of it on the current sign-up
sheet as well as the next sign-up sheet. Thanks!"

"You know, I've seen some people come in and look at
that sheet darn close to every morning they're here, and
some sign up and some don't. Some will even get their
coffee then stand in front of the sign-up sheet with a pen
in hand. Then after a moment or two, they'll put the
pen down and walk away," Tom said, shaking his head
again. "I really can't believe your experiment caught on
this well! I mean, I really thought you'd only have one
or two takers, and that'd be it."

"Like I said, a lot of tortured souls out there..." Steph
confirmed before taking another bite of her caramel roll,
but paused to continue, "Oh, and thank you, I think, for
that left-handed compliment."

"Do you think these confessions are as bad as what a
priest would hear?" Tom asked while Steph was
chewing.

After a moment of over-emphasizing her chewing to
point out to Tom he shouldn't ask people questions
while they're eating, Steph answered, "I don't know
what a Priest would hear since I'm not a Catholic, but if
I'm hearing, and continue to hear, what a normal
confessional reveals, I'm guessing there are a lot of 'Hail
Mary's' happening in this town!"

"That juicy, huh?"

"Juicy... sloppy... drowning... Pick an adjective.
Better yet, pick a number of adjectives. Then wait for
the book to come out!"

In another weak effort, Tom asked one more time,
"Are ya' sure you don't wanna tell your ol' Uncle Tom
any of what you're hearin' over at that table?"

"You're not my uncle and I'm pretty sure I'm not

going to divulge anything. Besides, they're not my secrets to tell!"

"I should call ya' *Boring Betty!*"

"Well," Steph said, spinning her stool around and beginning to set off to what was becoming her reserved table in the back corner, "*Boring Betty* will take an espresso today since *Boring Betty* didn't sleep all that well last night, for whatever reason."

"Sounds like *Boring Betty* is startin' to get clogged up and she should really start talkin'..."

As Steph walked away from the counter and through the tables, she answered in a singsong, "Not going to happen!"

It was getting close to ten minutes past the appointment time and Steph was wondering if she should think about packing it up and leaving, maybe getting to bed a little earlier tonight since she didn't sleep all that well the night before. Maybe this commitment to hearing all of these stories, confessions, whatever, would *actually* get to her... Or was starting to get to her? After another minute, she started to pack herself up. Getting some extra sleep wouldn't be the worst plan... Except she just drank an espresso, and that probably wasn't the greatest idea.

"Excuse me. Are you Steph?"

Steph looked up and saw a man standing by the table with a backpack slung over his shoulder and his long hair peeking out underneath a stocking cap. "Yeah, I am. You must be my appointment for today?" she answered with her hand extended but still sitting.

"Yeah, I'm sorry I'm late. Were you about to leave?" he asked while shaking Steph's hand.

"Well, I was thinking if you were going to be a no-show, I was going to go home and get some stuff..."

"Can we reschedule?"

"I'd rather meet today since you're here... would that work for you?"

"Yeah, that'll work. Truth be told, I have been sitting in my car over the past thirty minutes starting my car, then turning off the car, and then starting my car, and then turning it off... Wasn't sure if I should come in, but I figured I should. I need to get this off my chest and out of my head."

"What in the world are you keeping as a secret, so much, that you are out in the parking lot ruining your engine over?" Steph asked with a mix of concern and curiosity in her voice.

"Do you mind if I have a seat?"

"No, of course not... Please sit," Steph said motioning toward the chair, and moving her empty plate onto the window sill, so it wouldn't fall off the table when he sat down - in case his backpack swung off his shoulder. "By the way, what's your name?"

"Oh, it's Mike," he answered, pulling his left elbow across the table nearly knocking over the bud vase. If the plate had still been there, it would've now been on the floor in pieces. "Oops!"

"No worries. All is good," Steph assured him while she caught the vase and placed it on the window sill, too. "You sure seem like you brought in a lot of stuff for a one hour coffee chat. What's in the backpack?" Steph asked, smiling with a friendly voice in an effort to quiet Mike's noticeable nervousness.

"After I meet with you, I have some friends stopping here to do a study session tonight. Then maybe we will grab a late night dinner afterwards."

"I take it you're in college then?" Steph asked.

"Yeah..."

"What are you studying?"

Mike sat up a little straighter in his chair and said, "I'm in my last year of undergrad for Biology then it's off to grad school."

"Well, congratulations!" Steph said. "That's great!"

Returning the effort of small talk, Mike asked, "Where did you go to school?"

"The University of Hard Knocks," Steph said with the best smile she could keep up, despite her past education route being a sore spot in her life. "I didn't get anything past my Associates Degree... I got wrapped up in full time work and have been in it ever since. I've done well, though, all things considered."

"Oh," Mike said in a rather drab tone.

In an effort to get the conversation moving and hopefully have Mike become less nervous, Steph asked, "Well, what finally got you into this coffee shop after your half hour long decision-making process?"

"Have you ever seen anyone die?" Mike asked curtly while leaning into the table, staring intently at Steph.

Steph instantly sat up a bit straighter, cleared her throat and stated, "I think this would be a good time to go over my disclaimer, and make sure you understand it. Everyone should be on the same page moving forward."

"Uh, yeah... Sure," Mike said, leaning back off the table a bit.

"I'm a law-abiding citizen who would rather not hear about anything illegal done by you or anyone you know because I don't want to be put into the position of knowing something that should be reported."

"Okay."

"So, should we call this appointment off?" Steph asked, looking Mike square in the eye with all seriousness. "Maybe call it a day and I go home?"

"No."

"But you're going to tell me something about someone who has died? Did you have anything to do with it?"

With a worried look on his face, Mike fidgeted in his chair for a couple of seconds then looked down, then back up and said, "Yes, and no... Or at least I don't think so, but maybe I did?"

"No wonder you sat in the car for the past thirty minutes wondering if you should come in," Steph blurted out, overcompensating for the fact she didn't know what else to say at that moment.

"Yeah..."

Steph leaned into the table and in a hushed tone suggested, "How about we do this? I'll ask a question and you answer. At any time, if you think the answer you will give shouldn't be answered because it would go against my disclaimer, then all you have to do is tell me this conversation is over, and we will each go on our merry way, and that's it. Sound good?"

"I guess..." Mike answered, shrugging his shoulders.

"Good. Because I don't want to hear anything illegal; I'm sorry to put it this way, but do you understand? Have I made myself clear?"

"Crystal. You sound like my mom."

"You have a smart mom."

"I used to have a smart Mom. Sometimes..." Mike trailed off, looking back down at the top of the table.

"Is she the person you are speaking of who is now deceased?" Steph asked.

"Yes."

"When did she die?"

"About a year ago," Mike answered as he looked back up at Steph.

After learning the deceased was his Mom, Steph softened her somewhat reprimanding tone with Mike and said, "I'm sorry to hear that."

"Yeah..."

"Have you been doing okay?" Steph asked.

"Yeah... If I don't think about it," Mike admitted.

"Did she live around here?"

"Yeah, she lived here all of her life, and so have I."

"Were you living with her at the time of her

passing?"

"Yeah," Mike said quietly, looking back down at the table again.

"Oh. Oh, boy..." Steph acknowledged quietly and then asked, "Were you with her when she died?"

"Sort of..." Mike mumbled, looking back up at Steph with sorrow-filled eyes.

"How does this *sort of* thing work?"

"Well," Mike began as he resituated himself in his chair.

"You sure you're okay to answer this?" Steph interrupted. "Nothing illegal, right?"

"Yeah. It wasn't my fault."

"Okay, just checking – the *sort of* thing causes me to worry..." Steph said, leaning forward and resting her forearms on the table. With no change on Mike's face or in his actions, she gave him a nod and said, "Okay, keep going..."

"Alright... I had just turned twenty-one a couple of months before, and my buddies and I had this tradition of going out on Wednesday nights to play pool and have some beers and stuff, 'cuz none of us had any classes until Thursday afternoon. Wednesdays were an easy day for all of us to get that night off from our jobs, so that was the one night of the week we were all able to get together."

"Okay..." Steph said, gently nodding her head.

"Anyway, like I said, I'd just turned twenty-one a couple of months prior, so it was still a novelty to me to get stupid. Not totally drunk, but still stupid. And my friends would always drop me off since I didn't yet have a car, and..."

Steph couldn't help but throw in her advice of, "You don't drive when you're stupid, either."

"I know, and I didn't. And I haven't. I never will," Mike acknowledged, clarified, and agreed all in one breath.

"Sorry for interrupting. Drunk driving happens to be a sore spot in my world; a long story for another time," Steph said with a wave of her hand while she briefly glanced down at the table and shook her head.

"Sorry."

"No worries about me and my issues. We're here for you now."

Mike sat up straight in his chair again and said, "Okay. Anyway, my friends dropped me off that night. When I got into the house, I heard my Mom snoring on the couch with the TV volume down low. She often fell asleep on the couch, so I didn't think anything of it."

"Yeah..."

"Walking in, I glanced into the living room which was lit up only with the television and told her I was home. I also told her I loved her, then I went into my room which was the next room over, got into bed, and passed out myself."

"Did she wake up and answer you?" Steph asked.

Mike shook his head and answered, "No, she was out cold... When I walked past the living room, she was snoring."

"Okay."

"But here's the thing. When I got home that night, and I stopped by the living room to say goodnight and tell her I loved her, her snoring struck me as a bit... *off*. But I was so tired after a long day and four beers, I just went to sleep."

"What do you mean it was *off*?" Steph asked with a concerned look on her face.

Mike leaned back into the table and asked again, "Have you ever been around someone who is dying?"

Reassessing Mike's question, this time around, with the new information she was told, Steph muttered, "Oh, no..."

"You haven't?"

"No, I have," Steph said, looking Mike straight in the

eye again. "And I bet I know where this is going, too."

"Yeah, she was taking her last breaths," Mike confessed, staring back at Steph while moving his fingers around the table in a random pattern. "She wasn't snoring. But I fell asleep almost as soon as my head hit that pillow."

In an attempt to avert this appointment from plummeting into complete despair and to build up – or at least support - Mike's overall emotional-being, Steph asked, "You know it wasn't your fault, don't you?"

"Yes and no," Mike said as he began to tap his fingers on the table.

"It wasn't," Steph rebutted.

Mike inhaled and leaned back with his hands in his lap, "I have gone over this a gazillion times in my head, and everyone has told me that when the death rattle starts, it's pretty much a done deal."

"It is," Steph nodded in agreement.

"But could I have done more? I should have noticed the pill bottles on the table, the whiskey bottle dumped on the floor, but it was dark in the living room except for the TV over in the corner."

"It's not your fault."

"But she had been asking me to spend more time with her – maybe skip a Wednesday with the boys and go out on what we used to call a *Mommy – Son Date*," Mike said, leaning forward again with his hands still in his lap. "But we did that back when I was little and now I was older and going out with friends. I can't even remember the last time she and I just hung out together."

Steph feeling a bit overwhelmed with her personal skepticism of what *exactly* to say to Mike regarding this traumatic event in his life sputtered, "Can I just remind you that I am not a psychiatrist, by any means? Only someone who can give you a shoulder to cry on and a sympathetic ear who will take the time to listen to all you have to say?"

"Yeah, I know. I talked with the investigator when this all happened," Mike said, grimacing and bringing his arms up to rest on the table again, "after I found her in the morning."

"And what did they tell you?"

"The same thing you are telling me – it's not my fault."

"And it isn't," Steph agreed.

"But what if I had stayed with her that night? What if I had spent more time with her, over the years, rather than running off everywhere with my friends every chance I got? What if I had gotten home sooner? What if I..."

Steph took a deep breath as she sat up straight and said, "Yep, the 'what if?' game. I did that, too, when my stepdad was hit by a drunk driver four years ago. They were going home from my house. They were going to stay for dessert but then my stepdad got into another round of why I wasn't bothering to find a husband, and the fact that I was getting old and past my prime to give them grandchildren. So, he got upset and that ruined the evening. They both left my house to go home, and not even a mile from my house, a drunk driver plowed into them and that was it. My stepdad died at the scene and my mom was in the hospital for nearly a month. He left my house upset at me, and I wasn't too happy with him, either, and now it's over. For the past four years, no nothing. I can't fix it. He can't fix it. Things happen and I don't know why they happen, but they do and that's just the way it goes, and I'm sorry I'm not helping. I just don't know what to tell you."

"I know," Mike answered, pushing a spoon around the table. "I'm sorry to hear you lost your stepdad. Is your mom okay?"

"Yeah, she's good now. Her back and neck are screwed up and she still gets migraines, on occasion, but she's alive, and that's all that matters," Steph answered but then continued, "So, please *never* drive drunk!"

"Don't worry... drinking and driving is not on my agenda. My Wednesday night out with the guys has fallen by the wayside, too. I'm stuck in a funk. Wednesday nights are the worst because those always start the 'what ifs'?"

"If it helps, it gets a little easier with time," Steph offered up.

"I've heard," Mike agreed with another sigh.

In an effort to route the conversation away from the eternal 'what ifs?', Steph asked, "Have you spoken to a psychiatrist about any of this?"

"No..."

"Why not?" Steph asked with a look of concern.

"I just can't bring myself to really ever talk about this," Mike said, tapping his fingers on the table again. "I see it as being partially my fault..."

"But it's not."

"I'd like to be able to accept that, but with biology being what my entire schooling is about and I do know what a death rattle sounds like, I should have been able to put two and two together, and tried to stop it. Do CPR or something. Notice the pill bottles and the dumped bottle of whiskey on the living room floor. Call 911. But I didn't. Instead I stumbled into the house, carelessly told her I was home rather than checking in on her, and then passed out myself."

"Can I ask you a side question?"

"Sure. What?"

"Where's your dad?" Steph asked, curling up a napkin in front of her to soak up some of the nervous energy her own regretful family memories were causing.

Mike looked up at Steph and stated frankly, "He got into the car while he was drunk, started the car up and then passed out before he opened the garage door... Whether he intentionally did it, or accidentally forgot to open the garage door to go out drunk-driving, we will never know. I was 15 years old at the time."

Steph was really at a loss for words, now. She simply sat across from Mike, trying to formulate a question, a comment, something... But nothing came out.

Sensing the awkwardness of the silence in between them and knowing Steph was trying to say something... anything... Mike mumbled, "Yeah...."

Steph stammered out the first thing she finally thought of, "Did you see any of this coming on - any signs of depression with your mom?"

"Looking back on it now, yeah, I did. Did I do anything about it? No, I didn't. And that's what I'm ashamed of; I was a spoiled child who didn't give two shits about anyone else and was busy living my own life, not realizing my mom was depressed and lonely, and it's like I cut her out of my life... permanently," Mike stammered as his eyes began to fill with tears. "And I didn't mean to. I never wanted my mom to die... didn't want my father to die, either, although he wasn't the nicest guy when he drank. I wasn't there for my mom."

"I can give you the name and number of a friend of mine who is a licensed psychiatrist."

"Yeah, sure..."

"I'm afraid whatever I say is not going to help, and I sure don't want to make things worse," Steph said while looking through the contacts in her phone.

Mike started to nod his head and said, "Yeah, I'll take the number."

"For the fact you came in here today and told a stranger what has been bothering you, is probably a good indication that you are ready to start talking about what happened with someone who can better assist you."

"Yeah, I suppose."

"The only thing I can tell you is it wasn't your fault. It's a good idea for people to hang out with family every

so often, but you also need to live your own life. True, if
something sounded off, one should have investigated a
bit further. But if you're coming in already tired from
the day and heading for bed, you won't be in the best
state of mind to - as you stated - put two and two
together. But then again, most people don't expect to
hear a death rattle at any time of the day. Most people
would do just what you did... get in the door, say good
night as you walked past, and fall asleep. I would have
done that, myself."

"I know. But it's the 'what if?' game that gets to me.
And then I push those 'what ifs' back into the past
around the time my dad died, and then it just falls
apart. I should have been more aware, but I was
selfish. I was a selfish teenager who just didn't cue into
what was happening."

In another attempt to reroute the conversation again,
Steph asked, "Do you have any siblings?"

"I have an older sister who is close to ten years older
than me but lives in Germany with her military
husband," Mike answered.

"Was she and your mom close?"

"As close as they could be considering the lack of time
and lack of money with both parties. Mom worked two
jobs and never had enough money, and Sarah never got
back home very much... only once every two or three
years at the most, usually around Christmas."

After Mike finished answering, Steph slid a piece of
paper across the table, "Here's the name and number of
someone to call. Being you're a student, you may
qualify for his sliding fee scale. I don't know though –
You'll have to talk to him on that, too."

"Oh, thanks," Mike said, picking up the paper and
looking at it. "Okay."

"Are you close with your sister?"

"Same deal for me as it was with our mom. Sarah
said they should be back in the States in the next two

years or so, for good, but we'll see."

"Who do you live with now?" Steph asked.

"Since neither Sarah, nor myself, could afford the house, it was put up for sale and the money absorbed into her estate which paid off the bills, and her final expenses. The rest was divided up between Sarah and me," Mike explained. It's not a whole lot, but it's something. I live with roommates now. Two other guys..."

"Are these two other guys friends of yours, or just roommates?" Steph asked with concern.

"Oh, yeah... They're both good buddies of mine. We've all known each other since high school, and both their families have 'adopted' me since I'm pretty much flying solo these days."

"I'm happy to hear you have your friends as well as two families who have embraced you as 'one of their own'," Steph said with a smile. "It's good to hear you have support and love around you."

"I know I'm lucky to have these guys; they're like brothers to me."

As Steph was listening to Mike, she happened to see a few guys get out of a car, carrying backpacks, and start heading toward the front door of the coffee shop. Pointing out the window at them Steph asked, "Those guys wouldn't happen to be your friends, would they?"

Mike turned to look over his left shoulder, then turned back to Steph, and started standing up, "Yep, they're my friends... Well, thank you for taking the time to meet with me today..."

Steph stood up, too, and extended her hand for a handshake. "Thank *you* for coming in and talking about all of this today, Mike."

Mike returned the handshake before grabbing his bag and said, "Thank you again for waiting around for me. I'm sorry I took so long to get in here... I just wasn't sure if I could tell anyone this and if I did, would

I be able to get through it and what would the other person think?"

"I'm happy you came in to talk, and here... Don't forget this," Steph said, smiling as she handed Mike the piece of paper with the name and phone number. "Have a good evening with your friends... and know you *are* a good person."

"Thank you and you, too," Mike said before turning to walk away.

Steph quickly answered with, "You're welcome... And I'm just going home tonight – not hanging out with friends."

Mike stopped right as he had just begun to walk away, turned back around to face Steph with a smile and said, "No, I wasn't talking about you hanging out with your friends tonight. I was letting you know you are a good person, too."

Being at another loss for words, Steph simply replied, "Thank you."

Chet

Sitting in the warmth of the window at the coffee shop, waiting for the next scheduled person to stop in and tell her a secret, she started her habit of people-watching again. Two women had just gotten out of parked car which had arrived a few moments before; they looked like a mother-daughter duo, although the presumed 'mom' looked young and the 'daughter' looked older. Maybe they were sisters? No, from the way they were dressed, as well as the way they carried themselves, Steph settled on the two of them being a mother-daughter duo.

A few moments later, another car sped into the parking lot and parked at an angle in an available spot. Seeing this inadequate parking job, Steph bristled at the possibility this could be her next interviewee - if that were the case, she'd start off the appointment by making them fix their lousy parking job! She had seen enough of this type of parking in her lifetime, and was wondering if she was finally going to have the chance to confront someone who needed to retake the parking portion of Driver's Ed. But just as the driver was about to get out of the car, they pulled the door shut again,

started the car, backed out quickly, and drove away.
Steph watched the car as it made a right turn out of the parking lot and disappeared. Perhaps they decided they were in the wrong lot? After a few minutes of watching various people walk by, holding their different purchases, talking on the phone, getting in and out of cars, a Jeep pulled in and parked in the same spot the lousy driver had been in. A man probably in his mid to late thirties got out, made sure the doors were locked, and started heading toward the coffee shop. Steph decided this was probably her next interviewee. She watched him walk in and survey the restaurant. When he spotted her in the corner, she waved her plastic daisy-topped pen in the air and he set off toward her table.

"Hi. Are you Stephanie?" he asked with trepidation.

"Yes, I am. But you can call me Steph."

"Okay, I hope I'm not late."

"Not that I know of. I was busy soaking in the warmth of the sun," Steph pointed out the window. She pulled her crossword puzzle off the table, stowing it in her backpack on the floor.

"Good idea. It's pretty blustery out there today. I'm Chet, by the way. Nice to meet you," he said, leaning on the back of the chair across from Steph.

"Nice to meet you, too," Steph said, motioning toward the chair, still sitting, herself. "Go ahead and have a seat."

"I will in just a moment. I need to use the restroom first. I'll be right back," Chet said, starting to walk toward the bathroom.

"Okay..."

In the time it took for Chet to use the restroom,
Steph got up and refilled the coffee pot at the counter,
returned to the table with an extra mug and spoon for
her guest, and began perfecting her next cup of coffee
with her one sugar packet and just the right amount of
creamer.

"Okay," Chet said, returning to the table and pulling
the chair out to sit down. "This is weird."

"Weird?"

"Weird talking to a stranger about this," Chet
continued. "Then again, I haven't told anyone and I'm
certainly not going to share it with any of my family
members. So, I guess you'll do."

"Thank you?"

"Oh, no. I didn't mean it that way, but it's such an
awkward thing to talk about."

With a deep breath, Chet was about to reveal his
secret when Steph remembered her required
announcement to be given before all confessions.
"Apologies on interrupting, but I need to throw in my
disclaimer... I'm a law-abiding citizen who would rather
not hear about anything illegal done by you or anyone
you know because I don't want to be put into the
position of knowing something that should be reported."

"Nothing illegal... At least I don't think it's illegal...
Not completely illegal... *But it sure is disgusting*!"

"Oh! One other thing... I'm not a licensed
therapist," Steph reminded Chet, bracing herself for the
worst. "Okay, let's hear it."

Chet leaned in and whispered frantically, "My dad
looks at porn!"

Steph was at a loss for words. Trying to hide a smile,
she asked, "What?"

A little louder, this time, Chet repeated himself.
"My... dad... looks... at... porn!"

"Your dad looks at porn?"

"Yeah."

"I don't mean to be rude here, but what dad *doesn't* look at porn?"

"But it's not regular porn," Chet pointed out.

"There's regular and non-regular porn?"

"When you include animals, violence, and blood, yeah, then there are varying degrees of porn."

"Okay, yeah. I can see how you're a bit weirded out! How do you know your dad looks at this type of stuff?"

"Shortly before Christmas, my dad's hard drive crashed," Chet began.

"Oh, okay. I can see where this is going..." Steph nodded.

"Yeah, I'm into computers and I've always been the one my family members call before giving up on a computer, altogether. So, for Christmas, all of us kids agreed I would try to fix it, and we'd give dad his computer back so he could access all of the family pictures he stored on it after mom passed away a little over a year ago."

"Well, it was definitely a nice thought..." Steph said, sipping at her coffee.

"He had the porn hidden pretty well, too."

"How do you know it wasn't just a virus, or something on the computer? How do you know he was looking at the pictures?"

As Chet was pouring a cup of coffee for himself, he answered Steph's question. "It most likely *was* a virus he picked up on those sites that caused the crash. But the pictures that he had saved had his notes attached to them, along with a couple of pictures of him – full frontal, back, profile... Use your imagination..."

"I am, unfortunately..." Steph frowned, absent-mindedly folding and unfolding an empty sugar packet.

"Uh huh, and a few close ups of... Yeah. Use some *more imagination...*"

"Yeah. I can see why you wouldn't tell anyone about this," Steph said. "How did you happen to find these pictures if he had done a good job hiding them?"

"The recovery program I normally use had trouble pulling up the family pictures from MyDocs. So, I had it scan the entire hard drive for a single file type, and I got quite the eyeful!"

Steph still using her imagination, agreed, "I can only imagine!"

Chet continued, "I replaced the hard drive, backed up the family pictures and nothing else, and we all gave him his computer back as one of his Christmas presents."

"Do you think he was wondering if you saw anything?" Steph asked.

"I don't know, and I certainly didn't tell anyone else."

"Did he ask you anything?"

"He did ask me in a couple of roundabout ways if I had backed up *all* the pictures. Or did I see anything else that should have been backed up? You know, those kinds of probing questions."

"Probing…." Steph trailed off with a little laugh. "Oh, I'm sorry."

"No, it's funny, you're right. And maybe I *am* making a bigger stink out of this than I should be…" Chet trailed off.

"No, I think you might be justified in freaking out. Porn is one thing… Your dad watching animals is a…"

"Animals with humans…" Chet clarified.

Steph shuddered, "Yeah, that's a whole different thing…"

"I can't believe he was watching that!" Chet said, stirring the sugar into his coffee and shaking his head.

"Do you think he may have accidentally found this kind of porn, and out of curiosity, took a look?" Steph proposed. "I mean, how old is your dad?"

"He's seventy-nine. He'll be eighty in a couple of

weeks. I'm the youngest of six kids. I was the accident baby who showed up twelve years after the last planned child," Chet explained.

"Okay. So... maybe he *accidentally* saw an ad for something and out of curiosity, clicked on it and that's what led to the crash and everything."

"But you forget that he had notes attached to these pictures along with pictures of himself, all saved on the computer."

"That's right... By the way, how did he get so good at computers? I mean, my mom is only in her sixties and is lucky if she can find the power button on her computer," Steph pointed out with a small laugh.

"My dad used to work for a large computer firm back in the day, and I filled him in on whatever he didn't know. He's a rather savvy person when it comes to technology."

"Sounds like it..." Steph said.

"I was happy to give him back his computer for Christmas. All of us kids made a big to-do about it. But sitting in my sister's living room watching him open the box on Christmas Day, knowing what I had found on the hard drive, all I could think was 'Why are we giving him this computer back when that kind of horrid trash is what occupies his time?'" Chet said, stirring his coffee.

"I mean, I found myself playing 'parent' to my parent. Two of my sisters even picked up on how I was not my normal, jovial self that day. I told them I wasn't feeling well."

"May I suggest something?" Steph asked.

"Okay."

"Well, first of all, I have a few questions..."

Being open to whatever Steph had thought of, Chet asked, "What?"

"You mentioned your mom passed away a little over a year ago, right?"

"Yeah," Chet confirmed.

"Has your dad always been a good person to you and your siblings?"

"Yeah, we're a close knit family – always there for each other. We were closer when mom was here, but yeah, we're still close."

"Since your mom passed away, has your dad changed at all?"

"Well, he doesn't get out much. Sort of seems like he's given up on living, some days. I think he's lonely," Chet sighed.

"So, he hasn't taken up with anyone since your mom's passing?"

"No. He says he's too old and he doesn't want to get wrapped up in that nonsense again. So, he sits at home most of the time - might occasionally go down to the corner for a beer, but nothing too exciting."

"Well, then I can see where this might have become something of a pastime for him," Steph concluded. "Although a bit warped, it's still something for him to do rather than sitting in a chair waiting to die."

"Yeah, I guess. But why can't he just watch regular porn?" Chet complained.

"Maybe he does? Maybe he started out with that and then a sidebar ad popped up with this type of trash, and it piqued his curiosity?" Steph suggested.

Chet furthered his questions, "I get all of that, but bestiality? Violence? Blood?"

"It's not like your dad, in his seventy-nine years, has never heard of bestiality or has never seen violence that has resulted in blood being drawn…. One can barely even go to a movie these days and not see some type of bloody violence," Steph pointed out.

"I know. But why does he have to be into *this* type of trash?"

"My guess is he's trying to do something that keeps the brain active," Steph suggested. "Maybe he also doesn't have the control to *not* look at this stuff. Maybe it's nothing more than him trying to amuse himself while the rest of the world goes on about their own business, including his own family members."

"But I need to continue working in order to support my family. I can't sit around all day babysitting him, making sure he's not looking at this crap!"

"No one is suggesting that you do," Steph frowned.

"I have no idea what to do then."

"If it were my dad, I would do nothing."

"I can't do 'nothing.' This is disgusting," Chet retorted.

"Yes, you can do nothing by putting all of this out of your mind. Christmas was over four months ago. It's done. Put it out of your mind. He's a big boy who is making his own decisions, and if he wants to look at this stuff and share pictures of his body with others, online, then that's what he's going to do."

"I don't think he needs to do it."

"It doesn't really matter what you think, and he may need to do it. Humans are sexual beings from the time of birth to the moment they die."

"I don't want to think about my dad as a sexual being..."

Steph laughed and asked, "You're one of six kids – how do you think that all happened?"

Chet acknowledged, "I know. But -"

"But I bet your dad is doing this for validation of some sort. Maybe sending out his pictures to the virtual world in order to validate the fact that he is still alive, and is still attractive to females even at his age... You know, if he isn't hurting anyone, or any animals, or himself, let him be. It could be he did that once and couldn't figure out how to get it off the computer."

"One of the pictures he took of himself was on this past Thanksgiving Day... Time stamped for an hour after I dropped him off at his house," Chet revealed, dropping the spoon on the table like a microphone.

71

Deciding this was a good place to add in her unlicensed summary of the situation, Steph finished with, "So be it, then. He's an adult with all of his faculties intact. If this is what he wants to do, then let him do it, as long as he's not causing harm to anyone else, including himself. That would be my advice, if you are looking for an unbiased, and non-family member opinion."

"I suppose..."

"And I would not tell any of your siblings, either. Consider this secret off your conscious, and put it to rest."

"I have five sisters. There's no way I'm telling them!" Chet exclaimed.

"That would be a good idea. Plus, you don't want anything to change for your dad in a negative way. That would crush him. He's already lost his wife, recently. You don't want to be the person who winds up taking away his family."

"No, I don't," Chet said. "And I know two of my sisters would absolutely freak out. That's one of the biggest reasons I never told anyone, including any of them. Word spreads, and then people would be asking me questions, and I don't even want to think about it."

"Then don't; end of story," Steph nodded.

"I'll try..."

In an effort to change the subject, Steph asked, "Do you have fun things planned with your family, today? It would be a great day to fly a kite in the park!"

Chet looked at Steph, puzzled. "My kids are in school now, and I'm taking an early lunch. Why are you talking about kites? Did I miss something?"

"I'm changing the subject... I'm trying to help you move on."

"Oh. I get it. Apparently, I'm a little slow on the draw today."

"No worries."

"Actually, flying a kite would be fun today, but it will have to wait until I'm off work and the kids are home from school, preferably with their homework done," Chet said, finishing off the last of his coffee.

"Good ideas - both the homework and the kite," Steph agreed.

"And speaking of, I do need to get back to work. Thank you so much for doing this for people; doing this for me," Chet said, backing up his chair and standing.

"My pleasure," Steph responded.

Chet shook her hand and smiled, "Alright, you have a nice day, and thank you again. I'll take your advice to heart and be done with this matter. I'll start ignoring what I saw all those months ago."

"That would definitely be a good idea. You don't want this stuff to eat away at you, and ruin your life."

"No, I don't. Not anymore."

"And remember," Steph added, "I am *not* a licensed psychiatrist or anything. I was simply telling you what I would do if I were in your position as we talked over a cup of coffee at the corner table."

"I know, and I appreciate the help. Thank you again," Chet said, beginning to leave. After a few steps, Chet looked over his shoulder and hollered, "You have a good kite-flying day, too!"

Julie

"And... top o' the morning to ya', this fine day!" Tom said cheerfully as Steph walked in the front door of the coffee shop. "Who's up to bat today?"

Steph sauntered slowly up to the counter, as fast as her typical morning gait was going to take her anywhere. "Absolutely no idea... As a matter of fact, I'm not even sure what day it is, or what number appointment I'm on, this morning."

"Well, we'll start off with the basics then... What planet are you on?"

"Earth; I already figured that much out."

"Good deal. How 'bout, do ya' know who you are?"

"Yep, I recognized myself in the mirror," Steph answered with a glimmer of a smile.

"Alright! Two for two, so far!" Tom looked around and spotted Steph's coffee mug, then turned back to her and asked, "Do you remember what your coffee mug looks like?"

"Yeah, it's right there," Steph said, pointing to it.

"And what would ya' like in it, today?"

"Do you have a medium roast going?"

"Always!" Tom said cheerfully, taking her mug over to the correct urn and filling her cup. Heading back to the counter in front of her, he confirmed, "I just made that batch not ten minutes ago, so it's gonna be really hot. Don't burn yourself."

Steph started doctoring her coffee up while still standing at the counter, "So, why the chipper Irish morning thing going on today?"

"Last night, we found out we're gonna be grandparents at the end of November or early December!"

"But you already have a gaggle of grandkids!" Steph pointed out to Tom.

"But this one is the first grand-monkey from Annie and Rich!" Tom said, throwing his hands up in the air with excitement.

"So, they're finally giving in to the constant haranguing from the family about pitter-pattering feet, huh?"

"Yep! We all knew we would eventually wear 'em down!"

Steph tried to muster more energy than what she'd been exuding so far, "Well, congratulations!"

"I remember when Annie was just a lil' monkey! I'll finally get to pull the Santa suit outta the attic and wear it again!" Tom said with a twinkle in his eye.

"Will it still fit?"

"Are you implyin' somethin'?"

With a smile and a wink, Steph answered, "No, I'm merely inquiring..."

"Yeah, I might have to put another reindeer or two or four onto the line-up to pull the sleigh, these days," Tom said, patting his belly and still beaming from the news of an upcoming birth of another grandchild.

"Did they tell you the sex?"

"No, they said they didn't even know, but I bet they do know and just aren't tellin' anyone," Tom said, tapping his fingers on the countertop. "Damn kids!"

"Well, this is great! We will all have to throw you a

Becoming a Grandpa Again party!"

"They have those, these days?" Tom asked.

"No... but for you? Maybe!" Steph said with a smile.

"Oh, hey! In celebratory fashion and because I need to clean the pan out, here's the last slice of the coffee cake you love so much," Tom said, taking the last piece out of the bakery display and sliding it across the counter to Steph.

"Thank you, but it was already on the plate," Steph said, reaching for the piece of cake.

"Do you want it or not?" Tom asked with a smile, pretending to take it back. "I'm tryin' to be nice here."

As Steph succeeded in getting a hold of the plate she winked at Tom and said, "Thank you... and I know this is really a bribe from you hoping I will tell you about what is discussed at these appointments."

"Sure, it could be considered a bribe for that... Really hadn't thought about that idea. I was just tryin' to be nice," Tom said.

"Then we will stick with the *nice* theory and forget the bribe – which wouldn't have worked on me anyway!" Steph laughed, picking up her mug of perfectly made coffee to head back toward her now familiar table.

Steph happened to look up from her morning crossword puzzle at just the same time Tom was directing a woman in her early to mid-thirties towards her. Taking this as the cue her next appointment had arrived Steph put her crossword puzzle away in her bag, took a napkin out of the holder, and dried the ring of steam off the table top left by her coffee mug.

"Hi, are you Steph?"

Steph stood up and greeted the next guest to her back corner, "Yes, hi. Good morning! Please, have a seat," Steph confirmed as she gestured toward the chair opposite her at the table.

"Thank you! Everyone is in such good spirits here, this morning!"

"Legalized stimulants and the news of a soon-to-be grandbaby make things a bit sunnier around here!"

"Are you... having... a grandchild?"

"Me? Oh no! Heck! I still have to do the child thing first before we even get around to the grandchild part!" Steph said, waving her hand in the air shushing off such an absurd thought. "No, no! Tom, over there at the counter, the one you just spoke to... He's the one with the grandchild on its way!"

"Oh, okay. Yeah, that would make more sense... You don't look like you're old enough to be having a grandchild anytime soon... I mean if you were, you'd be aging really well!"

"Thank you and we won't mention that observation to Tom — about him looking more like a grandparent than me, although he is much older! By the way, you are?"

"Julie. I'm Julie, nice to meet you."

"And nice to meet you, too," Steph responded, sitting down. "Please, have a seat."

Once seated, Julie asked, "So, how has this experiment been going for you?"

"Surprisingly, rather well," Steph answered with a nod. "No one has stood me up yet, so that's good."

"It is. It'd be rude for someone to take the time slot, then not show up," Julie agreed.

"It would be, and I hope that doesn't happen. I'm taking time off from my job to sit in this corner and listen to the secrets people don't want to tell anyone else. So, yeah, I hope I don't get stood up," Steph confirmed, scrunching up the napkin she had been using earlier to dry off the table, and depositing it into her coffee mug.

"Oh, that reminds me," Julie said, pointing over her shoulder toward Tom, who was helping another patron at the front counter. "He wanted to know if you needed any more coffee, or are you good?"

Looking over Julie's shoulder, Steph shrugged, "Eh, I'm good for now, but thank you for relaying the message. So, what brings you to the dark corner of a local coffee shop, today?"

"My parents are cheating on each other and it gets worse from there," Julie said quietly while looking at the surface of the table.

"Well, okay. Boy... Ummm..." Steph said with widened eyes, trying to find the right words to say, but nothing was coming to mind.

"Yeah, I feel the same way. I need to talk about it to someone but it's so embarrassing... I can't even tell my husband."

"How about I'll be quiet over on this side of the table and you start talking? And if you'd like to have me say something, ask me a question. Otherwise, I'll simply listen," Steph suggested.

"Okay," Julie said, shifting in her chair. "We can try that route. Okay... Ummm, where to begin? Well, about three months ago, I pulled into a gas station and I saw a woman who looked a lot like my mom, getting onto the back of a motorcycle with someone who is *not* my dad, and he was *much* younger, too!"

"Okay..."

"But this person only *looked* like my mom and I only caught a quick glimpse of her before they pulled out of the gas station and were gone. So, I really didn't give it a second thought. I've heard we all have doppelgangers in the world, so, there you go... I'd found my mom's."

"Alright... makes sense..." Steph added for verbal support.

"And then about a month ago..." Julie said as she began tracing circles on the table top with her fingers, "I was sitting in a local restaurant with some friends, and I saw my dad walk in with another woman on his arm who was *not* my mom!"

"Oooooo, that doesn't sound good," Steph sighed, leaning back in her chair. "Are you *sure* it was your dad?"

"Yeah, I saw him clearly."

"Did he see you?"

"No, they came in with another couple and were busy talking and laughing."

Experiencing a continual lack of wisdom to share at this point in time, Steph only said, "Uh oh..."

"Yeah, no kidding, uh oh. My night instantly went into the crapper," Julie said.

"Can I ask how long your parents have been married?" Steph asked.

"Well, there's a good question!" Julie said, rolling her eyes and shifting in her chair. "It turns out my parents have never been married to each other!"

"I didn't expect that answer!"

"Yeah, the whole thirty two years I've existed, I thought my parents were married. No one ever told me differently! I don't think my younger siblings know, either... As a matter of fact, I'm not sure anyone really knows!"

Confused with where this conversation was going, Steph asked, "How could anyone not know?"

"Yeah... Especially since we've all seen the wedding pictures!"

"But they're not married, right?"

"Yep, not married, but they have *wedding pictures*," Julie confirmed as her circles on the table top turned into the tapping of her fingers.

"Well, there's a new one! How exactly does *that* work?"

"Hold that thought," Julie said, holding her right index finger up to pause Steph's thoughts.

"Okay," Steph said.

"So, one night I stopped by my parent's house and

confronted my dad on this situation, and *this* is where it gets weird... My dad confirmed he *was* on a date with another woman who he's been seeing for the past few months, and my *mom* introduced the two of them!"

"Yep, we've hit major weirdness," Steph verbally agreed.

"So, with nothing to lose, I mentioned how I saw her *twin* getting on the back of a motorcycle at a gas station a few months ago with some guy *a lot younger* than she was... She blushes then admits it was her, and the guy is her boyfriend named Scott! So, I asked her how old he was and she tells me he's 36 years old, so everything is apparently okay because he's actually older than I am!"

Steph wanted to say something but realized she should start following the suggestion she'd put out there at the beginning of the conversation, to keep commentary to herself unless asked since she was now completely without words.

"Aren't you going to say something?" Julie asked, interrupting Steph's wordless abyss.

"I'm sorry," Steph said. "I'm not sure what to say, here."

"It's okay. The look on your face, I'm sure, is what my face looked like when they told me all of this."

"I bet!" Steph agreed.

Julie then added with heavy sarcasm, "And to throw salt into the wound, my mom follows up with, 'You should be proud to have a mom who's a cougar!'"

To make sure she would say something to support Julie, Steph mustered out the words, "I'm still speechless. I'm sorry."

"Oh, it gets better..." Julie said, tapping her fingers a little harder on the top of the table. "As I said, like you, I'm sure I was just sitting there with a shell-shocked look; I must have asked something along the lines of how long this has all been going on? And that's when they told me they'd actually never been married - that it was never legalized - they'd lived the past years as married but were never officially *married...* I don't know, it was just one big blur of chatter while I sat there in a numb state, on their couch, petting Muffin."

"Muffin?"

"Yeah, my parent's dog... But then again, maybe they aren't my parents?" Julie summarized out of exasperation while she waved both of her hands in front of herself. "Hell, I don't know anymore! I don't know what to think anymore!"

To appear somewhat useful on the other side of the table, Steph straightened up, "What else did they say? Or what do you remember?"

"Apparently I was a result of a party, one night, when my parents first met," Julie divulged with a roll of her eyes. "That says a lot for my parents, doesn't it?"

"Well, those things happen..."

"Yep, they do – I'm living proof," Julie said while pointing to herself. "Anyway, my dad claims he did the *right thing* and married my mom. They were both going to school at UCLA at the time and decided to run out to Vegas for the weekend and have Elvis walk her down the aisle..."

"Okay..."

"So, they do that – they pay for the highest wedding package available to make it *all* seem legit, took the pictures, Elvis showed up and kissed the bride, etcetera. But the officiant, that day, wasn't feeling very well and after the ceremony, he just went home and forgot to file the paperwork with the State of Nevada!"

"Ah!"

"Yeah... Ah!" Julie repeated, growing louder while she spoke. "Yeah, none of this was figured out until they went in one day, about twelve years later, to set up some legal and financial structures for the future of the family and their two businesses. When it was required to cough up a marriage certificate, that's when they learned the certificate was never filed, and then they were told common-law didn't actually count, which meant they were never married!"

"Well, then, they just get married and laugh about it later, right?" Steph suggested half-heartedly since she knew there was probably a lot more unhappiness still to come with this confession.

"No, actually they were setting up these outlines and trusts as a precursor to filing for divorce," Julie countered, managing to somewhat relax and lean back in her chair.

"That's a new one – a couple securing the future of their businesses prior to filing for divorce," Steph said.

"My parents have always gotten along as friends and business partners, but there was never romantic love there," Julie continued to explain and then put her hands up in the air with her fingers representing quotes as she then said, "They got, so-called *married*, off the result of a one-night stand, but if I hadn't been conceived, they both told me they would have never married each other; they were too different."

"At least it sounds like they had everything in order, although this scenario is highly nontraditional," Steph announced, trying to help the mood of the conversation, perhaps unsuccessfully so.

"True, I mean if you're going to get a divorce, it's courteous to set up everything first before you file..." Julie began to explain, verbally working her way through her family's situation. "But then again, if you look at it, for the fact they were more interested in saving the businesses and getting those lined up prior to filing for a divorce - that only illustrates they were looking at this inconvenience as a mere bump in the road rather than a whole drama-filled event."

"Yep, there's that – that's good..." Steph trailed off, again trying to bring some type of positive into the conversation.

"If there had been love there and it was a typical filing with the heartbreak and the scorn, and such, I doubt they would've come together to set up the businesses so they were safe from all divorce filings," Julie summarized as she continued to parse through her thoughts, out loud.

"Yeah..."

After Steph's audible subconscious response, Julie continued, "So, when they found out they weren't technically married, they figured they would start living more as roommates with the occasional built-in 'friends with benefits' theme, keeping together for all of the efforts of merging their lives together over the past dozen years - not rocking the boat anywhere... the insurance benefits, and keeping up the ruse for the sake of the children."

"Well..." Steph said, continuing to try and insert words where she could, but Julie was talking nearly a mile a minute. Besides, Steph had no idea what in the world to say with all of this information; she thought it best for Julie to be able to work through this situation herself as she sat nearby, spectating.

"I remember the day my parents decided to have different bedrooms. My mom said it was a result of losing too much sleep because dad snored so much. I had no idea that it was because they had the convenient option of an under the table divorce since paperwork was never filed!"

"I think staying together for the kids had a lot to do with it, too," Steph added.

"It played into it, they said. But they also followed that bit of info up with the fact that they didn't hate each other - they preferred to live together as business partners slash friends. But if they had to do the whole marriage thing, then it wasn't going to work out; they never wanted to be married to each other. The only reason they were married was because of me – their *surprise* baby!"

"Well, I'm sure they didn't say that, did they? I mean, it's not your fault."

"No, they phrased it as making an honest woman out of my mom, doing the right thing, and giving it a go because it must have been *fate*... The only thing it was... was a one-night stand!" Julie exclaimed, dropping both her arms down to her sides as if she had hit her mental capacity with this entire situation.

Feeling as if Julie had said as much as she was going to say, or could have said with this divulged secret, Steph asked, "Has anyone told your siblings yet?"

"I don't think so. I mean, no one had said anything to me, and this is certainly not something siblings would avoid talking about if it were a known fact."

"Are you going to tell them? Or are you going to leave it up to your parents?"

"It's not my mess to talk about – I'm going to leave it up to my parents."

"Do you think your parents are going to tell them?" Steph asked.

"They should..." Julie said, bringing her arms back up and resting them in her lap.

"Are your siblings in town, too?"

"No, I'm the only one who lives nearby – it just happened to be pure chance that I saw anything at all. I was driving through when I stopped at the gas station, and my dad was at a restaurant in a city closer to where I live... I'm sure they would have kept it all going without ever telling anyone anything, especially us kids."

"How are you going to process this news?" Steph paused, rewording her question, "How are you planning on relating to your parents from now on?"

"Processing is exactly what I will be doing for a while. Imagine if your parents told you this information?"

"I'd be in the same boat as you, that's for sure," Steph agreed.

"I guess, at the moment, I will have to treat my parents as individuals instead of a duo. I mean, I've never really had a close relationship with my dad anyway - he always rode on the coattails of my mom when it came to any type of a relationship since he was out of town working all of the time..." Julie said, parsing through a different route of thoughts on this matter. "Oh! My! Gawd! How much do you want to bet his *so-called out of town on business stories* were of him leading a second life, elsewhere?"

"You would have to ask him that," Steph responded to Julie's indirect question.

"I don't want to ask him anything, quite frankly," Julie said, shushing off that thought entirely.

"The only way you are going to be able to get through this is to talk with each of your parents," Steph said in an attempt to take control of the conversation, and at least route the overall mood onto some level of moderation. "I may not be a psychiatrist, but I do know the only way to work things out with people is to sit down and have a long, dragged out conversation, and clear the air."

"Yeah, I know... But I'm having a difficult time stomaching all of this unexpected news. How can I even look at either one of my parents knowing they've lied to me all these years? How can I even think of them as parents? How can I trust them, moving forward? Why didn't they just get a divorce and leave it at that?" Julie asked in quick succession, getting louder with each question. "That would've been much easier!"

"Well, if you're interested in what I have to say, even though I am not a licensed therapist..."

"Yes, I'm listening," Julie said, trying to calm down.

"Take my advice for what it's worth then... In

answer to your questions, if you had a happy childhood free of divorcing parents, endless fighting, and both of your parents looking at you and your siblings more like property rather than humans, they made the right choice not to tell any of you and remain *married* keeping everything peaceful. A piece of paper doesn't make a marriage and a happy family. Happiness comes from people working together toward common goals. It sounds like your parents did their best to ensure you and your siblings had a good home and a good support system to grow in. Seriously, if you had a good childhood experience, you're doing a lot better than most children."

"I had a good childhood..." Julie quietly admitted, looking down at the table again. "Truthfully, I've had a good adulthood with my parents, too. This info just knocked my world off kilter."

"Not to sound like I am lecturing here," Steph continued, "But to answer another question you posed – actually two of them – your parents are still the same people you've always known, you just happen to know a bit more about them now. For example, tell me about your mom... What's she like? What kind of person is she?"

"What do you mean?" Julie asked.

"Tell me examples of her hobbies... Was she the instigator of fun? Or did she prefer to be quiet and reserved? What did she like to do?"

"Well, she's always been the one on the go; her schedule was always jam-packed, especially with all of us kids. We had one of the best moms... everyday was a party with a new adventure! She was and still is a social butterfly..."

"She sounds like she's young at heart," Steph agreed with a smile, hoping the conversation was now heading toward more of an upbeat mood.

"Definitely! She tells me she wants to be like me if

she gets around to growing up!" Julie confirmed with a little laugh.

"Now, tell me about your dad."

"Well, I guess I don't know him as well as my mom. He was never around – was either out of town, in the garage, out playing golf, fishing, hanging out with his friends... I definitely wouldn't refer to him as the social butterfly... I mean, he does talk and he can smile when talking with people, but he wouldn't be comfortable talking about anything with people he doesn't know, like my mom can do anywhere."

"Maybe these differences you've noticed are just the tip of the iceberg?" Steph suggested. "Give me examples of things you've seen your parents doing the most throughout your life. Like, looking back over your childhood, what memories stand out about the times they spent with you or your siblings?"

"Okay... Well, my mom would go to basically all of my concerts, at least," Julie pointed out.

"Your school concerts?" Steph asked.

"No, I'm talking about the rock concerts my friends and I bought tickets to," Julie clarified, beginning to smile more.

"Did she go as a chaperone?"

"That was her assumed role, as well as driver, but she was right there with the rest of us dancing in the aisles and body surfing in the mosh pits. We were mistaken more for sisters than a mother and daughter," Julie said with a genuine smile on her face as the memories came back.

"Now, how about your dad? What's he like?"

"Truthfully, I just remember him working at the house, working away from the house, reading the newspaper, or puttering around in the garage. He never attended any school related functions, and he sure as hell would've never been found at a rock concert, let alone in a mosh pit..."

"I thought you were kidding about that," Steph said with a small laugh.

"My mom? Oh no, she's been in several mosh pits. She always said she found it exhilarating!"

"It sure sounds like your parents are two completely separate people, right down to their likes and dislikes! What did they do together?"

"They both had their own business ventures, but they also worked together since she was usually PR and he was the accountant type. She brought in the money and he managed it."

In an effort to keep the conversation light-hearted, Steph asked, "What were their businesses, if you don't mind me asking?"

"She started an adventure event business which catered to businesses promoting teamwork with their employees, or taking their clients out on day trips for promotional purposes..."

"Cool!" Steph exclaimed.

"Yeah, that's where a lot of our adventures came from with the zip-lining, and rock climbing, and whitewater rafting and such – I had the best birthday parties!"

"Sounds like it!"

"My dad's business, on the other hand," Julie continued, "is consulting. He used to work at a Fortune 100 company until it folded in a scandal. So, to avoid being involved in another headlining mess, he branched off on his own and started using his visionary skills of organization, details, and non-stop work ethics to help other companies improve their overall bottom lines, and efficiency in global markets."

"Wow! Did your parents work together then?"

"Initially? No. My dad couldn't see where zip-lining would help his business. But eventually, he gave into my mom's suggestions about offering the idea of an employee morale-improving outing for one of his companies."

"Why?"

"Because every time he worked with them, it seemed all of his energy was sapped by the end of the day just from trying to bring a modicum of happiness into their office; the employee turnover was huge and their budget for new-hires was astronomical versus their output."

"I'm guessing it went well?"

"It went very well! The company was sold on these quarterly performance-based outings which all of their employees worked towards. My dad's client base exploded; he needed clones to keep up with the business calling in from all the referrals. And my mom's business, pretty much went global instantly!"

"That's great!" Steph exclaimed again, getting wrapped up in all of Julie's exciting descriptions of her parents' work. "So, they work well as business partners, then?"

"Yeah, but not as a married couple," Julie confirmed.

"But they worked it out and raised happy kids, right?"

"Mmmm hmmm..." Julie agreed. "But aren't opposites supposed to attract?"

"In some instances, they do, but not always."

"I suppose, but it's going to take time to get used to all of this."

"Well, that's understandable and it *should* take time, actually. It would be unusual to accept this situation instantly... I think it's healthier to take the time to understand this new information completely," Steph summarized. "As for the whole trust issue and how to view your parents from now on, I would personally look at it this way... If your parents have never done you or the rest of their kids wrong and have provided a happy home for everyone, then I wouldn't look at it as a trust issue, per se. I would view it as, I don't know, a sort of coping mechanism they created when they found they weren't a good match, then found out they weren't legally married, but decided to find another way to stay together, anyway, for the benefit of everyone else and their businesses. They could have blown the whole thing up, ruining other people's lives including yours. Quite frankly, I think they did everyone, including their kids and themselves, a great service by sticking together and coming to an arrangement for getting along and working it out."

"You sound like a shrink," Julie smiled, soaking in Steph's soapbox speech.

"Thank you, but I'm not," Steph answered, pushing her coffee mug around the table by the handle. "I've only lived through a lot in life, and have observed other people's situations. Of course, I can also speak to you as a child from a home ripped apart by divorce. So, take it from me – you got the better end of the deal. Your parents kept your family together. I think that's great! Were *able* to keep everything status quo for the benefit of others, and their businesses, and take care of their personal needs and desires on their own time. I would be viewing the both of them as incredible people who have unique outlooks on life with certain goals and made everything work.

"That's true... They did make everything work... perfectly, in fact. To this day, I would still know nothing if I hadn't randomly seen them out in public with their respective partners," Julie admitted. "But I will also say I'm not going to refer to someone barely four years older than me as my *step-dad* when my husband is two years older than he is."

"I don't think anyone is expecting you to," assured Steph.

"My mom said the same thing."

"Then there is nothing to worry about there!" Steph said, lightly clapping her hands together.

"What about my brother and two sisters? Who's

going to tell them?"

"You said it yourself, earlier... Leave that up to your mom and dad. But I would tell them to hop on it so you don't wind up giving it away and putting yourself in an awkward position, conversation-wise, somewhere down the road," Steph advised. "Now that it's out on the table, it would be best if it were out on the table with the immediate family, at least... less pressure on you that way."

"I'll share that idea with my parents this weekend. We are due out there for my dad's birthday. I have the next few days to put aside all of the weirdness and get comfortable with all of these ideas."

"I'm sure it'll be the same for them. I'm sure they're wondering how you're going to absorb this information, too. I would even bet they're a bit nervous and are hoping for a positive outcome," Steph suggested to Julie who was looking out the window, listening, intently.

Julie looked back at Steph then down at her watch. "Oh! I don't mean to be rude but I have to run! My daughter has a field trip today and I'm chaperoning. There are really only two of us who volunteer so I get to go on *a lot* of field trips!" Julie said, gathering her purse into her lap and looking for her keys. "Thank you so much for meeting with me and giving me a new perspective. I guess I really am being quite childish about all of this, but it's a helluva thing to wrap my head around, you know?"

"No problem!" Steph said, both her and Julie standing up. "I'm glad I could help with my non-shrink background. I don't know if I gave you the right advice, but from an everyday person point of view, I sure hope it helps."

Julie extended her hand toward Steph for a handshake, "I truly appreciate it, and I think you've done a lot to help calm my nerves... so much appreciated. Seriously, thank you!"

Steph smiled, "Again, you are certainly welcome and have fun on your field trip today!"

"Thank you," Julie said, slinging her purse onto her shoulder and grabbing her keys off the table, "Thank you again!"

Soon after Julie left, Tom came over with a pot of coffee. "Boy, you two seemed to be in deep with whatever you were talkin' about," Tom said, reaching the table and setting the pot of coffee down. "Did she ask you if you wanted more coffee?"

"Yeah, she did and thank you, but you were busy with someone and she got right into the meat and potatoes of why she was here."

"Are you gonna stick around for a while?" Tom asked.

"Yeah, I can. Have a seat," Steph said, gesturing to the other chair. "I take it this is the eye of the storm before the lunch crowd arrives?"

"Yep," Tom said, sitting down and looking at his watch. "Give it about a half an hour, then the party is gonna start up again."

"Going back to the good news, did Annie and her other half at least hint at the sex of the baby?" Steph asked.

"Yeah, just a bit. They told us they like the names of Noelle and Nicholas being the little one was due 'round December."

"They're mean," Steph said, laughing.

"Yes. Yes, they are," Tom confirmed. "By the way, what was covered in this last appointment?"

"I like how you slid that question in," Steph said, sliding her hand through the air to demonstrate.

"You noticed that, huh?" Tom asked.

"You being sneaky? Yeah, I noticed," laughed Steph.

"Can you divulge anything?"

"Elvis," Steph revealed.

"Elvis?"

"Mmmm hmmmm, we briefly spoke of Elvis," Steph confirmed.

"You're mean," Tom said.

"Yes. Yes, I am," Steph agreed with a kind smile.

Jimmy

"Sittin' back here in the shadows, I bet you're the lady listenin' to everyone's deep, dark secrets, aren't you?"

"That'd be me," Steph said, looking up from her tablet. "Is it that dark back here?"

"Well, for my eyes, yeah. But I'm sure everyone else can see you just fine."

"You must be Jim?" Steph asked.

"All my friends call me Jimmy."

"All my friends call me.... Well, they call me Steph..."

"Well, Steph... I have a story for ya'. Somethin' I've never told anyone in my life, even my Momma!" Jimmy confessed as he reached the table, pulled out a chair, and sat down with his sandwich and a can of soda. "But before I do, can I ask why you're doin' this? Or how'd you come up with this idea?"

"I've been coming to this coffee shop for the past three years and over the years, have become friends with the shop owner, Tom."

"Tommy! He's a good guy! I've known him since he was crappin' in his drawers!"

With a look of shock on her face, Steph exclaimed,

"Wow! I didn't expect to hear that!" Steph continued to laugh for a moment longer since she didn't think she would *ever* hear something like that during her little experiment. She was also *very* sure Tom would've never let her do this experiment in his establishment if there was ever a chance of *hearing* this type of information about him, either.

"Ah, you laugh, but I've been puttin' up with that lil' shit my entire life!" Jimmy continued, playing off of Steph's laugh.

Steph was looking at Jimmy and wondering if she was starting to see a resemblance with Tom... maybe? "Are you... Are you brothers?"

"Nah, we're cousins," Jimmy grinned, flashing clean and weathered teeth. "I've known that knucklehead since I was five years old, and he's been taggin' around with me ever since. I can't shake him!"

"Okay... Yeah, I can sort of see a resemblance..."

"Yeah, our moms were sisters... I'm the better lookin' one out of the two of us, though," Jimmy pointed out, sitting up a bit straighter and preening. "Back in the mid-fifties, Tom, his little sister Janie, and their mom moved in with my family since his dad took off on the three of 'em. He was a mean drunk; an absolute ass!"

"Oh, I'm sorry to hear that," Steph said, glancing over Jimmy's shoulder at Tom who was busy ringing up another customer.

"Ah, don't be. It was good he left. He drank himself to death and it was better for the rest of us that he took that last drink. He wasn't worth the air his body displaced!"

"Is this your secret? I should first..."

"No, this ain't no secret. Norman was an asshole! Everyone knew that, even Tommy."

Just then, Steph saw Tom weaving his way through the tables toward the back corner, coming up behind

Jimmy. "Who let this guy into this fine establishment? I should really hire better security!" Tom said loudly, walking over to the table and giving Jimmy's shoulder a friendly squeeze. "Alright, what's this bellowin' ol' geezer told you so far?"

Jimmy hunched over the table toward Steph and said in a loud whisper, smiling, "Tell him "Nothin'. I haven't told you nothin'!"

"Jimmy, here, has told me *nothing*!" Steph repeated, smiling and winking at Tom.

"Oh, it's Jimmy, I see! That means you two are already friends... he's told you darn close to everything, hasn't he?" Tom chuckled, throwing his hands up in the air.

"Not everything, Tommy... Only that you used to crap in your drawers, and I've been your idol since the day you were born!"

"Everyone starts and ends with crappin' in their drawers and since you're older than me, Jimmy, you're next!"

"Yeah, yeah, yeah..." Jimmy fake-scowled.

"Alright, you two... No fighting," Steph lightheartedly reprimanded, waggling her finger. "Break it up or I'll have to put you two in opposite corners of the room!"

"Yeah, listen to Steph here! Run along and leave us alone – I have to catch her up on all the dirt I have on you!"

"I'm the cleanest guy ya' know!" Tom exclaimed, throwing his towel over his left shoulder and backing away slowly. "And no tellin' her anymore of my secrets!!!"

"I thought *you* said you were the cleanest guy I knew? How could there be any secrets?"

"Exactly!"

"Run along. I'm sure there's another pot of coffee ya' need to make," Jimmy joked, shooing Tom away from behind him.

"I'm watching you!" said Tom, holding two fingers up and gesturing that he had his eyes on Jimmy.

Jimmy retorted in a loud singsong voice and without turning around, "Watch me all you want – I can't see your ugly mug and that's all that matters!"

Tom turned and started walking away, loudly muttering about installing a better security system to keep out the riff raff.

"You two sure *sound* like brothers!"

"Well, we grew up in the same house for a while... Shit! We drove our mothers crazy!"

"How did you know about this little experiment of mine? Do you frequent this fine establishment?" Steph asked.

"Nah, I'm not a coffee kinda guy. Every Wednesday mornin', Tommy and I get out on the greens and rip 'em up!"

"Oh, you two are good at golf?"

"No. We're both good at creating divots and tearing around on my golf cart!" Jimmy admitted with a loud, boisterous laugh, causing Tom to look up from behind the counter on the other side of the restaurant with a definite look of concern.

"Sounds like you play golf like I did that one time I tried, but I didn't get to drive a golf cart..." Steph confessed. "What's that one line? *Golf is a good walk spoiled...* Yeah, that's sort of how I see that waste of time."

"Ah, you know some golf lore, do you?" Steph could detect a hint of surprise in his voice.

"I come from a long line of 'goffers' and none of those talents made it into my DNA; neither the talent nor the patience! I can't even stand mini-putt, it's that bad!"

"I hear ya'!" Jimmy snorted. "I only got the golf cart 'cuz I thought it would be fun to screw around on!" Jimmy confessed. "But the only place I can drive it is out on the golf course now 'cuz I once had it out in my neighborhood, and wound up having a sneezin' fit which caused me to drive the cart onto someone's lawn and land on top of a prized rose bush!"

"Oh!"

"Yeah, everyone got into a big ol' stink about this thorny monstrosity over in some jackass's yard! So, my wife told me I'd better keep to a golf course so I don't piss people off!" Jimmy chuckled, slapping a knee.

"How did the rose bush fare?"

"Ah... I tore it up pretty good; shredded it, actually!" Jimmy continued. "Drivin' over it didn't do it any good, and then tryin' to get off of it, well.... That definitely finished it off! Had to pay the neighbor five hundred freakin' dollars to ensure they didn't make a stink out of it with the cops. Friggin' blood money, that was!" Jimmy said, leaning back in his chair. "If that's what those damn bushes truly cost, no wonder long stemmed roses are always an arm and a leg when ya' have to buy 'em!"

"When you *have* to buy them?" Steph asked with an arch of her eyebrow.

"Yeah, ya' know for Valentine's and when you get into trouble and ya' wanna smooth everything over with the wife," Jimmy admitted.

"I wouldn't know," Steph answered, reaching for the coffee pot.

"About Valentine's Day? Don't ya' have anyone givin' you any roses?"

"No, not about Valentine's Day... I'm talking about being in trouble with the wife!" Steph laughed.

"Well, if ya' ever get in trouble and roses are required, a trip to the jewelry store is a good add-on for extra insurance, too!" Jimmy suggested, pointing his finger at Steph and winking, driving the point home while spoken from pure experience.

"So, is neighborhood vandalism with your golf cart

your deep dark secret?" Steph inquired.

"Nah... My secret is a bit more, I don't know... more sinister than tearing up rose bushes. It's ummm, hmmmm..."

"Well, before you start," Steph said, holding her hand up, "I'm first going to state my disclaimer so you don't tell me anything I shouldn't hear."

"I already told ya' Tommy used to shit his drawers!"

"Well, yeah, that... But I'm talking about illegal things."

"Oh, yeah. Some of this is illegal..." Jimmy said, nodding his head.

"About Tommy? I mean, Tom?" Steph asked with a worried look on her face.

"Nah, he's a good kid. I'm talkin' 'bout someone else."

"You?"

Jimmy crossed his arms in front of him, "No, not me. I'm no angel, but I'm not the devil, either."

"Okay, well.... I will tell you my disclaimer and then you can figure it out from there."

"Okay, shoot."

From absolute memorization, Steph quickly rambled off her disclaimer, "I'm a law-abiding citizen and would rather not hear anything illegal done by you or anyone you know because I don't want to be put into the position of knowing something that should be reported."

"Well, what I have to say is about someone who is long gone. I don't think it would make much of a difference, these days, if I told you what he did fifty or so years ago."

"Okay, well... I will listen and if everyone is gone and there's nothing to worry about, then so be it."

"Alright... so, here goes..." Jimmy said, exhaling deeply.

"Okay," Steph said, readjusting herself in her chair, getting comfortable for what was sounding like a good story from someone who was excellent at telling long tales.

"Well, like I told ya', Tommy's father Norman up and died one night when he took his last drink..."

"Yeah," Steph said, adding her one cream and one sugar to her coffee.

"And with no money in the bank, Tommy's momma along with his little sister Janie, moved into our house... We had a big house out by the park and more than enough room to spare, so it was all good."

"Yep..."

"Okay... So, both our mommas were good-lookin' women - there was no doubt about it! I mean, that's why Tommy and I are such handsome men, right?"

"Definitely!" Steph agreed with a smile and a wink. "Well, you being the better looking one, of course!"

"Ah, you shouldn't be winkin' at me so much... My wife might get jealous!"

"I'll smooth it all over with some long-stemmed roses and a trip to the jewelry store!" Steph said as she was enjoying Jimmy's candor.

"Oh, we have ourselves a smart one, over here, Tommy!" Jimmy shouted while glancing over his shoulder at Tom standing behind the counter.

"I know! That's why we're friends!" Tom shouted back to Jimmy.

"Alright, where were we?" Jimmy wondered out loud. "Oh yeah! Okay, so our mommas were good-lookin' women and now that Tommy's momma was a widow 'cuz Norman dropped, the men came a-callin'. Good lordy! They came in droves to the doorstep of my parents' house! Talk about a woman gettin' more long-stemmed roses than any other woman ever had in the history of this world!"

"How many men were lined up in the yard?" Steph asked before taking another sip of her coffee.

"You would think a ton of them by the number of roses, but over time, the number of men flockin' out in the yard went from darn close to twenty down to just one, but the roses stayed plentiful."

"Did this particular one own a greenhouse?" Steph quipped.

"Yeah, it was green... Full of green, but there were no plants!"

"Huh?"

"His name was Santo Kaczmarek, but his nickname was Sam," Jimmy said, sitting up in his chair and resting his forearms on the table top.

"How do you get Sam out of Santo?"

"Santo is Italian for Sam."

"That last name didn't sound Italian," Steph said.

"Good ear.... Nah, his momma was Italian and his papa was the Polish immigrant fresh off the boat who fell in love with an Italian bird! She was a breath of fresh air and he'd certainly never seen a woman with such a vibrant personality... Sammy showed up about 14 months later."

"So, he went by Sammy instead of Sam?"

"He went by many names: Mr. Kaczmarek to those who respected and looked up to him in local business and in church. Sam to his friends outside of business, and lastly, Sammy Slick to those who cavorted with him in his separate life not many people knew about, locally."

"Sammy Slick?" Steph asked eyebrow arched. "That sounds sort of like a mafia nickname."

"Yeah, it does, doesn't it?" Jimmy said, smiling coyly at Steph.

"Is it?" Steph asked.

"Well, Sam had some uncles he grew up with who ran the neighborhoods of New York – he was raised in that environment. So, when he became of age 'round his early teens, they started takin' him out and teachin' him the ways. He was big for his age, and that got him the position of sentry when there was a job to be done."

"Oh...." Steph chimed in with concern.

"And when a job was goin' down, he observed and learned."

"Ohhhh...." Steph said, the concern growing.

"So, fast forward twenty five or so years, and Sammy hears through the grapevine about Norman droppin' and realizes Tressa is up for grabs..."

"Grabs?"

"She's available, that's what I mean," Jimmy clarified.

"That sounds much better."

"Anyway, he blocks off some time to go a-courtin'..."

"Wait... now how does Sammy know Tom's mom?" Steph asked, trying to make sure she had all the facts in Jimmy's story.

"He really didn't, but had seen her with Norman and had no idea how those two ended up married. He had always thought it was an arranged marriage, or somethin', because Tressa was way too good for Norman. And Sammy knew Norman through business dealings..."

"Mr. Kaczmarek business dealings, or Sammy Slick business dealings?"

"Sammy Slick dealings," Jimmy confirmed.

"Ah."

"Yeah, so, Sammy always admired Tressa from afar. But, when Norman dropped, Sammy turned up his game and positioned himself for the number one applicant to be considered..."

"And you said Norman died because of drinking?" Steph asked.

"Yeah..."

"Was Norman involved with Sammy at the time of his demise?"

"The question should be, when was Norman *not* in trouble or involved with Sammy, in some capacity?"

"Where was Norman found?"

Jimmy leaned back in his chair again and asked, "Why all of these questions?"

"Well, I have a hypothetical I'm working through at the moment," Steph admitted.

"Okay, well... Let's see... If I remember correctly, he was found behind a dumpster out on Clark and Henry..."

"Was the dumpster behind a building?"

"Yeah, it was behind one of the Kaczmarek properties, actually. Huh... Small world..." Jimmy mused.

"Did he die of anything else? Was he shot, or hit by a car, or stabbed, or die of hypothermia?"

"No. He just drank himself to death. Everyone always wagered he would meet his demise through a bottle of booze, and that's what he did."

"I'm wondering if he didn't actually die of alcohol poisoning?" Steph suggested.

"Well, yeah... He drank himself to death."

"Yeah, but if he was used to being drunk all the time and didn't die of anything else..." Steph said, piecing together the clues, "I'm wondering if he wasn't intentionally poisoned with *a lot* of alcohol to make him die, in order to get him out of the picture if Tressa was a fine woman... who was admired from afar... as his body was found on a Kaczmarek property?"

It took nearly a minute for Jimmy to process what Steph was suggesting, but then he slammed his hand on top of the table, "Oh!!! Oh! Holy shit! Oh! I had never put those two pieces together!!! Holy shit!"

"Uh huh...." Steph said with a hint of a smile on her lips.

"Well, shit! That wasn't my secret, either, but holy shit! If *that's* not a secret!!!!!"

"Doesn't Tom know where his dad died?" Steph asked.

"Nah, he was only four years old and doesn't

remember much about his father. I think he's blocked out all of those early memories, which is just as well."

"Well," Steph chuckled still a little shocked at her revelation, "What was your secret?"

"Well, my secret pales in comparison to your hypothesis, that's for sure!"

"Sorry about that... Maybe I am too skeptical of everyone, but the info was sure matching up. Did the cops ever ask around about Norman's death?"

"Sammy owned the cops so, I doubt it."

"Well, that answer sure ups the percentage of my hypothetical being right, doesn't it?"

"It sure does, and no tellin' Tommy 'bout that, either. Tommy looked up to Sammy especially since Sammy treated him, and his momma, and his siblings so well. Any of this conversation would probably crush him."

"I promise none of this will get to Tom through me. I don't tell him anything about the conversations I have with people," Steph assured Jimmy.

"Oh, that must just drive him crazy!" Jimmy said, bursting into laughter once more, his slight beer gut shaking with glee. Tom looked over again and just shook his head.

"It does. He tries, every time I see him, to get me to give up the goods. But I know his tricks," Steph grinned.

"Yeah, since that morning of golf when he told me 'bout this idea of confessions and I told him I had one, and to sign me up, he's been losin' his mind about what I was going to say! I just love torturing that lil' shit! Payback for all that babysitting I had to do with him while I was a teenager and he was a tagalong!"

"Well, what was the secret you were planning on telling me?"

"Yeah, okay.... Hold on, I have to remember where I was before we took a detour from my mental path..."

Steph tried to help Jimmy along with where he left

off, "Sammy was trying to get Tressa's attention and..."

"Oh yeah, Sammy had positioned himself as the prime candidate for Tressa's now empty dance card," Jimmy said, sitting up straight in his chair again.

"Did Tressa know what was up with Sammy?"

"I remember hearin' my momma tellin' Auntie Tressa that Sam Kaczmarek was not someone she should hang around with because she had *heard* things. She didn't know if these things were *true*, but she had definitely *heard* things."

"So, what did Tressa do?"

"She went out on a couple of dates with him, and he treated her like a queen."

"Did she ever find out what was going on?"

"No, not that I know of and I know Sammy was very good at keepin' his two lives separate; Tressa would really have had to do a lot of sleuthin' to learn anything about Sammy."

"And she didn't look into it?"

"No, and really, why would she?" Jimmy asked.

"I guess out of caution, and curiosity, and peace of mind especially since she had two kids," Steph suggested.

"Back then, women didn't really ask questions, and with two kids to look after and support... You know, if you've got somethin' good, you don't rock the boat."

"I guess..."

"And Sammy was a one-eighty compared to Norman. Oh, he treated her and those kids very well. If the subject of Tom's childhood ever comes up, he will have only the greatest things to say about his stepfather and his momma!"

"So, they got married, then?"

"Yep, they got married. Had a set of twins a couple of years into the marriage, too; the picture perfect family of two parents and four kids. They were all very happy... Sammy made sure of it," Jimmy said, pulling his cold grilled cheese and soda closer to him.

"He seems to have been very devoted and insistent on making her happy, like it was his life's mission, or something," Steph observed.

"He once told me and Tommy he wanted the same love his parents had. The same set up; the picture perfect life... and for him, Tressa was the one. He said she was a bit stubborn to begin with, not falling for all of his smooth talkin'. But he also said that's what made her more interesting – she was a challenge. She didn't fall for the shiny loot and the flowers and the sweet talkin'. She was a seasoned woman with her head on straight and didn't take crap along with bein' gorgeous. He was in love. I think Tressa and the kids were probably the only people he truly loved, besides his parents and family members who didn't piss him off. Everyone else was expendable."

"Ah, well there are definitely some days I feel the same..." Steph nodded.

"Me, too."

"So, okay... on with your story," Steph said, gesturing for him to continue and picking up her cooling coffee.

"Okay, yeah.... Anyway, there was one week during the summer when I was eleven years old and Tommy was almost six years old, and our mommas had gone upstate to visit their other sisters and attend a funeral for a past classmate. My dad couldn't get away..."

"What did he do for a living?"

"Construction... And when it's sunny, you make hay! Well, in his case it was buildings, but if the sun was shining, you don't go on vacation, you stay home and work."

"Yep, that makes sense," Steph nodded.

"So, Sammy agreed to watch the kids, since his schedule was a bit more lax due to his *self-employment*."

"Okay..."

"Well, most of the time we were hangin' out with Sammy and he took us down to the boardwalk, out to the beach, that kind of thing. But one day, he had to work. So, he got us kids some babysitters..." Jimmy explained, picking up his sandwich.

"Okay..."

"So, yeah.... Shirley took the train over and babysat the twins, and Gus picked Tommy and me up for a day of fun..."

"Who were Shirley and Gus?"

"Associates of Sammy's," Jimmy said, biting into his grilled cheese.

"What did they do?"

"Well, Shirley was given a couple of nights off to come over and babysit the babies..." Jimmy said with a full mouth.

"She worked nights doing what?"

Still chewing, Jimmy smiled, "What do *you* think she did at night being an associate of Sammy's?"

Catching on, Steph gasped, "Oh!!!!"

"Yeah, she came into the house all decked out! My gawd! You could put her out on the dance floor and shine a light on her and she would twinkle like a disco ball with all the shiny stuff she wore, all glitzed up and displayin' her wares!" Jimmy said, wiping his mouth. "And I can still smell the overwhelming amounts of perfume she wore! I want to say it was 'Evening in Paris' – that perfume that came in a blue bottle... A little bit of it was fine, but I'm still convinced she used half a bottle every day, and whenever I smell that scent or somethin' close to it, I still remember Shirley strollin' into Sammy's and Tressa's house all decked out like she was goin' to the Met for an opera!"

"She was all dressed up to go babysitting?"

"Sammy figured since she was a female, she would know what to do with a couple of toddlers, but he assumed wrong – especially when she showed up in a glitzy evening gown and an ostrich feather boa!" Jimmy explained between short bursts of laughter.

Joining in with Jimmy's infectious laughter, Steph asked, "What in the world was she thinking, showing up for a babysitting job all dressed up?"

"I'm sure she thought with an invitation out to Sammy's house away from the city, she should make a good impression. But she forgot about that *tiny detail* of babysitting three small kids... I'll never forget the look on her face when the kids were introduced to her and she remembered why she was there in the first place!"

"And what time did she get there?"

"About eleven..." Jimmy started laughing again and pointing toward his half-eaten grilled cheese, "You know, just in time for lunch!"

"Let me guess... Peanut butter and jelly was being served up for lunch and she was the one making them... in an evening gown?" Steph asked, still laughing.

"Yep, she didn't know a thing about kids and Sammy didn't tell her much, especially since kids weren't exactly his forté, either. By the time we got home from an interesting day with Gus, there were ostrich feathers all over the house!" Jimmy said, now slapping his knee and laughing nearly to the point of falling off his chair. "Lord! That woman was pissed! She stomped right past us when we got back, met Gus out on the front porch, and demanded a ride, *immediately*, back to the city! Tommy and I got stuck cleanin' up the house before Sammy got back home later that evening...
There were toys and food everywhere! We found Janie makin' cookies in the kitchen, the best way a four year old could without supervision. Betsy was nappin' in the tub, and Bobby was covered in powder and runnin' around butt-naked upstairs!"

"Did Sammy ever find out about any of this?" Steph asked.

"Yeah, we were still cleanin' as best we could when

he got home. When he realized Shirley wasn't there watchin' all of us kids, he hit the roof!"

"I bet he did!"

"I don't know whatever happened between everyone later, but I'm thinkin' that's the day Sammy realized just because a person has lady parts doesn't mean that person knows what to do with three little kids throughout the day!"

"And there's the fact she showed up in an evening gown and a boa... That boa is just asking for trouble with three kids!"

"Oh, that's an understatement! You wouldn't believe how many feathers it takes to make one boa!" Jimmy exclaimed. The people at other tables were glancing their way, attention drawn by Jimmy's raucous laughter.

"How was your day out with Gus?"

"Well, he had some errands to do on our way out to the beach that afternoon..."

"Like what?"

"Well, he had some debt-collecting to do..."

"Ohhh," Steph said, amusement shifting to concern, once again catching onto what Jimmy was hinting at..

"Mmmm hmmmm.... When we first got into the car, he asked me if I could whistle and I showed him I could, rather proudly. Then he asked me if I could do it louder, and I did. I was thinkin' we were gonna go whistle at all the girls out on the beach..."

"Why did he want you to whistle?"

"He had me do what ol' Sammy Slick did for his uncles back in the day," Jimmy said.

"You had to stand guard?"

"Yep..."

"Where was Tom?"

"He stayed in the car playin' with some toys he'd brought along. He was only five or six at the time," Jimmy explained.

"How many stops did you wind up making?" Steph asked.

"We had five stops altogether... he was supposed to do those errands the day before but he screwed around and figured he'd just do 'em on the way out to the beach instead," Jimmy said, taking a long drink from his soda. Steph noticed it was a ginger ale and wondered briefly if he had gotten it at the coffee shop.

"What happened at these stops?" Steph asked.

Placing his soda back on the table, Jimmy continued to explain, "Four of them were rather quick, what with the threats and the brandishing of Gus' gun, but the fifth one erupted in gunfire and we ran for it! I had to jump in the car while Gus was already drivin' it!"

"Seriously?!?" Steph asked in amazement.

"Yeah, Gus came flyin' out of that building and ran right past me – I didn't even know it was him when he ran by. He forgot I was standin' guard, jumped into his car and then took off!"

"He *forgot* about you?!?" Steph gasped, leaning into the table.

"I s'pose ya' forget about things when people are shootin' at ya'..."

"I suppose so!" Steph said, eyes wide with disbelief.

"When I recognized him - since two hours prior was the first time I had ever seen him in my life, I started runnin' toward the car but saw him get in and take off, completely forgettin' about me!"

"What did you do?" Steph asked, now hanging on every word.

"I stopped altogether, wonderin' what to do, and turned around just in time to see someone runnin' toward me. But as soon as they saw I was a lil' punk-ass kid, they swerved and ran right past me realizin' I wasn't Gus. All I can say is thank the sweet lord I turned around and they realized I wasn't Gus or another adult who could have been working with Gus..."

"No kidding!"

"So, this guy takes off down the street runnin' in the same direction Gus took off in the car, and I just stood there wonderin' what to do!"

"Oh, my gawd!"

"About half a minute later, from the intersection behind me, I hear a car horn and a whistle... It was Gus wavin' at me to haul ass to the car! So, I took off runnin' as fast as I could, came 'round the back side of the car, and he started movin'!"

"You weren't in the car yet?!?" Steph asked, realizing she probably hadn't blinked yet since her eyes were getting dry.

"I don't think he cared! I jumped onto the running board of the front passenger side and dove into the open window, landin' my face down by his right foot pressed on the accelerator, and puttin' my nose up close and personal to the razor he had along his right ankle underneath the cuff of his pants! My legs were still hangin' out of the window as he held onto the back of my shirt while he careened around corners makin' sure I didn't fly out of the car!"

"Pardon my French, but... holy shit!"

"No shit, holy shit!" Jimmy nearly shouted, getting wrapped up into his story, too.

"What was Tom doing?" Steph asked.

"Oh, he was on the backseat floor the entire time, laughin' at all of the fun and playin' with his toys. He didn't have a clue!" Jimmy explained, shaking his head.

"So you all got out of there okay?" Steph asked.

"Yeah. We finally got to the beach, had an ice cream cone and went back home... We didn't get a chance to whistle at any girls, either," Jimmy smiled, snapping his fingers of an opportunity missed.

"Did word get back to Sammy about Gus taking you out on some *errands*?"

"Yeah, 'bout a week or so later, Sammy pulled me

aside and asked if Gus drove us straight out to the beach like he was supposed to, or if he made some stops on the way?" Jimmy recollected, leaning back in his chair with his arms folded. "I told him that he ran five errands on the way out to the beach because Gus said it made more sense to do it that day while we were drivin' by rather than the day before when he wasn't even out in that neck of the woods."

"And?" Steph asked impatiently for the rest of the story.

"And I never saw Gus again, either."

"Well, there you go... So, no one except you, Gus, and Sammy know what went down?"

"And now you," Jimmy pointed out, gesturing toward Steph with a nod.

"No worries, I won't tell anyone," Steph promised.

"Good. To this day, Tommy continues to hold Sammy in great regard. Sammy was everything to him, and Tommy was everything to Sammy. Tressa, Tommy, Janie, Betsy and Bobby gave Sammy the chance at a family he always wanted but never thought he'd get..."

"Didn't Tom ever figure out what Sammy did on the side?"

"Nah... Shortly after that whole fiasco, I think Sammy realized if he wanted the wholesome family thing, he couldn't be livin' that kinda life and bringin' it around so close to home. He would never forgive himself if somethin' happened to Tressa or the kids. So, he groomed his youngest cousin to come in and run the different avenues of the family business with the understanding he would still be actin' as the 'Chairman Emeritus' of the entire operation, and was gonna live in a retirement status to do the 'family-man' gig, from there on."

"Did Tressa ever ask where the money came from?" Steph asked.

"It was understood by all that he and his family had

hotels and other commercial properties which brought in money, and he had a diverse portfolio of investments, and that was all there was to it," Jimmy said, clapping his hands together.

"And there you go."

"Yep, there you go..."

Steph straightened herself up in her chair, inhaled fully and then said with a smile, "Well, we have definitely covered quite a bit, haven't we?"

"Yeah, and then some!" Jimmy gathered his empty soda can and napkin onto his plate. "Thanks for that theory I'd never even thought of.... I mean, I have no idea as to what went down all those years ago. But I do know both Tressa and Sammy were very happy and they raised four great kids."

"Well, that's all that counts, as far as I'm concerned," Steph said, smiling and pointing to Tom, who had been walking up behind Jimmy. Jimmy swiveled in his seat, spotting Tom.

"So, you two have been over here long enough! Do you want to fill me in on anything?" Tom asked, suave smile at the ready.

Jimmy looked at Steph, "Do you have anything to tell Tommy?"

"No, I don't have anything to tell Tommy..." Steph smiled, then returned the question to Jimmy, "Do you have anything to tell Tommy?"

"Nope," Jimmy answered with a shrug of his shoulders, looking back at Tom. "Well, it looks like we have nothin' to say over here... Do you have anything to say to us, Tommy?"

"You're just as stubborn as *she* is, you ol' coot!" Tom said.

"You two remind me of that movie, 'Grumpy Old Men'," Steph laughed, watching the impromptu comedic sketch unfold between Tom and Jimmy.

Jimmy snapped his fingers and pointed at Tom,

"That's what we should do instead of golf!"

"What?" Tom asked, slightly taken aback.

"We should pull a couch out to the lake and go fishin' on Wednesday mornings!" Jimmy exclaimed.

"And I'll bring the bacon and the beer!" Tom offered.

"Are you bringin' the couch, too?" Jimmy asked.

"No! If I'm supplying the bacon and the beer, we're usin' your couch!" Tom said with another laugh.

"Nah... The missus would never allow that... so much for that idea!" Jimmy said, shaking his head and throwing his hands up in the air.

Steph, enjoying the back and forth banter, suggested, "Why don't you two use Jimmy's golf cart?"

Both Tom's and Jimmy's attentions were immediately captured by Steph's viable idea, "She's a smart one, Tommy! That's a great idea!"

"Yeah! We could rotate golfin' and fishin' on Wednesday mornings!" Tom suggested while lightly punching Jimmy in his right arm.

"Yeah," Jimmy agreed, starting to laugh again. "We could play an honest golf game one week, and then be honest with our fishin' tales the next week!"

"Sure, yep.... An honest game of golf! *That's* what we call it!" Tom mocked.

Jimmy turned back toward Steph, "Alright, young lady! Daylight's a'wastin' and I still need to find some trouble to get into today!"

Steph stood up, and looked over Jimmy's shoulder as he was also getting up from his chair, "Tom... Thank you for telling your cousin about my little experiment." Then looking back at Jimmy, Steph smiled, "Jimmy... Thank you for being a part of my little experiment. I enjoyed our conversation today and thank you again for all the inside dirt on Tom!"

With a wink, Jimmy replied, "My pleasure, dear," and turning to Tom, "I'll see *your* so-called honest arse out on the greens next Wednesday mornin', bright and early!"

"Yep, sounds good!" Tom said while Jimmy walked past him, heading for the front door.

When both men got to the front of the store, Tom headed back to the counter and Jimmy aimed for the door. On his way out, Jimmy turned to Tom and loudly said, "And don't forget your balls like you did yesterday!"

With a smile, Tom waved his towel at Jimmy and shouted, "And don't come back in here again, riff raff!"

Brant

Steph arrived to the coffee shop early Wednesday morning, her first sales appointment of the day having rescheduled for the following week. She figured she would spend her downtime working on her schedule for the rest of the work week. After ordering a blended Turtle Mocha and a piece of cinnamon spice cake, she wandered through the empty tables and chairs of the coffee shop over to what had become known as *her corner*. She'd become used to sitting back there, and laughed to herself when she thought about asking Tom to put up a 'Reserved' sign for her to keep other people out of the area. She laughed a bit more, thinking about how she had finally made it in the world by having a 'table in the back.'

Once seated and settled in, she took out her tablet and turned it on. As she waited for the desktop to load, she surveyed the restaurant and noticed a guy staring at her. She knew he wouldn't be looking at anyone else behind her since she was backed up into the corner. It also didn't appear he was looking out the windows to the right of her... Yep, he was definitely looking at her. So for fun, and being the brazen sales person she was, she got up and walked over to him, "Yes? Can I help you?"

"Maybe," he answered, catching her off guard. "Are you the person doing those confession things?"

"Ah... Yep, that would be me. Are you my ten o'clock?" Steph asked.

"No. But I have seen you here on other days talking with people."

"Yep, the schedule filled up quick. Who knew, right?" Steph smiled, sitting down on the arm of an overstuffed chair next to her.

"I think what you're doing is a great idea!"

"Well, thank you. I'll be bringing in another sign-up sheet tomorrow... This concept seems to be taking off."

"You're sort of like Lucy from the Peanuts cartoon strip who offers psychiatric help for five cents."

"I suppose I am," Steph said, "I had never thought about it that way. Of course, Lucy had the forethought to charge five cents... I'm doing this for free."

"Why *are* you doing this?"

"Sheer curiosity... I'm starting to prove my hypothesis correct on most people having little secrets they need to talk about but haven't because of fear, public acceptance or the lack thereof, or whatever."

"My guess would be all people have at least one secret."

"I'm sure you'd be correct about that," Steph confirmed. She glanced up and down, noting his closed off body language, yet hopeful eyes, "Do you have a secret?"

"Yes, and I would like to tell you about it, but none of the dates and times you had available on your list worked for me."

Steph stood up and gestured toward her back corner of the restaurant. "Well, you're here now... would you have the time to talk, if I opened up 'Lucy's Psychiatric

Help Stand' early today?"

"Yeah, would you? Is that okay?"

"Yep, no problem... I was just going to do some busy work before my ten o'clock."

"Cool! Okay, let me gather my things and I'll be right over."

"Yeah, just follow me over to the table in the back corner," Steph said, starting to walk away. "I can finally say I have a *table in the back*... pretty funny!"

Once they were both settled in at the table, Steph looked at her unexpected appointment, "By the way, what's your name?"

"Oh, it's Brant. Nice to meet you," he said, offering his hand for a shake.

With a smile, Steph shook his hand and answered, "Nice to meet you, too. My actual name is Steph, not Lucy, and I'm ready to hear your secret... Well, first of all, I will go over my disclaimer with you - the same one posted on the sign-up sheet - ready?"

"Yep..."

"I'm a law-abiding citizen who would rather not hear about anything illegal done by you or anyone you know because I don't want to be put into the position of knowing something that should be reported."

"Yep. Got it."

"And one other thing - I'm not a licensed therapist, either. This is just free conversation over a cup of coffee. Cool?"

"Yep, got that too," Brant said.

"Okay, so we're all good? You're not going to tell me anything illegal, right?"

"Nope, I won't. But it's sad."

Steph took a deep breath and looked at Brant sitting across from her, his face already remorseful. Exhaling, she said, "Okay, let's hear it."

"Back when I was around eight years old, I'd found my grandpa's lighter on the kitchen table when I went into my grandparent's farmhouse to get a Popsicle out of the freezer..."

"And you took it off the table, right?"

"Yeah, I did," Brant confessed. "I stuck it in my pocket, and walked back outside to the picnic we were having out in the yard."

"Were you staying out at your grandparent's place? Or did you live there?" Steph asked.

"I was staying out there for the week. My parents would drop me and my two little brothers off there every so often so they could actually get work done; three boys underfoot doesn't really lend itself to getting anything done."

"I can imagine. How old are your little brothers?"

"We came in a neat little package of eight, six and four. My mom, at that time, was pregnant with our little sister."

"No kidding, nothing ever got done!" Steph shook her head, smiling.

"Yeah, well I picked up Grandpa's lighter, put it in my pocket and forgot about it," Brant confessed again, looking down at the table.

"Why did you pick it up?"

"It was one of those cool silver lighters that had the hinged top on it, and I thought it was neat. I admired my grandpa and I wanted to be just like him and back then there were all the commercials for smoking – if you wanted to be cool, you needed to smoke."

Trying to figure out where this obvious admission of guilt was going, Steph asked, "Did you try smoking at the age of eight?"

"No. Actually, I've never tried smoking and I doubt I ever will."

"Good."

"Yep, that's a good part. Maybe the only good part..."

Brant said, still looking down. "Anyway, later that day, around late afternoon but before grandpa got back in from the fields, I got bored of watching cartoons and wandered outside to find something else to do."

"Uh huh..."

"I wandered out to the fence separating the garden from the pasture and tried to get the horses to come over so I could pet them, but I didn't have anything interesting to offer them, so they stayed out in the pasture and continued eating."

"Okay," Steph said, waiting for the sad part.

"So, I walked back through the garden, picking some raspberries off the bushes to eat as I walked by," Brant said, looking back up at Steph. "Then I wandered over to the machine shed and peeked in there at all of Grandpa's things. The machine shed, at that time, was akin to a man cave, these days. It had all the coolest stuff in it, and he had it packed with everything imaginable; tools and parts on every surface, and hanging from every rafter in the building. He had a really, really old snowmobile in there. That thing was never going to run again, but he kept it around. He always said he was going to get rid of it *one of these days*. Everything was going to happen *one of these days*, according to him, but he worked so much, nothing ever really happened."

"I don't mean to be rude," Steph interrupted Brant as she pointed to her watch. "But you have about twenty minutes left before my ten o'clock appointment gets here."

"Oh, right. Sorry... I was just walking down memory lane over here," Brant said, sitting up straighter in his chair. "Okay, I'll get back to my secret."

"No apologies needed. I just want to make sure you don't cut yourself short on time."

"Yeah, okay. Anyways, I was tinkering around in the shed and when I bent down to pick something up off the floor, something sharp pressed into my leg and that's when I remembered I had the lighter in my pocket. So, I took it out, found somewhere to sit down next to the door since it was so stuffy further into the building, and began to play with the lighter. I was trying to see how many times in a row I could successfully get it to light."

Steph now realized where the story was going, "Oh, no!"

"Uh huh…. Stupid me," Brant said while he began to push an empty sugar packet around the table with his finger. "I was going for my fifth time in a row when a gust of wind came in the door, and I seriously don't know what happened next. A piece of twine, hanging from the ceiling, and about ten inches away from me, lit up instantly. I looked up to where the twine was hanging from and the dried boards and the other stuff my Grandpa had tucked away up in the rafters started on fire, and flames started jumping around up there."

"You got out, okay, right?" Steph said, leaning closer.

"Yeah, I stuffed the lighter back into my pocket knowing I'd screwed up big time, and ran out of the shed and up to the farmhouse as fast as I could, yelling for Grandma."

"Oh, no…"

"Grandma was telling me to settle down; that nothing could be that important to cause the amount of ruckus I was creating until she caught a glimpse of the shed on fire through the kitchen window. Then all hell broke loose!"

"I bet it did!" Steph exclaimed, realizing she was literally on the edge of her seat.

"She got on the phone, dialed 911, and then shoved it into my hands and told me to tell whoever answered that our shed was on fire and to get out there fast! And then she ran out the door and across the yard to look for Grandpa."

"Was he still out in the fields?"

"He was on his way back from the furthest field when he saw the smoke."

"Did you tell the 911 operator to send help?"

"Yes, I did. I told them to hurry!" Brant said, looking up at Steph with red eyes.

"Did you tell them you lit the shed on fire?" Steph asked.

"No. I told them to hurry then I got off the phone with them. I was about to run out the door but then felt the lighter in my pocket. So, I put the lighter back on the kitchen table *exactly where I had found it earlier that day*, then I ran out the door."

"Ah... So you saved your butt..."

Brant looked back down at the table, "Yeah, I did." His voice was quiet and a little shaky.

"What happened next?"

"The fire department arrived and did their best to put it out, but that shed burned so hot and fast since it was literally oil-soaked from decades of machinery. Quite frankly, I'm surprised it didn't blow up and leave a crater in the ground for as fast and as hot as that thing burned."

"Were your brothers still in the house?"

"Yeah, my grandma yelled at me to get back in the house and stay in the house with my brothers until they came back."

"So, you three kids stayed in the house, then?"

"Yes, with our noses pressed up against the screens watching all of this, and hearing the roar of the fire, and people shouting at each other. It was so hot... A neighboring fire department showed up with their larger pumper truck about ten minutes later, but it was a complete loss. The fire trucks spent more time spraying the perimeter to make sure the flames didn't spread rather than trying to save the building. It was gone."

"What happened once all the fire trucks left?"

"Grandma occasionally checked in on us while the fire departments were still there, reminding us to stay inside and *NOT* come out, at all!"

"I bet she did!"

"When she finally came inside for good, she bee-lined for me and started questioning me in every possible way on what I was doing outside, and how I noticed the shed on fire..."

"What'd you say?"

"I told her I was out talking to the horses at the pasture gate in the garden, and then I stopped to pick raspberries. Then I wandered over to the shed to see if Grandpa was in there and saw the flames and that's when I ran into the house, screaming her name."

Steph leaned back in her chair again and folded her arms in front of her then said, "You left out the lighter part..."

"Yeah, I did. My alibi was the raspberry stains on my face. My hands were too dirty to truly be red, but if you looked close enough, you could see a little raspberry streaking on them, too."

Before Steph could ask another question, one of the coffee shop employees approached the table, "Your appointment is here."

Steph looked at her watch, then back up at the employee, "He's early, by about ten minutes."

"Yeah, but what do you want me to tell him?"

"Please tell him he's early, and I will be right with him after I finish talking with this gentleman."

"Okay, sure."

Steph looked back at Brant who was sitting across from her, looking out the window with glassy eyes. "Okay, where were we in your story?"

"My alibi was raspberries," Brant said quickly, disappointment in his voice.

"Right... So then what? What did the Fire Marshal declare as the origin of the fire?"

"I didn't hear the end result of the investigation until I was already home, but my mom said it was determined to most likely be linseed oil-soaked rags he used in the shed when he built or refinished wood furniture in his spare time during the winter. The Fire Marshal told my grandpa that it only took the right conditions – warm air and pressure of rags stored together in a closed space to cause linseed oil-soaked rags to spontaneously combust. No flame was needed."

"Did your grandpa buy that theory?"

"My mom said he told the fire department that he was always careful with the chemicals and never bunched rags together; that he always hung them up. He eventually admitted that maybe he had forgotten just this one time."

"So, he wound up blaming himself..." Steph said, leaning back in her chair.

"Yeah, and although I didn't admit to causing the fire, nearly every night I had a nightmare about things catching on fire."

"Mmmm hmmmm," Steph nodded. "You were feeling mighty guilty!"

"Yes, I was. My mom even told me I would occasionally wake up screaming and crying, saying I had started the fire, but since it had already been officially blamed on chemicals, my mom said I was just shook up over what I'd seen that night."

"Did your grandparents have the shed covered by insurance, at least?"

"Yeah, they did, but not to the amount of all that was in there."

"Oh, that's not good," Steph confirmed.

"No, it wasn't. My grandpa had been working on a

century old armoire for my grandma who had inherited it, through the generations of her family for as long as anyone could remember. Grandpa was repairing it for her upcoming birthday. That's actually the piece of furniture he was working on when he wasn't out planting, so he could get it done for her. That inherited piece became an object of contention between the two of them, rather than the gift it was intended to be."

"Wow," Steph said.

"None of the tractors were in there, but most of grandpa's tools were. Lots of memories were lost that night, too. My grandparents had also used the shed for storing some things my mom and her siblings had made when they were growing up - 4H projects and the like."

"Yeah, that's quite a secret."

"Yeah," Brant said, slowly gathering his things to leave.

To offer a silver-lining to this story, Steph said, "From a person-to-person, or I should say a kid-to-kid point of view, you did the smart thing about not telling the entire truth, otherwise you probably wouldn't be sitting here right now."

"I wouldn't be able to sit, ever, if I had told the truth."

"No kidding! My parents probably would have taken me out, altogether, with the household I grew up in!"

Wrapping up the conversation, Brant decided to open up the floodgates with all of the remorse he had pent up over the past forty years, "I knew I had screwed up big time! And I truly am sorry for what happened, and for the loss of everything that was in that shed. I thank God on a daily basis, even to this day, that those flames didn't leap and take out the barn or the house, or anything else!"

"Did you ever get a chance to tell anyone else?" Steph asked.

"No, I haven't even told my wife or kids. You're the

first one I've ever told, and please don't tell anyone," Brant requested with all the sincerity he could muster.

"Why haven't you told your wife?"

"Because she and my mom talk at least once a week, and if she should ever get really mad at me -"

"Oh! Got it... Smart move..."

Brant finished gathering his things off the table and started standing up, "Thank you for letting me get this off my guilty conscious; it's been so long. Nearly forty years... You won't tell anyone, will you?"

Steph followed suit and stood up herself, assuring Brant with a smile, "It's not my secret to tell and I don't know your mom. As a matter of fact, Brant might not even be your real name!"

"People give you fake names?" Brant asked with surprise, pushing his chair in.

"I don't know," Steph shrugged. "I don't ask for ID, I just take their word for it."

With a smile, Brant quickly said, "Okay, then my name is Brian, not Brant!"

"Well, thank you for the visit Brant-Brian, or Brian-Brant, or whatever. Stop worrying about this. There was no loss of life, you were eight years old and did something stupid. What eight-year old hasn't done something stupid? I'm glad I could help you get this off your brain..." Steph finished, reaching for a handshake.

"Thank you for your time," Brant said returning the handshake. "It looks like I'm already making you late for your real appointment. Take care."

"You're welcome, and you take care, too. Stop being so hard on yourself - it was forty years ago!" Steph reminded him, following him up to the front of the store to meet her ten o'clock.

Pete

With one last goodbye to her impromptu confessee, she greeted her next one. "Hi, I'm Steph. Thank you so much for waiting..."

"Hi Steph, I'm Pete. No problem on the waiting, I'm the one who was early, and it's only been a few minutes."

"Thanks for understanding. The guy who just left was an unexpected appointment. He just happened to be here when I got here. He had something to tell me and I had some extra time. So, I squeezed him into my 'oh so busy' schedule," Steph pointed out with a smile.

"That was very nice of you to do."

"Well, it's your turn now. Come on back to the *dark corner of secrets*," Steph said, gesturing toward the back of the coffee shop.

"Lead the way," Pete said, getting up from his chair and following her to the back table in the corner. Once at the table, both Steph and Pete sat down, but Pete was having difficulty getting his legs to fit comfortably underneath the table.

"Are your legs going to fit under there?" Steph asked, watching Pete try to tuck his legs under the table top. "If it would help, you could keep your legs out in the aisle. Being I'm back here in the corner, no one walks by."

"Yeah, that would probably be a better idea," Pete answered with a relieving sigh, moving his long legs out from underneath the table, crossing them at the ankles as he positioned them in the aisle. "Ah, that's *much* better!"

"How tall are you?"

"Six feet, six *and* a quarter inches tall," Pete said proudly.

"Yeah, you are! Did you play basketball in school?"

"No, not basketball... Wasn't quick enough, but I did get to play football in high school and college. I was more of the scary offensive lineman type who stood in one place," Pete answered, grinning proudly. "Between my height and my girth, I blocked out the sun and anyone who tried to tackle me wound up on the ground. Plus... I have a heck of an arm, and can catch the higher passes to send the ball flying back down the field toward a receiver."

"Did you get to play in the NFL, too?"

"Unfortunately, no... During tryouts, I blew out my knee right in front of the scouts," Pete said, shaking his head and looking down at the edge of the table. "Boy! That still really pisses me off!"

"Yeah...." Steph started to answer in agreement when Pete cut her off.

"Oh, my apologies... I didn't mean to swear."

"You swore?"

"Yeah, I just said the 'p' word."

"You did?"

"Yeah, how I still feel about blowing my knee out in front of the NFL scouts."

Steph sat there for a moment looking at Pete with a puzzled look on her face while mentally rewinding through the few lines they had exchanged since he'd just sat down not ten minutes earlier, and then she figured out what he was talking about. "Oh, you mean *piss?*"

"Yeah, I'm really sorry about that. I should have said it *angers* me," Pete said, sheepishly looking back up at Steph, who gave him a kind smile in return.

"That's not a swear word," Steph said, waving her hand through the air as though she were shooing away such nonsense. "You certainly didn't offend me. Don't worry about it... I'd be pretty torqued myself if that had happened to me. By the way, how'd that happen?"

"We were all running through some basic plays, and one of the guys decided to be funny and tackle me just when I caught the ball. I wasn't expecting him to do that being he was nearly twenty feet to my right a few seconds earlier. But when he ran into me, he fell in front of me just as I was stepping into the throw, and I wound up tripping over his body, landing just the right way to shatter my knee cap."

"Oh, that sucks!" Steph agreed with Pete again.

"That was the 's' word," Pete announced, once again looking flustered.

"What?" Steph asked, even more confused since they were just talking about football plays.

"Sucked... That's the 's' word."

Steph paused and smiled, "Did you grow up in a strict house?"

"Yes. My momma made sure all us boys spoke correctly, and could spell, and hold an intelligent conversation," Pete again answered proudly, sitting up a bit straighter.

"Ah," Steph acknowledged with a smile. "In the household I grew up in, your version of the 's' word was not the same as our 's' word... and no one had any problem using the more extreme version of the 's' word, either. But I will do my best to not offend you with my polished ability of being able to swear sailors underneath the table."

"Alright..." Pete agreed, hesitantly.

"Weren't you wearing pads and stuff when you were playing, though?" Steph asked while using her hands to motion around her body to suggest various football safety gear.

"Oh yeah, I was. But for whatever reason, I managed to hit my knee at just the right angle at just the right place, and with all of my weight behind it.... Well, it just shattered and that was that. The ambulance came and scooped me up, and that was the end of my possible football career, and here we are thirteen years later."

"What do you do now?" Steph asked.

"I work in the financial industry."

"Oh! That's definitely different than a sports-related career. Do you like what you do?"

"Yeah, yeah..." Pete said, looking out the window at nothing in particular then looked back at Steph. "Every so often, I think back to what could have been. But then again, maybe it was better I wound up going this route rather than putting my body through all of that battering. I still have my brain and spine somewhat intact versus if I'd been playing pro-ball all these years..." Pete began to trail off with his thought, and then with a wave of his hand and a long sigh, Pete affirmed his own destiny, "Ah, no complaints."

By the look on Pete's face, Steph realized he was sliding into the glory year memories of his youth, so she took the opportunity to change the subject. "So, what brings you to this fine coffee shop to meet with me, I mean besides reminding me of my swearing problem?"

"Oh, yeah!" Pete exclaimed, snapping back into the present and straightening from his slump. "Yes, I'm here to tell you about what I did, back in high school, which enabled me to stay in sports for so long."

"Did you inject horse testosterone?" Steph asked with a wink.

"What?"

"Isn't that what some athletes do to gain an edge over their competition?"

"No..."

"It's not?" Steph asked. "Or was it horse piss?"

"What?"

Steph caught herself and exclaimed, "Oh, I just said the 'p' word. Sorry..."

On the verge of getting up and leaving since he had no idea as to how the conversation suddenly got routed to the bodily fluids of horses, Pete decided to give Steph one more chance to explain. "I'm not following. What are you talking about?"

"Extreme steroids... Isn't that what you're talking about?"

"No. I'm talking about -" Pete started explaining only for Steph to cut him off again.

"Hold on!" Steph said, holding her hand up suddenly. "I have to tell you my disclaimer first before you go any further... I'm a law-abiding citizen who would rather not hear about anything illegal done by you or anyone you know because I don't want to be put into the position of knowing something that should be reported. Cool?"

"Yeah, I didn't do anything illegal," Pete confirmed.

"Well then, good! So, okay..." Steph said somewhat apologetically for interrupting him earlier with her disclaimer, but now ready to hear all Pete had to confess.

Pete, still smiling at Steph, continued with his confession. "Okay, I used bribery... Well, not really bribery... More like blackmail, but not really blackmail, either."

Steph sat back in her chair. After a couple of seconds of trying to figure out what he was trying to say, she suggested, "Why don't you just start from the beginning?"

"Okay. Good idea," Pete nodded, ready to begin. "I

grew up in a small town in Minnesota while my cousin grew up in one of the suburbs of the Twin Cities.

During our junior year in high school, she had a friend who wanted to go to prom but was without a date, so I was volunteered."

"That was nice of you."

"I didn't mind. I liked getting dressed up although trying to find a tux was a challenge... but I got to get all dressed up, go out to eat, ride in a limo... the whole nine yards. It was fun!"

"Sounds like it!"

"So, this prom took place in the Twin Cities at a hotel down by the airport, I think it was the Marriott, maybe?" Pete pondered for a moment before continuing with his story. "Anyway, it was on a Saturday night in April. My cousin and her date, along with my cousin's friend, and I all arrived to the prom... We went in, ate dinner, and like most kids when it came to dancing, we sat around a lot more than we were actually on the dance floor."

"Yeah, I remember sitting through my prom, too," Steph chimed in.

"Anyway, an hour or two into the dance, we decided to wander around the hotel rather than continue to sit in the ballroom. Just as we were walking through the hotel's restaurant lounge area, my eyes met the eyes of my married, *pillar of society*, high school math teacher who didn't particularly like me, and was in the process of flunking me for the year."

"Uh huh..."

Mmmm hmmm, and my Mom had been threatening me to pull up my grades or she would have yanked me out of sports for my senior year. If that had happened, I would've never been able to play college ball, let alone be scouted for the NFL."

"So, you saw your math teacher - from your high school in northern Minnesota?" Steph asked.

"Yeah, my high school up north," Pete confirmed.

"Okay... So, she was on a weekend getaway?" Steph asked.

Pete leaned forward and said, "*He* was on a weekend getaway and was apparently also on a date being he had a woman on his lap, and his hands were all over her!"

"So, you saw him on a date, being inappropriate in public with his wife?"

"Yep, he was drunk and being inappropriate, but she wasn't his wife..."

"Oh," Steph nodded and then after his last sentence really sunk in, she followed her initial confirmation with an even bigger and louder, "Ohhh!!!"

Pete agreed with Steph's acknowledgment of what had just been revealed while nodding his head.

"Blackmail... No kidding! You walked in on the perfect mix to pull off the perfect blackmail, didn't you?"

Pete agreed again while still nodding his head and smiling.

"Did you know what blackmail was at the time? I mean, did that cross your mind?"

"I knew what it was, but I'm not sure it immediately crossed my mind. But I did know and clearly understand what I was looking at, and so did he."

"I bet he did!" Steph exclaimed. "Were any words exchanged?"

"After the initial shock of the both of us seeing each other – and especially for him, he stumbled on his words but greeted me," Pete said, chuckling.

"Do you remember what he said?" Steph asked.

"If memory serves, I think he told me the lady sitting on his lap was his little sister and then she called him 'silly', and introduced herself as his *special friend* for the weekend. She was a tad drunker than he was, and I don't think she caught on to what was happening, exactly."

"So, what happened next?" Steph asked excitedly.

"Not much happened next except it was understood who saw who, and what it meant and could mean going forward once everyone got back home at the end of the weekend."

"Did you tell your parents?" Steph asked.

"I told my mom. My parents were divorced and my dad wouldn't have cared anyways."

"Well, what did your mom say?"

"She started laughing," Pete said.

"I'd be laughing, too!"

"She was also curious to find out what he was going to say to me on Monday in math class? How it was going to turn out with the guilty, caught-red-handed teacher when we met face-to-face back in real life, outside of the hotel bar..."

"Well, what did he say when you walked into class on Monday?" Steph asked impatiently.

"Not much actually. He looked at me and I looked at him, and it was if there was a silent and mutual understanding; he wanted it to stay a secret, and was willing to help me keep it a secret, too," Pete said with a chuckle.

"How'd he help you keep it a secret?"

"From that day forward, and everyday throughout my entire Senior year, would you believe I magically went from failing my math class to becoming a straight 'A' student?!" Pete asked, now laughing wholeheartedly. "That straight 'A' grade sure helped the rest of my GPA, and even got me some scholarships into college! Talk about being in the right place at the right time!"

"No kidding being in the right place at the right time! Very cool!" Steph exclaimed with a big smile, getting all caught up in Pete's excitement then added, "I'm still waiting for my lucky life-experience of being in the right place at the right time!"

As soon as she said that last comment, Steph made the involuntary mistake of placing too much personal thought into what she had just said while looking at Pete. Something in her brain triggered her mind to focus solely on him, more so than earlier when he had initially sat down and the conversation had begun. Steph could hear Pete talking in the background but everything faded out around him, and a barrage of thoughts and questions started to fly through her mind at breakneck speeds: What in the world is going on? He's intelligent and well-spoken! Where did the rest of the coffee shop go? He is definitely handsome. He's not short like all of the other men I know. I wonder if he's dating someone, at the moment? He has a great laugh! At least nod your head to appear that you're listening. He has nice arms - I bet he gives good hugs. I like his cologne. I'm sure he's dating someone right now. He has great eyes... and they're looking at me! Stop thinking about all of these random thoughts and get back into the conversation! I bet he's a good kisser! Nod your head again and smile - stop staring at him with no facial expression - you look catatonic. That was so stupid to bring up horse urine - where in the hell did that come from? You seriously need to snap out of this! I really like his cologne! I could always say I was trying to be funny to cover up my nervousness. His blue shirt goes nicely with his blue eyes! I hope he picked up on my effort to be funny when I brought up the horse urine... That was so stupid! Get back into the conversation now!

Pete was still talking away when the coffee shop reappeared around him, in Steph's view. "...I mean, I wasn't too bad in math, but anything below the grade of a 'C' was considered failing in my mom's eyes. So, she'd been threatening me to pull up my math grade or be pulled out of football. I'd been trying, but this instant 'A' worked out really well for me!"

Since she really had no idea what Pete had said for the minute or so she was busy 'evaluating' him, and to save face for the mistake of momentarily wandering away from the active conversation, Steph managed to ask the generic question of, "Did anything else happen?"

"No, not really... He backed off and stopped picking on me in class, and I got a great grade throughout the rest of high school when it came to math."

Although Steph was still personally embarrassed about what had just happened over on her side of the table, she could tell Pete hadn't picked up on her wandering thoughts - thankfully - and jumped back into the conversation fully, "Oh, I bet your math teacher was absolutely mortified, not to mention terrified, of what you or your family could have done to his family, and social statuses!" Steph suggested.

"Well, he made sure it stayed a secret between just the two of us - and my mom, indirectly. And, as they say, the rest is history!" Pete smiled.

Steph could feel herself slipping back into the happy state of simply watching Pete smile, and listening to him talk, and she took the proactive stance of making sure that didn't happen again. Whatever was happening to her was certainly uncharted territory; she was a great conversationalist and was always an active participant in every conversation - both listening and conversing. Yeah, he was handsome and smelled great, and had gorgeous blue eyes and was tall, and she would place high stakes on the fact that he probably gave great hugs - and was probably a good kisser, too - but this thought wandering and lack of participation from a conversation had never, ever happened to her... especially with a man! Steph put on her best game face to quell the emotions inside her and asked, "And nothing else was ever said?"

"Nope, not really," Pete answered.

That was not the answer Steph was hoping for. She was looking forward to the conversation continuing so she could keep enjoying the view. However, since her emotions were still bubbling over and she was having trouble concentrating and couldn't come up with any more questions, Steph threw out, "Well then, thank you for coming in today and telling me your secret... You're right, it was pretty funny!" As soon as she finished her last comment, she noticed Pete shift in his chair and his smile lessened a bit. Steph was worried he'd finally begun to pick up on her nervousness, although she was doing her best to control her blushing, and her loss of coherent thoughts and words, and her heart rate...

"Oh, yeah!" Pete said as he pulled his legs in, out of the aisle. "Thank you for listening to me, too. I really haven't told anyone over all of these years since it was an assumed mutual understanding between Mr. Heggeland and I..."

Steph, believing Pete was getting ready to leave since he had changed the position of his legs and had started thanking her for listening to his secret, began to hear her subconscious reprimand her for having her thoughts go astray during the conversation. To maintain some type of personal pride, although she was quite sure Pete had seen through her and picked up on her lack of professionalism, she began to gather her things in order to leave the area of her self-induced idiocy, and let Pete off the hook of having to sit across from her while she was having an apparent starry-eyed, teenage moment in her early thirties. "I would imagine your math teacher has retired by now, right?"

"Yeah, I think he retired about a year or two ago."

"Is he still married?" Steph asked, standing up and slinging her backpack over her shoulder.

"No, they got a divorce about six years ago, according to my mom," Pete answered.

"Who knows? His wife probably caught him in the next hotel bar he decided to weekend at, unfortunate as it may be," Steph suggested, pushing her chair in, and grabbing her coffee mug to bring to the counter.

"Yeah... Okay, I see you're getting ready to leave, huh?" Pete asked, still sitting.

What was originally a preferred desire to get out of that coffee shop two minutes ago was quickly becoming a mission of life or death. After a couple years of being single and not really placing a whole lot of energy on anything to do with the opposite sex, Steph was really having a hard time concentrating. She knew if she didn't leave right that moment, she was most likely going to embarrass herself greatly by spewing forth *every* thought in her mind. Falling back on her solid excuses surrounding her work schedule, Steph answered, "Yep. I have some appointments this afternoon and have to drive a bit to get to the first one. But it was nice meeting you today, Pete."

"Okay," said Pete, standing up and stepping back to allow Steph to walk past. Following Steph up to the front counter, Pete asked, "What if I come up with another secret? Can I meet with you again?"

Steph stopped and turned around to face Pete, nearly causing him to run into her. "Do you have another secret?" Steph asked excitely.

"Well, no. Not that I know of, but I might remember something else... although nothing else spectacular has happened in my life," Pete answered rather sheepishly since he'd noticed his close proximity to Steph.

"If you come up with another secret, then you know where to find me," Steph smiled warmly, turning back toward the counter.

"But your schedule is already filled up. Are you always here on Wednesday mornings at ten o'clock?" Pete asked, still following her up to the counter.

Steph placed her mug and garbage in the designated bins and turned to face Pete, who wasn't standing so close this time. "Do you *think* you might have another secret to tell me sometime soon?"

Pete looked down at the ground, then back up at Steph. With a smile, he asked, "Would you meet with me this Saturday afternoon around one o'clock if I promised to come up with another secret?"

Making a concerted effort to keep her head in the game and her mind on the conversation, Steph answered with a beaming smile and a crooked brow, "Well, I was going to stay home all weekend and clean... But if you think you might have another secret to divulge by Saturday afternoon, I suppose I could make room for you in my very busy schedule of cleaning in order to stop in and hear another confession."

Pete continued to look at Steph, trying to gauge if her agreement was genuine. Once he felt she meant it, Pete nodded, "Alright. I'll see you here this Saturday afternoon at one o'clock with a doozy of a secret to make it worth your while."

"Sounds good," Steph said, offering up a handshake.

Slightly blushing, Pete returned the handshake and smiled, "I'll see you then, Steph," before he turned and walked out the door of the coffee shop.

While standing there watching Pete walk out to his car, Steph wondered if she hadn't just experienced her lucky moment of being in the right place at the right time.

Ralph

Busy reading an article about the newest weight loss fad in a week-old celebrity magazine, Steph practically jumped out of her chair, and nearly knocked the coffee mug onto the floor when she heard the monotone voice behind her. "Good afternoon, you must be Stephanie..."

"Holy sh!!!! Yes, I'm Steph!" she yelped, quickly looking up to the left to see a person hovering to the side of her. "I'm guessing you are Ralph? Oh, my gosh, you scared me!"

Ralph moved around her left side and positioned himself, silently, across from Steph while she got herself situated back into the chair and moved the teetering coffee mug away from the edge of the table. Once organized, she looked up at her appointment.

"May I sit..." Ralph asked in his continued monotone and computerized voice.

"Yeah, sure," Steph answered quickly, gesturing to the chair across the table. "I'm sorry to have not greeted you properly. Yes, I'm Steph and thank you for joining me today," she said, offering a handshake.

"No, that's okay... I have a phobia of germs," Ralph said, pulling out the chair with leather-gloved hands and sitting down.

For what seemed longer than the few seconds she spent staring at her next appointment, she finally blurted out the most obvious questions, "Why are you changing your voice? And how are you doing it?"

"I'm in disguise," Ralph answered without blinking.

"No kidding!" Steph forced a smile - quite sure her unease was evident to the robot-like stranger. "But how are you changing your voice?"

"I have a small implant underneath my skin which changes my voice," Ralph continued in his monotone voice.

"What do you mean *underneath* your skin?"

Ralph smiled slightly while he brought his right hand up to his jawline just below his right ear and gently pinched some skin causing that particular area of his face to stretch and contort. Then he carefully pulled the small area of pinched skin away from his face, revealing a barely noticeable edge of a mask.

"Are you wearing a latex mask?" Steph asked with complete surprise.

"Yes..." Ralph answered, the smile on his face disappearing.

"Your hair... Is that even a real beard, then?" Steph asked.

"No."

"Is this like all of the spy movies?"

"Yes," he confirmed.

"Well, you definitely take first place for people who want to stay anonymous! Most people might only change their names if they want anonymity... or might not divulge everything during their confessions! You really put some thought into this, didn't you?"

"Yes."

"Okay. Well then, since you are in disguise, I will no longer continue to ask you about..." Steph paused and exhaled shakily - dumbfounded anyone would go to such great lengths to remain anonymous. Lightly clapping her hands together, she sat up a bit straighter in her chair and asked, "So, you are here to confess today?"

"Yes," Ralph answered. Then out from underneath the tabletop, he pulled a folded piece of paper and laid it on the table before shoving it across to the other side, motioning for Steph to pick it up and read.

Steph followed the movement of the paper in her peripheral sight but couldn't take her eyes off Ralph's realistic, yet eerily wrong, face. Once his hand left the piece of paper and disappeared in his lap underneath the table, she looked down and picked up the note, unfolded it, and looked back up at Ralph.

"Please read it," he said, observing her from over the top of the typewritten story she now held up.

Steph looked back down at the paper and started reading it to herself, as she had been requested to do.

"Please read it aloud, but quietly," Ralph requested.

Steph cleared her throat and began, *"I am what is known as a ghost."* Steph looked up at Ralph with a smirk and put the piece of paper down. "Are you serious? Now you're going to tell me you're a vapor or something my mind conjured up?"

"Please keep reading," Ralph requested, nodding his head toward the letter on the table.

With an exasperated sigh, Steph picked the piece of paper back off the table and kept reading aloud, *"A ghost is someone who spends much of their entire life undercover for any government agency, carrying out specific missions or tasks. I am hired through classified referrals on an anonymous basis. I don't meet my clients and they don't know who I am, specifically. I go in, do my job, and I get out without a trace. If I get caught, I am a nobody and I simply disappear..."* Steph paused again in her reading and looked up at Ralph. He stared back with dark blue eyes. "If you get caught? And what do you mean you don't have any family?"

"Yes, I have a family. But as far as they know, I died

in combat during the Vietnam War. I haven't seen them since I shipped out in the early 70s. But please keep reading," Ralph requested.

"Okay," Steph said as she drew her attention back toward the letter she had in her hand. "Where was I? Oh, here we go, okay…. You simply disappear… *"No government or organization claims responsibility for me in any way, shape or form.* Okay…" Steph interrupted herself to quickly glance up and look at the ghost sitting across from her, with bewilderment. After a held moment, Steph looked back down and continued to read aloud again, *"I have the highest form of security clearance created. I know of, and am involved in, matters even the President of the United States doesn't know about nor would he have the security clearance for me to tell him. There are a handful of people who run this entire world, and those are the people I take my cues from. They point me in the direction I need to go, and I get the job done. I have never met them and they have never met me. We converse in code via secured electronics."* Steph put the paper down on the table again and looked at Ralph. "Are you telling me the whole Mission Impossible thing is true? You're living James Bond's life? The Illuminati really do exist?"

"Please keep reading," Ralph requested again.

Steph continued, *"During my recovery after being minimally injured in Vietnam, the military decided to put my sniper skills to use in a different arena with different rules. My superiors were given the orders to generate my death certificate and take me off the roster of active soldiers. In essence, I disappeared. My family was told I had died and there was not much of a body to be sent back for a burial and I was no longer, technically, part of the military. But under the American government's umbrella of think tanks, a handful of organizations were developed to expand on the talents of soldiers who fit a certain profile… who exhibited the right type of criteria - I was basically turned into a spy. Spies have been around a lot longer than I have been alive, but as technology has advanced and people are more mobile, the rules of the game are continually changing. The spy who wants to stay ten steps ahead, needs to continually change, too."*

Steph stopped reading and took a moment to look up at Ralph again. Before looking back down at the literal task in her hand, she asked, "So, I suppose you are going to tell me *Ralph* isn't your real name then?"

"Correct."

"Okay... Do you remember your real name?"

"Yes," Ralph replied curtly with his monotone, computerized voice, signaling he wasn't planning on offering up anything else beyond that one word answer.

"Good. Just checking," Steph replied with a bit of a smile. "Alright, continuing on... *After signing on, I began strictly as a mercenary sniper on covert operations. If the American government needed someone taken out, I was one of a handful of individuals they could call on to get the job done. As a civilian or even in the government, if you don't have the security clearance, you aren't going to know about what's going on in the world; a lot of it is on a 'need to know' basis. A lot of it doesn't make it to the evening news. The people who control the governments of the world, and who control the media outlets of the world, make sure civilians only know the latest news on what so-called reality television celebrities are wearing, who is sleeping with who, and what the latest trend is in the superficial lifestyles spoon-fed to the masses. There's so much going on in the world, affecting everyone's everyday-lives, but ninety-nine percent of the population is oblivious. People have no idea."*

Steph stopped reading and looked up again. "You know, I'm inclined to believe you on all of this. Not questioning your spy status, but what you write in here about the garbage spoon-fed to the masses by media outlets."

"Good," Ralph continued to stare at her. Steph really wasn't sure he had blinked at all since he first sat down... Maybe he was blinking when she was reading and not looking at him? She wasn't really sure and this was definitely the oddest confession thus far; the irony of this appointment becoming the most memorable although it was designed to be quite anonymous was not lost on Steph.

"Moving on," Steph looked back down at the letter. After locating the spot she'd left off at, she took a breath and began reading out loud again, *"Since I began my career as a ghost, I have been to nearly every country on this planet and the only continent I haven't been on is Antarctica. I am fluent in twelve languages and can handle myself in a host of others. Most of my business is conducted in those languages as I really don't converse with my targets."*

With this, Steph looked up again, only to be met with Ralph's persistent stare. As it began to sink in who she was sitting with, Ralph brought a single gloved-hand out from underneath the table and gestured for her to go on. Steph complied. *"Below are listed five questions. You may choose three to find out more information."* Steph smiled after she read this. Although she was a bit spooked about sitting across the table from a contract killer, she was also having a bit of fun with this nearly one-sided conversation - appreciating the fact that someone would either bother to tell her this info, or on the other hand if it wasn't true, go to all the work to make this confession probably one of the best confessions she will have during the two months of her experiment.

Steph begun reading all the questions aloud, looking for three she'd ask, *"What brought you to participating in this experiment at this coffee shop? Tell me about some of the countries you have been to? What do you like about your job? Say something in the twelve languages you know, fluently. If you had a chance to do it all over again, what would you have done differently?"* Steph paused briefly and then chose the first question.

Looking her interviewee in his unblinking eyes, she chose her first question, "So, what made you come into this coffee shop and be a part of my confessional experiment?"

Ralph sat there for a second, looking at Steph, then brought five pieces of folded paper out from under the table, holding them up as one would a hand of playing cards. After a moment, he chose one of the papers and laid it down on the table.

Steph picked up the folded square and saw the number "1" neatly typed in the center. Familiar with Ralph's procedure now, she began reading aloud again, *"I have been stopping in at this particular coffee shop, every so often, for the past three years. As soon as the sign for your experiment went up, I decided to participate. Although I was the first to sign up, I purposely scheduled myself to be the last confession of your initial eight available time slots, in case I changed my mind. I'm happy to be here. Besides divulging what I already have, there are other things I've done that I'm not too proud of, but it has all been in the line of duty, if you will. For example, doing things I didn't think were moral - although I'm not one to talk. My profession, to most, is not remotely considered moral. But besides the overall picture, such things as going in and essentially looting my target's home, hideout, office, etcetera, to recover important documents, electronic files, and other relevant items; during my younger years I would also take their valuables. Ultimately, you could say I was burglarizing... but my actions were well hidden within the folds of the various governments and organizations."*

After reading this part out loud, Steph looked up at

Ralph realizing she had forgotten to mention her legal disclaimer. But who would believe her if she tried to report any of this? What would she even say? That a man who'd been legally dead for decades, with a security clearance higher than the president, was telling her things she shouldn't know over a cup of coffee? Silently thinking to herself about how ludicrous any of this would sound, she noticed Ralph was still staring at her and continued reading. *"During various wars and conflicts all over the world, I have witnessed our own troops desecrate the bodies of America's slain "enemies."* *Kicking decapitated heads around like they were soccer balls, using the butt of their firearms to knock the teeth containing gold fillings - quite violently - out of the heads of the deceased, dismembering parts of both the male and female bodies and feeding the sexual organs to stray dogs in the area, the act of necrophilia... When I saw this, I walked away. I didn't participate, but I didn't try to stop it, either. I let the others burn off their energy and I walked away. Those people were in a certain frame of mind where they wouldn't have listened to me anyway, and I didn't want to be on the receiving end, so I simply walked away. I have worked through all of this over the past few decades and have finally... mostly... come to terms with what I have seen in my lifetime. I am fortunate to know I wasn't capable of desecrating a human body. I may have brought death to many, but I never mutilated my fallen targets. I know I have done many immoral things in my life, but at least I drew a line somewhere."*

Steph paused again to catch her breath and let some of it sink in. She felt unease swirling in her stomach, but she pressed on. She no longer needed to look up to know Ralph would be staring her down with his expressionless fake face and knife-sharp eyes. *"Throughout my career, I've been involved in several secret military operations where I go in and do my part with the information I've been given at the coordinates provided - prior to anyone else being involved. When people wake up the following day, their morning news will report a bombing which took out a key individual or military sect and the world will continue to go on about its business. I'm sure you're familiar with conspiracy theories? To some degree, those stories are mostly true; very few people on this entire planet have the full story of what happens on a daily basis. This information, along with what you first read in the main letter, is two of three reasons I am here today. If you ask the correct question out of the five questions listed, I will tell you the third reason."* With that, the answer to her first question was complete. Steph raised her eyes to her confessor and saw him, still observing, still holding up the remaining squares of paper. "I'm sorry you had to witness, first-hand, the cruelty of the human psyche. Well, beyond the level of cruelty you dispensed, yourself."

"Thank you."

After a moment of returning Ralph's stare, Steph looked back down to choose her next question. "Tell me what you like about your job? That would be the third question."

"Correct," Ralph pulled the square with a "3" typeset on it from his hand and placed it on the table between them.

Once Ralph's hand left the piece of paper, Steph reached out, plucked it up, unfolded it, and began to read aloud, *"First and foremost, I enjoy the travel. I've been to so many places, have met so many people, done so many things, and eaten all sorts of cuisine. I enjoy the anonymity in my life, and I can come and go as I please. As a tech-geek, it's great to work with all the technology and the gadgets. And finally, I've never minded being alone. I think that was part of the reason I was vetted for this job. That, and I'm a sure shot. I don't miss."*

After reading those last three words, Steph again was reminded of who, or what, was sitting across the table. She cleared her throat and continued to read, *"The money is good. Early on, I got by, but once I gained more experience and proved my worth, the money definitely improved and I managed to retire many years ago, well before the retirement age of most people. Since then, I have had the privilege of living wherever I choose. I have the ability to tell anyone, anywhere about anything I choose to divulge, or not divulge. I can be anyone to any person, be it the truth or a lie, or any degree in between."* Steph looked up again at Ralph and asked, "Do you live locally?"

"No."

"Then why in the world do you come to this particular, hole-in-the-wall, small town coffee shop?"

"I found this place and the customers interesting," Ralph answered in his still monotone voice.

Steph swore she saw a twinkle in his unmoving, deep blue eyes. Why did he visit Tom's? She could tell she wasn't going to get a straight answer out of him on that count. So, she moved on to her third and final question to ask. "Hmmmmm, let's see... One more question to ask, so it better be good... How about you tell me something in the twelve languages you know fluently?" she looked up at Ralph expectantly.

Ralph sat there for a moment then started speaking in his disguised voice. "Mi è piaciuto finalmente incontrarvi oggi. Hai maturato in una bella persona. Vi auguro tutto il meglio della vita."

"Sounds good," Steph said with a smile, "but I have no idea what you just said. It sounded nice and I don't think you were being mean, so that's good. What language was that?"

"Italian."

"Can you say the same thing in Spanish?"

"Yes. Do you understand Spanish?" Ralph asked.

"No. Well, I can count to ten, thanks to a childhood full of Sesame Street."

"Finalmente le gustó mucho conocer hoy. Usted ha madurado hasta convertirse en una persona hermosa. Le deseo todo lo mejor en la vida."

"That was the same thing?"

"Yes."

"Sounded nice... Again I have no idea what you said, but okay."

"Ich genoss das Treffen mit Ihnen heute endlich. Sie haben in einer schönen Person gereift. Ich wünsche Ihnen alles Gute im Leben."

"Was that German?"

"Yes. Do you know German?"

"No, but it sounded German from any of the German I've ever heard in my life."

"Do you hear much German in your life?" Ralph asked.

"No," Steph said, waiting for the next language.

"YA s udovol'stviyem , nakonets, vstretit'sya s vami segodnya. Vy sozreli v krasivogo cheloveka . YA zhelayu vam vsego nailuchshego v zhizni..."

"That one went right over me," Steph said, running her left hand over the top of her head and grinning. She was beginning to have fun with this despite her lingering unease.

"Russian," Ralph answered.

"Of course," Steph nodded.

"Main ant mein aaj aapako baithak ka aanand liya. aap ek sundar vyakti mein paripakv ho chuke hain. main aap sabhee ke jeevan mein sabase achchha chaahate hain."

"Yep, you are definitely losing me, but I'm impressed."

"Hindi."

"Ah," Steph said, nodding her head in agreement once more.

"Wǒ hěn xǐhuān jīntiān zhōngyú jiàn dào nǐ. Nǐ yǐjīng chéngzhǎng wéi yīgè měilì de rén. Zhù nǐ shēnghuó zhōng suǒyǒu de zuì hǎo de."

"Where are we in the world now?" Steph asked.

"China."

"Jeg likte å endelig møte deg i dag. Du har modnet til en vakker person. Jeg ønsker deg alt det beste i livet."

"I heard the word 'person!' Did you say the word 'person' in there, somewhere?"

"Yes, and that was Norwegian."

"Okay, back to Europe we go."

"Cuối cùng tôi rất thích gặp bạn ngày hôm nay. Bạn đã trưởng thành thành một người đẹp. Tôi muốn tất cả các tốt nhất trong cuộc sống."

"That doesn't sound very European, but then again, what do I know?"

"Vietnamese."

"Jumping back to Asia," Steph smiled again, fascinated.

"I naneaʻo ka hope ka halawai ana me oukou i keia la. Oe iʻoihana i loko o ka nani kanaka. I makemake oukou i ka momona a pau i loko o ke ola."

"Somewhere in Asia?"

"Hawaiian."

"Hawaiian? I suppose they have their own language, don't they?" Steph mused.

"Yes," Ralph confirmed.

"Huh... Realize something new every day!"

"Nautin vihdoin tavata tänään. Olette kypsynyt kaunis henkilö. Toivotan teille kaikkea hyvää elämässä."

"That's Finnish! I heard the word 'beautiful' in there! Was that Finnish?"

"Yes. Do you know Finnish?"

"No, no... But my grandma, well my honorary grandma taught me a few words. 'Beautiful' was one of the words she would use, and I can count to ten in that language, too!"

"Why is she an honorary grandma?" Ralph inquired.

"Well, *was* an honorary grandma," Steph clarified. "She died a few years back. She was one of my mom's friends - an older lady who didn't have local family of her own so my mom designated her 'an honorary member' of our family and we all enjoyed having her around. She seemed to enjoy having all of us around, too. She was included in all of our family holidays, and she kept up with the birthday cards and such."

Steph paused when she realized she was rambling. She looked up to apologize when Ralph said, "Go on."

"Sorry. I so rarely talk about her, especially now that family functions are few and far between. Once we lost her, family life just sort of fizzled out," Steph frowned, readjusting herself in the chair. Pins and needles crept up her legs from sitting too still. "Anyway, her name was Lillian, and she loved to wear over-sized hats and white gloves when she got dressed up, which was often. Darn close to everything was a dressy affair for her, too... Thinking back on it now, she sure seemed to have a lot of money for a single lady living alone all those years... Maybe her family had money... who knows?"

"Your mom sounds like a kind person to have included others like that," Ralph pointed out.

"Thank you, I'll tell her you said so, though I'm sure she'll think I'm joking when I tell her a spy paid her a compliment!" Steph laughed.

Ralph observed her for a moment before continuing on with his demonstration. "Bhain mé taitneamh as cruinniú ar deireadh tú inniu. Tá tú tar éis aibithe isteach dhuine álainn. Ba mhaith liom tú go léir is fearr sa saol."

"Drawing a blank on that one I'm afraid," Steph said.

"Irish."

"Do we have one more or have we already done

twelve?"

"One more," Ralph confirmed.

"Okay, let's hear it."

"J'aimais enfin vous rencontrer aujourd'hui. Vous avez mûri dans une belle personne. Je vous souhaite tout le meilleur dans la vie."

"Oh! That's French! I know that! And... and..." Steph stammered as she looked up in the air and snapped her fingers, trying to recall Mrs. Moreau's high school French class. "I have absolutely no idea what you just said, but I know it was French! I took French in high school and didn't keep up with it, and I could kick myself, and shit! Say that again!"

"Merde?" Ralph asked with a slight smile on his life-like face.

"No, no, the statement you said, but slower.... S'il vous plait?"

"Touché," Ralph said with what could have been a little chuckle if he hadn't been wearing something to mask his voice. "Alright... Once, again... Last time..."

Just as he was about to speak, Steph whipped a pen out of her backpack along with an envelope which looked to be a bill she forgot to put in the mailbox, "Okay, I'm ready."

"J'aimais enfin vous rencontrer aujourd'hui. Vous avez mûri dans une belle personne. Je vous souhaite tout le meilleur dans la vie."

Rather than saying anything right away, she hastily scribbled out any words she thought she heard without much success. Knowing she was beat, she looked up at Ralph to find him still staring at her intently, but with a noticeable twinkle in his eye and a ghost of a smile on his latex face.

"Thank you for your time Miss Stephanie. We are done here today and I must go," Ralph said, abruptly collecting all the papers from the surface of the table. Crushing them tightly into a wad in his left hand, he stood up, pushed in his chair, and shoved the ball of paper into his coat pocket. "Have a nice day," Ralph said. He turned and walked straight out of the coffee shop before Steph could say another word.

Denyse

"What number confession is this one, today?" Tom asked, setting down Steph's coffee cup on the table while she situated herself in the chair.

"Number ten today," Steph answered, looking up at Tom. "Wanna join me while I wait for her?"

"Yeah, sure... I'll sit down for a spell." Tom pulled out the other chair at the table and sat, relieved to get off his aching feet.

"How was the morning rush, today?" Steph inquired as she set about perfecting her morning brew with the right amounts of cream and sugar.

"Oh..... Pretty good all things considered," Tom sighed, leaning back in his chair and watching Steph's specific mix of sugar, cream and coffee come together. "Erin didn't come into work this morning. I think she's having trouble with her boyfriend. She did the fake cough thing and I could hear her boyfriend shouting in the background."

"What's going on with all that?" Steph asked, looking up from mixing the concoction of sugary goodness in her coffee cup.

"From what she's said in the past, he comes home

late from playing board games with his friends... Or so he says.... And that interrupts her sleep schedule because he bangs around when he gets home at night."

"Board games? She's falling for that excuse? Sounds more like he's cheating on her... I don't buy the 'board game' excuse. Does she?"

"She says he plays a game involving dungeons, and all of his friends sit around drinking beer while they do this," Tom answered, tapping his fingers on the table, irritated at the thought of this lazy loaf.

"Oh, that's Dungeons and Dragons, I bet," exclaimed Steph. "Yeah, I could see how that would take people into the wee hours of the morning playing, especially if they were drinking beer, too. Doesn't he have a job? Doesn't he do construction or plumbing - something in that area?"

"He used to. He used to work for Mielke Construction but wound up getting his ass fired because he was spending too much time screwing around on the job and then told Scott Mielke where he could shove his nail gun," Tom answered with a chuckle.

"Ah," Steph confirmed while she nodded her head. "I would have to agree. Scott's a bit of an ass and if I had the chance, I would tell him he could stick his Sawzall up there, too!"

"I agree wholeheartedly, but Erin's guy wound up getting fired anyway, so he's been spending his days watching cartoons on the internet and his evenings drinking beer and playing that game with his friends, then coming home way too late and messing with Erin's schedule."

"Sounds like she needs to clean house," Steph said after she took a sip of her coffee. "Especially if he has no interest in getting a job anytime soon... how long has he been unemployed?"

"Almost three months," Tom answered with a look of disappointment on his face. "He keeps promising he'll find a job, but there he sits, watching cartoons all day."

"Yep, she needs to kick the garbage to the curb," Steph shook her head.

"She's an awesome employee and the customers love her, but I can't keep picking up shifts for her when I have stuff to do, too, especially at the last moment leaving me shorthanded for the morning rush," Tom said, forlornly pushing a spoon around on the table.

"Erin's been working here for a while, hasn't she? I mean, I'm pretty sure she's been here the entire time I've been coming here over the last three years, right?"

"Yeah, she started here when she was 16. She's been here four years."

"Well, then I would expect she'd understand if you pointed out how this little issue can't continue. It messes with your ability to run your business," Steph suggested.

With a troubled look on his face, Tom answered, "Yeah... Yeah, I know. I might come across as a blustery old man, but truth be told, I really don't like being the meanie."

"Meanie?" Steph laughed, unsure if she heard Tom correctly. "If you seriously just said 'meanie,' you're more like a big teddy bear. I haven't heard anyone say that in a while!"

"I couldn't think of the right word," Tom blushed. "I still can't think of the word... It's a 'con' word... Convection.... No, that's not it. Conviction? No..."

"Controversy?" Steph asked with a smile.

"Yeah, that's it. I don't like controversy. I'm a lover, not a fighter."

"Alright," Steph said, sitting up straight in her chair, and looking over Tom's left shoulder, "I think my appointment just got here." Looking back at Tom, Steph chuckled, "Oh, and about you being a big teddy bear?

Your secret is safe with me."

Tom looked over his shoulder at the woman walking toward the table, and then stood up. As soon as Steph's appointment was in hearing range, Tom pointed his finger at Steph and smiled as he said, "And let that be a lesson to you!"

Steph, still seated, grinned and saluted while her appointment came up from behind Tom. "Hi, I'm Denyse. Am I interrupting something?" she asked hesitantly, peering around Tom's body toward Steph and trying to gauge the situation.

"No, you're fine," Steph said, still smiling, "Just joking around with the cranky, old guy who owns this establishment."

Tom stepped aside and pulled the chair out for Denyse, motioning for her to sit down. While Denyse was settling in at the table, Tom looked at Steph with mock seriousness, "I've got my eye on you!" He then flipped his hand towel over his shoulder and walked back up to the front counter.

"It looks like you two are good friends," Denyse said to Steph as she adjusted herself in the chair, and put her purse on the floor next to her feet.

"Oh, we've been bantering back and forth for years since I first stopped in," Steph answered, moving her coffee cup a little closer to the wall. "My name's Steph, and you said your name is Denyse, right?" Steph asked, offering a handshake.

"Yes, its Denyse and it's nice to meet you, Steph," she answered, returning the handshake with a smile.

"Do you want some coffee?" Steph asked, gesturing to the empty cup on the table she'd had waiting for her next interviewee.

"No, that's okay. I've been drinking coffee since six o'clock this morning. Any more caffeine and my vision will start getting jittery!"

"That happens to you?" Steph asked incredulously.

"No, but I wouldn't be surprised if it did," Denyse answered with a smile. "I've been up since five-thirty... Actually, earlier than that, couldn't really sleep last night."

"Why?"

"Because I knew I was coming in to meet you this morning and confess, out loud, something I've been doing to avoid something I really should do... should have done years ago. Maybe I shouldn't have done it in the first place, really."

With Denyse's last statement, Steph held her hand up and said, "Okay, looks like we are going to plunge right in. So, before we do, I'm going to share my disclaimer with you."

"The same disclaimer as the one on your sign-up sheet?"

"Yep, but I am going to say it, too, just so we're all on the same page," Steph confirmed.

"Okay, let's hear it," Denyse said, pulling over the empty coffee cup, having decided coffee was a good idea after all.

"I'm a law-abiding citizen who would rather not hear about anything illegal done by you or anyone you know because I don't want to be put into the position of knowing something that should be reported."

"No worries, nothing illegal here," Denyse assured Steph, shaking her head.

"And I'm not a licensed therapist, either," Steph added.

"Got it."

"Alright then, let's keep going. Why couldn't you sleep last night?"

"I've been married for a little over five years now, but..." Denise trailed off and paused.

"But what?"

"But I don't want any kids..."

"Okay..."

"But my husband does."

"Ah...." Steph said, grasping the idea of this particular confession. "Does he know this? Or are you hiding this important detail from him?"

"Hiding it," Denyse confirmed, holding her gaze to the table top.

"Hmmmm... Well... Well...." Steph stalled, trying to come up with something to say.

Denyse interrupted Steph's thought process, "We've been *trying* to get pregnant for the past year, but I haven't told him about how I got a birth control implant in my arm two years ago while he was out on a hunting trip in Montana for a few weeks. That type of birth control lasts for three years."

"So, you got the implant around your third year of marriage?" Steph asked.

"Yeah..."

Doing the math in her head between years married and the two years of birth control, Steph managed to unsuccessfully pose her next few questions, "Were you... No, why were you... Why did..." to Denyse who was looking at her for some understanding until she finally concluded she couldn't find the right words for the question she wanted to ask. So, in a tactful way, Steph settled on the statement of, "I'm confused."

Denyse coming to Steph's rescue from the confusion set into explaining why she didn't want to have kids, "It's like this... When we got married, we had planned on waiting for five years before we started to try for kids. At the time, five years seemed like quite a long ways off and being we were both in grad school, I didn't think much of it; I didn't think much of anything at all except homework and getting my doctorate."

"Okay..."

"A couple of years into marriage, and after we had finished school, both of us had become absorbed in our respective fields," Denyse continued. "About a year into

our careers, I had noticed we were growing apart..."
Well, maybe not apart, but he was certainly more
absorbed in his work than coming home to hang out
with me."

"Uh oh..." Steph interjected.

"Well, no... There's no *uh oh* as you might think. He
really *is* a workaholic. Actually, we probably both are...
I'm as guilty as he is, at times."

Finally, Steph came up with a coherent response to
Denyse's situation, "Why don't you talk with him and
readjust your schedules then? Either make more time
for each other and future kids, *or* agree to hold off on a
family for another set amount of time, or possibly not at
all, depending on where life takes the both of you."

"That would be the easier thing to do," Denyse
agreed. "However, there are the anxious future
grandparents to contend with..."

"Well, you both need to tell all four of them to wait,"
Steph stated, refilling her mug.

"Yes, we have, but my husband's father has been
haranguing him over the past few years about growing
up and taking on the responsibilities of being a family
man," Denyse said, starting to stir her coffee again with
the spoon she'd left in it. "Being a family man... Like
him. Like how he was and for the most part, still is."

"That doesn't sound good, the way you put it... What
does a family man *like him* mean?"

"My husband assured me going into marriage that he
wouldn't turn out like his dad. That he didn't
appreciate how his dad treated his mom, or he and his
brothers, and his one sister," Denyse explained.

Steph realized out loud, "Oh, I can see how this is all
coming together."

Denyse nodded her head and continued, "Yeah...
Without going into the particulars of past behavior, I
have overheard my father-in-law telling my husband
that although he thinks it's *cute* that I achieved my

PhD, it's high time he put me in my place and *make* me assume my wifely duties of kissing my husband's feet and changing diapers – apparently the sole purpose of all women in existence, according to him."

"What does your husband think of this suggestion? Does he tell his dad to stick his antiquated ideas up his antiquated ass?" Steph asked with a little laugh, attempting to lighten up the tone of the conversation.

"No, but he gets quiet for the rest of the day. Very sullen, in fact, when he is normally a very happy person... And if we're still at their house past that, for Thanksgiving or for a birthday dinner, his dad will pick up on his quiet behavior and go after me about how it's my fault his son is so unhappy since I haven't done the responsible thing of foregoing my life - as the good Lord intended in the Christian wedding vows - to support my husband fully."

"Seriously?"

"Mmmmm hmmm..." Denyse continued, "Yep, I'm supposed to submit to my husband, a.k.a. drop everything to kiss his feet, pump out babies, and tend to his beck and call should he remember that I still exist for any reason at all."

"And I can now see why you're on birth control... What's your mother-in-law think of all of this?"

"She stopped thinking a long, long time ago... As a dutiful wife should," Denyse answered sarcastically. "I'm surprised she isn't a complete mute. I definitely know she's not happy... She definitely doesn't *look* happy!"

"Have you tried talking to your husband about this at all?"

"Yes, but he shuts the topic down immediately and is either quiet the rest of the day, or talks about something else."

"Do you think he understands your unhappiness about your father-in-law's opinions?"

"Oh, yes. He is quite aware of what I think his blowhard father can do with his opinions!" Denyse said, violently picking up her cup and taking an angry sip.

"Does he share in your opinion? Or is that the time he avoids all opinions, and either goes quiet or talks about something else?"

"Sounds like you've figured out my conundrum," Denyse nodded.

"It sounds like he needs to break away from his father and his opinions and live his own life. What does he think about his mom in all of this?" Steph asked, hoping to shed light on a new angle to the problem.

"I know he loves her, but when we first got together, he told me the one thing that just sparkled about me was the fact I was independent and spoke my mind and knew what I wanted to do in life and how to get there. He told me he admired my determination, and how I wasn't afraid to speak up for myself – the one thing that drove him crazy about other women he'd met in his life, including his mom and his sister."

"But he gets quiet when this all comes up because he wants to show respect to his dad, right?"

"Exactly, and to add more fuel to this fucked up fire, pardon my French..." Denyse trailed off, glancing at Steph to make sure she hadn't offended her.

"No, don't worry about me..." Steph said with a reassuring smile, "Keep going."

"To add to the fun, when we first got married and his dad started in with the grandkid thing, and the wifely duty thing, my husband got away with telling his dad that we were waiting on the family-planning due to school. Of course, that translated to my father-in-law's ear as, my husband was waiting until he was done with school and was established into a good paying job."

"Okay, yep... Sounds like the neanderthal approach," Steph said.

"But now that he has been in a good job for the past

handful of years, the pushing has become damn close to incessant. As of this past Christmas, my husband informed me that his father is now urging him to go out and find a new bride who can pump out babies being his first wife can't even seem to do that... let alone tend to her Christian wifely duties of kissing her husband's ass."

"He told you this?" Steph asked, completely disgusted with what she had just heard.

"Yes. So can you see why I hide the fact that I'm on birth control, and have strong feelings about not getting off of it anytime soon?"

With continued disgust, Steph asked, "Did he at least tell you about his father's suggestion with an air of disbelief?"

"Yeah, but why would he tell me that in the first place?" Denyse asked.

"Good point," Steph said, doing her best to quell her anger over a situation she wasn't even involved in. "But no matter what, you two seriously need to sit down and have a long, drawn out conversation about all of this - regardless of whether he wants to go quiet or you would rather keep secrets, you two need to go back to the drawing board and figure out your futures minus everyone else's beliefs."

"I know. This is getting ridiculous," Denyse agreed.

"Do you two love each other? I mean, do you at least get along? Or has all of that flown out the window now?"

"As far as I'm concerned, we're still in love. But it's easier when other people are kept out of our relationship. If any overly anxious, wannabe grandparents come around, then everything goes silent and it takes around twenty four hours to get out of that funk."

Steph pointed out, "Although I am only here to listen to whatever you want to confess, I would strongly suggest you two sit down and have a heart to heart."

"Yeah, I agree."

"And you two need to come clean on all of your thoughts and birth control secrets…"

"Yeah, I know that, too," Denyse frowned, anxiously tapping her fingers on the table.

Continuing from up on her soapbox, Steph added, "And you two need to leave the rest of the world out of your conversations and plans regardless of how much others would like to sway either one of your opinions, and overall life decisions."

"And I know that, too. Could be I just wanted to run it past a stranger before I opened up that can of worms with my husband," Denyse suggested with hope in her voice.

"Oh, I think that can is already open and you two now have to catch the worms that are inching out of it at a rapid pace!" Steph said with another little laugh and a faint smile, again trying to lighten up the entire conversation, or to at least end on a somewhat even-keeled note.

Denyse paused for a little bit to let the conversation fully sink in.

Steph, seeing Denyse was mulling it all over, stayed silent and tended to her coffee. Just as Steph was about to finish off her coffee, Denyse snapped back to reality. "Hey! Thanks for today's talk. Very much appreciated!"

"You are certainly welcome!" Steph replied.

"Well," Denyse said, smiling as she slid her chair out and stood up, "I have to run… I have a client lunch today, and I will *definitely not be drinking* any coffee there! I think it will be water for me for the rest of the day!"

Steph stood up while Denyse was gathering her purse and searching for her keys. "Thank you again for stopping in and chatting. I hope my random, stranger advice was useful to you."

Keys in hand, Denyse looked at Steph and smiled. "You *have* helped and you've also confirmed what I'd been thinking this entire time... Just need to sit down with my husband and have a long, long conversation about how I see my life going and how it doesn't include *anything* my father-in-law wants!"

With a smile, Steph extended her hand for another handshake and added, "I hope this all works out well for you two."

Denyse met the handshake, "Well, if it doesn't... At least there won't be any kids involved when this all ends..."

"I hope that's not the case," Steph said, reaching down to pick up her backpack.

"Me neither, but... I guess we shall see," Denyse sighed, starting for the door.

"Have a good one!" Steph called out.

"You, too and thank you again!" Denyse called back, over her shoulder.

Steph got up to the front counter where Tom was waiting for her. "That was a short conversation!"

"Short, but definitely in-depth. We covered a lot of intense emotion in the last twenty minutes."

"May I ask what it was about?" Tom asked.

With a smile, Steph answered, "Yes, you may ask... But no, I'm not telling you anything."

"You're such a buzz kill!"

"I am ethical, YOU are nosey!"

Tom smiled, knowing he wasn't going to crack Steph today. "So, where are you off to now?"

Digging around the bottom of her backpack for her car keys, Steph looked up at Tom, "I have an appointment with that new water park opening up on the outskirts of town. They would make a great addition to the magazine for families visiting this summer, especially when the state fair is happening!"

"Oh, yeah," Tom said, wiping off the counter. "When does that open again?"

"The first of June... I think that's three days before the end of school, around here. That place is going to be packed during the beginning of summer!"

"I'll wait until the end of summer before I visit then," Tom said as he started refilling the napkin dispenser.

"You do waterparks?" Steph asked, pulling her keys out of her backpack and looking at Tom with a disbelieving smile.

"Yeah, the grandkids and I enjoy hurtling our bodies down twisty slides and through dark tunnels in a rush of water!"

"Well," Steph laughed, "each family has their own thing, I suppose!"

"That we do!"

"Alright, I'm off! Have a good one and I'll see you tomorrow afternoon," Steph said, pulling her backpack over her shoulder and starting to turn toward the door.

"Won't be here myself, but the coffee and your corner table will be waiting!" Tom called out, watching Steph go.

"Sounds good - see you next week then!" Steph called back with a wave before she walked out the door.

Stella

Stella was Steph's eleventh appointment. Although appointments were scheduled for four o'clock on Thursday afternoons, Stella had crossed out the '4pm' and written in '4:30pm' instead. True to her word, Stella arrived at the coffee shop at exactly four-thirty, and paused right inside the door, silently commanding the attention of everyone inside the establishment. Eventually, Stella saw Steph sitting in the back corner of the shop, waving her pen with the oversized, white, plastic daisy.

As soon as Stella had entered Tom's shop, Steph knew she'd seen her around town before. Some of Steph's friends referred to her as 'Cruella de Vil' for her apparel and statuesque form. As Stella waltzed down the length of the café toward Steph's corner, Steph took in the details of her. She wore a three-quarters length black dress which highlighted her toned figure, and a stole of what appeared to be mink, though Steph wasn't entirely sure if it was real. She didn't exactly consider herself a connoisseur of animal coats and skins. For accents, the woman wore a pillbox hat with the netting partially covering her eyes, and conservative diamond studs for earrings. Glancing down briefly, Steph

wagered her heels were at least four inches, if not
higher, and were made out of crocodile. Again, Steph
was not entirely sure, but she subconsciously pulled her
own modest two-inch heels under the table while she
considered it, just the same.

"Good afternoon," Stella said, extending her hand,
palm down. "Would you be Miss Stephanie?"

"Yes, I am, and you're Stella?" Steph stood up and
met Stella's hand with a regular handshake.

"Yes, I am," Stella said, quickly conforming to the
common handshake, then let go and clutched her
handbag to her midriff, waiting.

After an awkward moment of looking at each other,
Steph motioned to the chair across from her and said,
"Please, have a seat."

"Yes, I will have a seat," Stella replied while she set
her handbag down. With her left foot, she moved the
chair away from the table as if she was shoving an
unwanted item out of her area. She sat down with a coy
smile leaving Steph standing awkwardly. "Thank you
for asking."

Steph, feeling a bit uneasy, sat down and nervously
responded, "I'm sorry. I didn't ask."

"Precisely," Stella replied in a calm, collected voice
while gazing into Steph's eyes.

Flustered, Steph asked, "Precisely, what?"

"You didn't ask; you commanded," Stella said calmly,
still holding Steph's gaze.

"I did?" Steph asked, starting to realize maybe an
appointment with this formidable woman may not have
been a good idea.

"Yes, but that's not why I'm here today - to banter
back and forth about how I came to be sitting in this
chair, am I?"

"Not really…"

"Good," Stella found a comfortable posture in her
chair and continued, "I believe I am here to share with

you a deep, dark secret about myself or someone I know, but it can't be illegal. Is this correct?"

"Uh huh," Steph replied while mesmerized with Stella's posture, mannerisms, and the absolute ability to take over a conversation; a style which was different from Patti's (or whatever her name was...) approach. Steph decided she would overanalyze the entire situation at another time since she was too wrapped up in her current interviewee's presence at that moment.

Receiving the all-too-familiar gaze of yet another person dumbfounded by her, Stella continued the one-sided conversation. "Would you like to ask me questions? Or do I start talking?"

Steph snapped out of her quasi-trance and replied, "Yes, I actually have some questions. Are you ready?"

Stella was tempted to state how she had already been there for roughly seven minutes and had only covered how she had come to be seated in the chair, and put up with someone staring at her, similar to the *deer in the headlights* look, but she refrained. "Yes, that would be good," Stella said.

Steph straightened herself in her chair in an attempt to take back the conversation she knew she had lost control of somewhere between the observance of crocodile shoes and Stella's last sentence. With an unexplained urge to put everything on the table, and after a deep inhale, Steph began, "Okay, first thing's first, my disclaimer: I'm a law-abiding citizen and would rather not hear anything illegal done by you or anyone you know because I don't want to be put into the position of knowing something that should be reported. Also, I am not doing this for any educational purpose, I'm not a licensed therapist, and I won't be taking notes. And why am I doing this? Because for the last fifteen years I have been in sales, in some form or another, and I have met quite a number of people realizing everyone has a story. Everyone has done something, or is doing something, or has something about them that not a lot of people know about - nor is there a need for a lot of people to know about this information - but what they do or have done is what makes them the person they are today. We all have backgrounds, we all have stories, and over the years, I have become intrigued with this idea. So, for my own, personal research if you want to call it that, I thought I would set times to sit down with people I don't know, and I could hear about some of their experiences which make them tick."

"Well, that's quite a disclaimer, and this certainly is a unique idea! I admire your interest in learning people's stories for your own *research*," Stella smiled. "I believe I have a unique experience to share with you. So, what's the first question?"

"It's actually a two part question, but it should get us off to a good start," Steph said, returning the smile. The compliment had put her a little more at ease. "What would you like to tell me? And why are you choosing to tell me?"

Stella answered, "I'm a Dominatrix." Pausing for a few moments so Steph could process this statement, Stella continued, "I am telling you this because I will never be able to tell my family being I was raised a strict Catholic. My family would most likely disown me and I would be ousted from the inheritance I am due to receive upon my parents' passing."

Steph stared at her confessor for what felt like minutes before realizing she was being rude. Taking a deep breath in, Steph nodded, "Yep, you're probably right. I would say you are *definitely* correct in that assumption." Then Steph exhaled.

"Do you believe me?"

Steph frowned, "Why wouldn't I believe you? Are you lying?"

"Not lying. I actually do this type of work," Stella confirmed calmly.

"But I told you I didn't want to know anything illegal; this puts me in a weird position."

"It's not illegal, though."

"Yes, it is. Having sex with people for money is illegal."

"But I don't have sex with them."

To avoid another set of roundabout answers similar to the conversation she had with the con-artist-best-selling-author at the beginning of this experiment, she asked Stella outright, "Well then, what exactly *do* you do for money?"

"I provide a service for my clients. A fantasy, if you will. And yes, they do pay me in various forms, but I don't have sex with them."

"What type of services do you provide if you don't have sex with them?"

"A Dominatrix provides dominance for people who crave it," Stella explained. "Whether or not they're personally dominant in their own lives doesn't matter. What they're looking for is to be dominated by someone else, usually in a sexual context, but not always. Whatever type they may be seeking, ultimately they want to submit."

Steph leaned back in her chair, slightly confounded. She had so many questions running through her head she really didn't know where to start. "Okay, and I do apologize for anything I might say here, but I need to get this straight..." she said, leaning in again. In a hushed voice, she began to recap. "So, people who crave dominance come to you for their fantasies of being dominated, but you don't have sex with them, but they pay you in various forms? Is that correct, so far?"

"Yes, it is," Stella said proudly from the other side of the table. "People pay me to dominate them but I don't have sex with them."

In a continued hushed tone, Steph asked, "What kind of domination are we talking about here?"

"Well... with my current clients, sometimes there's pain... perhaps humiliation, sometimes verbally, or through demeaning tasks - maybe both, service, etcetera," Stella clarified. Then with a coy smile continued, "I do have a couple of full-time house boys, as well."

"What?"

"What part do you have a question about?" Stella asked, although she knew full well what Steph was asking about.

"What are house boys?"

"Men who live at my house and earn their keep by obeying every one of my commands, whether they want to or not. Essentially, they are my live in help at my beck and call."

"Every woman could use a few of those in their home..." Steph remarked, trailing off with thoughts of buff men tending to her every wish.

"Precisely!"

"Well, at least you aren't married. That would be odd to have men running around your house when your husband walks in the door."

"I *am* married."

"You're what?" Steph asked incredulously. "How did you arrange that?"

"I have been married for nearly seventeen years, happily, I might add. About fourteen years ago, we discovered we couldn't have a baby. One of us was barren. We were planning on going in and figuring it out and deciding on a remedy such as in-vitro fertilization, but with the way our work schedules were at the time, the years passed and we never got around to doing anything about it..."

"Okay, but that doesn't explain how you provide men fantasies, have house boys, *and* are still married."

Sidestepping Steph's interruption, Stella continued, "So, anyway, about ten years ago, we had a few friends over for dinner one night and one of my husband's friends remarked on how he was attracted to my domineering personality. My husband made some smart-ass remark and shrugged it off as a joke. But then a few days later, his friend approached him while sober, and asked if he could be dominated by me. At the time, I had never done anything close to what he was suggesting I do to him. But after my husband and I talked about it, and the green-light was given, his friend said he would give me explicit directions for what he was looking for and I told him I would give it a whirl - just for fun, because you only live once, right?"

"Is your husband's friend one of your house boys?"

"Heaven's sakes, no!" Stella said with a little laugh. "No, no… He still is a client, but only comes over once a month with the schedule I keep these days."

"Who are these house boys, then?"

"Both are college students who needed somewhere to live, and I offered them the opportunity to enter my employment with some strict rules and an understanding of what was expected of them. We signed some contracts, we toasted with champagne, and then they assumed their roles, and we've been one big happy family since!"

"From what you've told me so far, I can understand why you haven't told your family!" Steph marveled.

"Would you like to hear more?" Stella asked coyly, trying to make Steph indulge her.

"Uh huh…." Steph said, then immediately corrected her faux pas, "I mean, yes, please."

"Now you're catching on…"

"Catching on to what?"

"The 'yes, please.' All you'd have to do now is put a 'Ma'am' or 'Madame' after those two words, and you'd be set."

"Yeah, but I'm not a guy."

"You don't have to be a guy."

With wide eyes, Steph realized what she was getting at, "You have women doing this, too?"

"Yes. Whoever has a craving for one of my services and has the time to spend, I can be whatever Domme they are looking for."

"What do you do, specifically, to these people? I mean, and if you don't mind me asking... What do you do with your current clientele?"

"Well, I typically work Monday through Friday, but I do offer the option of spending either an overnight or a weekend with me."

"What do people do overnight or over the weekend with you and your husband?"

"Hold on, I'm getting there," Stella said, waving off the question with a manicured hand. "Monday through Friday, I have a regular who comes in at eight o'clock in the morning and makes me breakfast; he serves me in bed when I wake up around nine o'clock, or so. He is *thee* best chef in town - his wife is so lucky!"

"You have married men as clients, too?"

"Yes, and I also have married women as clients. I have met and spoken with each of their spouses and through transparency, everyone knows what's going on. I have an open door policy so the spouses can observe, if they would like to.... No secrets here. Nothing illegal and I want everyone to be happy. Happy people are better to deal with than not-so-happy people, if you know what I mean."

"So, you have spouses come in and watch you get served breakfast in bed?"

"There have been times, over the years, she has come in and had breakfast served to her in my bed, too... But his wife is rarely in town due to business and he is retired and likes to cook for beautiful women; I'm the lucky winner of his culinary talents on weekday mornings... He makes the best eggs benedict!"

"Does he also make your other meals? Or does he

cook for other women throughout the rest of the week?"

"I have no idea what he does the rest of the week. But would you like to hear more?"

Steph leaned in again and rested her folded arms on the tabletop. "What does the rest of the week hold for you, then?"

"Do you want to hear about the rest of Monday?"

"There's more? Where's your husband when all of this is happening?"

"Yes, there's more… and my husband now works from home and is generally with me nearly every hour of the day since both of us spend so much time at our residence."

"Okay, so the rest of Monday brings you what? Or I should say, who? Or maybe who and what?"

"Monday afternoon, I have another gentleman who comes over about two hours after my personal chef leaves, and insists on having his… ummm…" Stella shifted in her chair a bit then in a hushed voice asked, "How are you with… *body things*?"

"What do you mean body things? What kind of *body things* are you talking about?"

"Well, some people really enjoy pain. I mean, they get off on it. They sexually enjoy it. Do you want to hear more? It's going to get explicit."

Steph squirmed a little in her chair, but pushed on, not sure what she'd hear next. "Okay, tell me."

"Okay. This particular gentleman enjoys CBT… a lot!"

"What's CBT?"

"Cock and ball torture," Stella quipped.

Steph nearly fainted. "What?"

"Cock and ball torture," Stella repeated.

"I heard what you said. But what I am asking is, guys like having their junk tortured?"

"Yes. Well, some guys do and some guys don't," Stella clarified.

176

"What exactly do you mean by the term... *torture?*"

"Well, I cause them pain. A lot of pain, but they enjoy it, and... put it this way, you'd do best to Google it, and we should move on."

"Okay... Ummm... Yeah, okay..." Steph said nodding her head while her mind ran wild with ideas of what Stella did to men's anatomy.

After a few moments of observing Steph's bewildered look... and enjoying every bit of it, Stella continued,

"So, by the time this gentleman leaves, there's only an hour left before one of my house boys - I'll call him by his first initial 'R' - gets home from school. 'R' works Mondays, Wednesdays, Fridays, and every other Saturday. My other boy 'J', works Tuesday, Thursdays, and Sundays, with every other Saturday."

"What do those two do for work at your house?"

"Everything: Housework, shopping, cooking, lawn care, daily pool maintenance, laundry, and upkeep of my dungeon and supplies, and basically whatever else I come up with on a whim. Our residence is my office and workspace, and it must be immaculate at all times."

"Did I hear the word *dungeon?*" Steph asked.

"Yes."

"You mean the basement, right?"

"It is located in the basement, but for the most part, it really is a dungeon."

"Oh, for all the torture you inflict..." Steph nodded, realization dawning on her.

"Yes, for all the torture I inflict," Stella confirmed with a smile. "The best part is that the screams of pain are muffled because it's in the basement. And of course, I have the egress windows blacked out so prying and peeping eyes can't see what's going on down there."

"So everything happens in the dungeon?" Steph asked.

"Well, not everything. My kitchen isn't down there. My morning meals are made on the main floor and served to me upstairs in my bedroom," Stella said. "And 'R' and 'J' have full run of the house, naturally, since they are solely responsible for the upkeep and the cooking."

As a joke, and with a little laugh, Steph asked, "I suppose you're going to tell me you dress them in little French maid outfits when they clean the house?"

"No, no... nothing that complicated," Stella said with a coy smile and then continued, "Their uniform consists of only a sheer chiffon apron."

Steph sat straight up in her chair, "*Really?*"

"*Really...* I mean, if you are going to have two well-built young men living in your house, catering to your every whim, you might as well have fun with it, *right?*"

"What if someone comes to the door?"

"The only person who answers the door is my husband."

"What do they wear when they're outside... when they clean the pool?" Steph asked, still in a state of disbelief.

"Their swimsuits, of course... 'R' wears Speedos and 'J' wears swim trunks. Their choice outside as long as the job gets done. But inside, it's the chiffon apron."

"And they go for this? The apron and that's all?"

"They do if they like the free room and board, and the monthly stipend I pay them for their housekeeping service."

"Do they have jobs elsewhere?"

"I believe so - my husband keeps track of all that," Stella said, leaning luxuriously back in her chair. "*J* puts together websites on the side, and I'm pretty sure *R* still has a part time bartending gig at some club downtown. Otherwise, they're both in college, too."

"Do they get to have friends over... or girlfriends? Or maybe it's boyfriends? Whatever?"

Stella looked stern at this, and in a very businesslike manner explained, "No. That's one of the rules of my house. No friends over regardless of the relationship. Unless you're a client, an employee, or you own the house, you're not coming in. Trust is everything. If I didn't invite you to be there - you're not coming in... period."

Steph leaned back in her chair again, "Makes sense."

"So, where'd we leave off?" Stella asked with her voice slightly less formal again. She reached for the clean mug next to the coffee pot.

Steph pointed to the coffee pot, "It's nearly full. I only had one cup out of it right before you got here."

"Thank you," Stella said then asked again, "Where were we in the conversation?"

"Oh, yeah... Ummm... someone gets home on Monday afternoon from school."

"Okay, yes, that's right," Stella said, pouring a cup of coffee for her own self. "So, *R* gets home from school, gets into his uniform, and begins work."

"And so he does the dishes and makes dinner?" Steph asked, waiting her turn to fill her mug.

"Eventually... but first he likes to start in the basement and work his way up. His first task is to clean up the... *mess* of my noon appointment, and then he preps the dungeon for my Tuesday afternoon appointment. He takes any linen from there and gets a load of laundry started, then out to the backyard to make sure the pool is clean. Once back inside, he changes into his uniform again..."

"Does he just walk in and drop his swimsuit right inside the door?" Steph interrupted, pointing to the cream and moving the dish toward Stella.

"No, thank you... I prefer straight black," Stella responded then continued, "No. He goes into his room and changes. I'm all about privacy... Sort of..." Stella winked.

"So, then 'R' does the housework?"

"Yes, he tidies up and gets dinner started, then tends

to the laundry, etcetera. The house is really never too messy since it's tidied up every day."

"When is he done for the day?"

"He generally gets back from school around three in the afternoon, and works until eight in the evening, or thereabouts... It's not too long... We eat dinner at half past six. A handful of hours a day, a couple of days a week for somewhere to live, something to eat and a little money on the side. A rather good deal, if I may say so myself."

"Obviously your two house boys know each other. Do they know who your clients are?" Steph asked, taking a sip of her new cup.

"No. Again, privacy is of the utmost importance. Another rule in the house is they can only go into the dungeon when there are no appointments over." Stella then paused for a moment and held up a finger as she corrected herself. "Actually, I'll back up. The only person they know is my morning chef. But the lack of anonymity has been approved by all parties, and it's been going on for years. So all is good there."

"Does your morning chef have a uniform?"

"Yes. He has his own French maid outfit he likes to wear."

"Of course..." Steph laughed before she took another sip.

Stella smiled at that answer and continued. "On Tuesday afternoon, I have an extended appointment for a couple who come in every other week. They're both masochists and enjoy exhibitionist and voyeurism play, as well."

"So, what happens with this couple?"

"The short answer? I string both of them up and they each watch the other one be tortured for a bit until it's their turn to start screaming."

Steph squirmed in her chair, once again, with the mention of the word 'torture.' She also reminded herself, for the umpteenth time since Stella had started talking, that this wasn't exactly the type of conversation she would normally partake in on an average Thursday afternoon. Truthfully, it was surreal to be having a Dominatrix sitting across from her, filling her in on all of the things she does for a job. A helluva career, that was for sure! "Should I ask what you do to these two? Or should I use my imagination?"

"It's your choice. Which would you prefer?"

Steph thought for a moment while she poured a little more coffee into her cup and decided she'd already heard quite a bit – it wouldn't make any sense to not find out a bit more, "Alright, let's hear it..."

"Are you sure?" Stella inquired, sensing Steph's hesitation. "Okay, one thoroughly enjoys whips and the other one is really into electricity. So..."

With a wave of her hand, Steph interrupted, "Electricity and whips? Okay, I'll use my imagination from now on... But my other question is, how do you find your clients? Do you put out an ad or what?"

"No ads. I am very lucky not to have to do that. Do you remember earlier when I mentioned my husband's friend who requested I dominate him?"

"Yeah?"

"Well, after that became a regular appointment and we all realized I had a bit of a sadistic streak in me which some people really appreciate, my husband started to pay more attention to the testosterone-filled banter of his friends at the country club, at work, and at after-hour business and community events. He discovered a lot of his friends had either toyed with the idea of visiting a Dominatrix, or had already been to one when they were on a business trip out of town, or whatever," Stella explained, warming up her coffee. "Being he already knew these guys, he would chat them up a little bit more, get a feel for them. Once he was comfortable with it, he would invite his friend and his wife, if he had one, over for dinner. At dinner, the idea would be brought up, and we would all go from there. That's where the transparency of having the spouse know came into the mix. If it's a girlfriend, or they weren't in a relationship at the time of the original commitment, then they weren't required to be transparent. However, if the girlfriend were to become a fiancée, then there needs to be a talk."

After Stella finished her explanation, Steph immediately began to repeat everything she had just learned, "So, clients don't know other clients. House boys know each other but *not* the clients, except for your breakfast chef. Your husband knows *all* of the clients because he found all of them for you, and you know everyone, too, because you torture them."

"My husband didn't find all of them for me. Some were referred."

"But I'm guessing your husband still interviewed them, correct?" Steph asked.

"Yes."

"Okay, just making sure we're all on the same page, here," Steph said with a smile.

"And I don't torture all of them - only the ones who look for sadism. My chef doesn't want torture, he only wants to serve. I also compliment him and tell him how nice he looks in his French maid outfit. I mean, I sure don't want my five star breakfasts to be scared off!"

"I'm guessing it's been a long time since you've had a bowl of cereal for breakfast and you probably don't want to go back down that road, huh?"

"Exactly! So, you treat them nicely. Well, it depends on their version of 'nice', I suppose." Stella said with a devious twinkle in her eye.

"So, what do Wednesdays hold for you?"

"Oh, let's see," Stella mused, looking off into space. "Wednesdays see me spanking all of the naughty school boys."

"You spank your house boys?" Steph asked, setting her coffee mug back down on the table.

"Only if they're deserving of such a punishment, but no, I'm talking about a group of guys who stop by after they get their round of morning golf in - complete with lies about how many strokes it took to get the ball into the hole, lots of foul-mouthed language out on the greens, etcetera. So, they come to me for their weekly spankings concerning their behavior out on the course, and for any other indiscretions they may have had over the past six plus days."

"What do you mean spankings? Like real spankings?"

Stella smiled, "Yes, real spankings."

"So, they just line up and wait their turn?"

"Yes. They all wait their turn and watch when one comes up to me and lists out all of their sins for the week. I count up the number of spankings to be doled out based on a point list we all came up with when they first started with me, and then they drop their pants and underwear down to their ankles and get over my knee and I spank them."

"Just like you would do to a child? Well, when parents could do that to a child?"

"Yes. Just like what you and I grew up with."

"How hard do you spank them?" Steph asked, involuntarily wincing.

"I leave marks. Sometimes their skin splits open. They all definitely get bruised and I'm sure the pain reminds them of how naughty they were for a few days afterwards..."

"You do all that with your hand?"

"No. I use a hairbrush for the lighter penalties, and a leather strap for the more severe penalties."

Again, Steph squirmed in her chair, but this time with the memories of being spanked herself as a child, and couldn't possibly imagine that would be something to look forward to each week.

Stella could sense Steph was growing a bit more uneasy with each weekday she described. "Would you like me to continue? Or should we call it a day?"

"No, no, that's okay. I just can't imagine people looking forward to having this done every week. But, you know... *to each their own*, I suppose. Why do you call them school boys? How old are they?"

"They span from their late-fifties to mid-sixties."

"That's not exactly school aged... so, why the term *school boys?*"

"Because part of their fantasy is to have me administer the spankings as a headmistress or governess, but with a twist; I dress the part complete with the tight bun hair-do, the spectacles with the neck chain, the slightly see through white blouse with the first three buttons undone, a short pencil skirt, and my four inch heels. Of course, *every* school teacher dresses this way," Stella said sarcastically with another coy smile. "But that's the fantasy they have in their heads. That's what they crave, and that's what I provide."

"Well, what do they do when they're done getting spanked?" Steph asked peeking into the pot of coffee to check on how much was left. Only a few sips, it seemed, which she poured into her mug.

"I make them face the corner with their pants still around their ankles so they can think about how they will correct their actions over the next week to avoid this happening again."

"But you see them every week..."

"Exactly! That's the fun for them... Well, that and getting spanked by the *sexy school teacher* each week," Stella explained. "They come up with every imaginable indiscretion they can think of to get spanked: Didn't change the toilet paper roll when it was empty, left dirty dishes around the house, left the toilet seat up, that kind of thing."

"Are these guys married?"

"Three of them are, the other one is an eternal bachelor."

"Then why don't their wives spank them?" Steph asked.

"One of their wives has fibromyalgia and she's unable to do this type of activity. Another one couldn't imagine swatting at a fly much less spanking her husband. And the last one is not interested in dressing up, so she allows her husband to get his spankings elsewhere with someone who will wear the costume."

Leaning forward into the table, Steph asked, "How about the guy who likes to be tortured on Monday afternoons?"

"What about him?"

"Does he have a wife?"

"Yes, he does. As a matter of fact, they just celebrated their thirtieth wedding anniversary," Stella said with a genuine smile.

"Why doesn't his wife torture him the way you do?"

"Because everyone has their limits and she can't get over some of the stuff he wants to have done, especially with the CBT. So, she has me do it. But their relationship at home is a Master/slave dynamic and she dominates him in other ways throughout each day."

"So, she has him do the dishes and laundry at their house?" Steph asked as she sat up straight again.

"Yes, along with the whips, blades and electricity... She's rather wicked with the hardware she possesses."

"Blades?"

"Yes, blades. Some people enjoy knife play."

Shifting around in her chair again, Steph frowned, "Spanking doesn't seem all that bad now..."

Stella smiled and asked, "Shall I continue?"

Knowing there were only two days left of Stella's *interesting* work schedule, Steph answered, "Sure. What happens on Thursdays?"

"I have a lady who comes in and gives me a manicure and a pedicure each Thursday at noon," Stella said, displaying her fingers on the surface of the table.

"Well, that's not bad. Is she into service, too?"

"Yes, and she also likes to be tortured while doing my nails."

"Of course," Steph said, feeling stupid. "But why do you torture her when she's doing your nails? Wouldn't that cause her to *not* do a very good job?"

"That's part of the problem she has to work through. If she doesn't do a good job, for any reason, such as being a good conversationalist, getting any polish on anything else besides my nails, etcetera, she prefers to be whipped as a punishment."

"What?"

"It's all part of their fantasies and that's what she requested of me when we first met a few years ago. Actually, when we first started, she was coming in just for the masochist end of things, but she noticed my nails and asked where I was getting them done," Stella explained, lazily surveying her nails with mild amusement. "After I told her where and how much I was spending on them each week, she requested I consider her services, since she had worked in a nail salon before and wanted to show her gratitude to me. So, as long as I supply the polish and such, she comes in each Thursday and does all twenty of my nails. I've been quite pleased."

"How do you torture her when she's doing your nails?" Steph asked hesitantly.

"Ah, well that's the fun part! We incorporated the mani/pedi in with her weekly sessions. So, instead of sitting on a comfy padded stool, I have her sit in two minute intervals on a... Well, something that is not a comfy padded stool. I also have special techniques for getting her attention if she starts to zone out."

"What does she sit on?"

"Again, are you sure you want to know?" Stella grinned.

Steph, not entirely sure she actually wanted to know, shook her head, "Got it. I'll use my imagination."

"Would you like me to continue?"

"Yes, please... Yes, I'm just trying to keep up with everything you're telling me... please, keep going," Steph assured with a wave of a hand, urging Stella to continue.

"Very well... On Fridays, there's a rotation of a few people throughout the month who enjoy flogging, spanking, fire play, knife play, rope and latex bondage, that kind of stuff, or some who find interesting things in books or off the internet and want to try something different."

"Should I ask what the different stuff is?"

"If you'd like..."

Pausing for another moment while she finished off her coffee, Steph decided to resort back to the self-directed growing list of terminology to look up on Google when she got home that evening. "You know, on second thought, never mind. I'll use my imagination."

"Okay. Well, there's one more type of dominating I provide. Do you want to hear about that?"

"Yep. We are here to let you air out your secrets, and I have to say, you *definitely* have some secrets!" Steph chuckled, wondering what could be coming next.

"I also provide the service of what I refer to as 'captivation.' People can stay one or two nights through the weekend, in captivation, at my house."

Steph had already heard quite a bit and her mind was running wild. When she heard the word *captivation* however, Steph nearly burst out with laughter. She gracefully managed to keep it at bay with just a smile, "You *captivate* them? Like an animal at a zoo?"

Stella pursed her lips and gave a reprimanding look,

all business again. "Yes. I have a few cages around the house so I can keep an eye on them. Most of them wear a gimp hood for both sensory deprivation and to conceal their identity, but some choose not wear it. For those who choose to go without the hood, they are required to wear a blindfold at all times..."

Picking up on the change of tone, Steph interjected with, "I'm sorry. I didn't expect to hear the word *captivate*..."

"I understand," Stella nodded calmly, then continued in a professional manner, "Either way though, they stay in their cages except for eating - which they do in the dungeon out of dog food bowls - or when they have to use the bathroom. At night, they sleep in a cage underneath our bed. During the day, they're either out in the great room or in the dungeon if I happen to have an extra appointment over for some play. And that's about it. Do you have any questions?"

Wanting to make sure she hadn't offended Stella, Steph cleared her throat, "I truly am sorry... I seriously didn't expect to hear that word. You took me by surprise... Actually, you've had me surprised this entire appointment and I guess my surprise level just bubbled over when you mentioned your last service..."

"I understand," Stella said, putting her unused spoon and napkin into her empty coffee mug. "No need to apologize."

"I feel I should, though," Steph shook her head and placed a hand on the table. "I seriously wasn't laughing at you... I think I may just be... maybe nervous? No, nervous isn't the right word..."

Stella interrupted Steph and put her hand on top of Steph's hand, "It's really okay. I'm sure you *are* nervous... I make people nervous - I know that. And I understand that what I've told you isn't the everyday banter you're used to, either. It's okay... It's really okay. I understand and I accept your apology.

Everything is good."

"Alright," Steph said, pulling her hand out from underneath Stella's hand gently. "As long as you know I wasn't disrespecting you. But, if it helps, I can honestly say you've had the wildest confession, so far!"

"I'm sure you've definitely heard some great secrets..." Stella said standing and extending her hand for a handshake. "Thank you again for this opportunity. It was a pleasure meeting you, Miss Stephanie."

Steph stood up and met Stella's hand with a confident handshake, "You're welcome and thank you, as well... Actually, I do have one more question..."

"What might that be?" Stella asked with her devious smile again.

"How did you find out about this *little experiment* of mine?"

"One of my clients frequents this coffee shop and told me of your idea. I thought it was interesting so, I had one of my house boys stop in and sign me up."

"Ah," Steph said, wondering to herself who it could be.

"And I can see from the look on your face, you're trying to figure out who that person is... would I be correct?"

"Is it *that* obvious?" Steph smiled sheepishly.

"Yes, and I cannot tell you. Privacy is of the utmost importance in my line of work," Stella reminded Steph, turning around and heading toward the door.

"Of course..." Steph said to herself, quietly, watching Stella navigate, effortlessly, through the tables and chairs, and out the door in her four-inch crocodile heels.

Iona

Steph got into the coffee shop just seconds before it started raining heavily. She gave a loud sigh of relief and walked up to the counter. "Is Tom in this afternoon?"

"No, he had to bring his wife to the eye doctor, today," Erin said. "She's getting those drops in her eyes so she won't be able to drive afterwards."

"Ah, yeah... I hate those. Do you have my coffee cup back there, somewhere?"

Erin turned around to look on the shelf labeled 'Loyal Beans'- the shelf where the regular customers got to store their favorite coffee mugs. "What does it look like again?"

"It's ivory in color... Over-sized... Stripes," Steph described, peeking around Erin to help locate the mug. "Oh, there it is!"

Erin picked the mug off the shelf and gave it to Steph, "Here you go."

"Thanks..." Steph said, looking up at the menu board, trying to figure out what she was in the mood for, if anything, since she had had a rather large lunch.

"How's the interview thing going?" Erin asked.

Her attention diverted from food, Steph frowned,

"What interview?"

"The appointments you have with people back in the corner..." Erin answered with a puzzled expression on her face.

"Oh! Sorry, kinda spaced out there for a second. Those aren't interviews... At least, I don't call them interviews... They are more along the lines of appointments or confessions," Steph explained.

"Cool... so, how are the confessions going?"

"Well, yesterday I had my first no-show. That was a bit of a bummer, but otherwise, they've been going pretty well. It's been two months solid of people getting things off their chests, and out of their closets... Lots of skeletons out there, I tell you!"

Erin looked down at the counter, then back up at Steph, "Yeah, I was thinking about putting my name down and coming over to talk to you, but between work and life... and not being sure if I want to talk about it since I see you a lot, and I don't want to have you think differently of me... I haven't put my name down yet, and now it's too late."

"It might not be," Steph answered with hope. "I know Tom doesn't mind having the extra income with more people stopping in, and I might do this again in a couple of months. There certainly seems to be a need for it, or at least I seem to get a lot of people who want to sign up..."

"When would you start the interviews again, then? I mean confessions?" Erin corrected herself.

"Oh, probably around September and October... Between Labor Day and Thanksgiving, or so... I don't want to be doing this during the holidays - too many people are too busy, including myself."

"Yeah, me too," Erin agreed. "Maybe over the next few months I can figure out if I'm good with talking to you about my problem."

"You know I'm not a licensed therapist, right?" Steph

cautioned. "I'm just an ear to listen... a shoulder to cry on..."

"Yeah, I know that..."

"Okay... just so we're all clear," Steph said with a relieved smile. "I don't want to have any confusion."

Erin smiled and shook her head, "No confusion over here, I just have to figure it out. By the way, didn't you want to order something?"

"Yeah, do you have any of that Italian Dark Roast today?"

"Yep, it's in that farthest urn... Just made it about twenty minutes ago; seems to be the popular one this week," Erin pointed down the line of coffees.

"Oh, it's very good - especially with just the right amount of sugar and cream!" Steph smiled, starting to move down to the urn to fill her cup.

"Who's your appointment with today?" Erin asked.

Just before Steph could answer, a voice from behind her asked, "Is Stephanie Dean here yet?"

"I think I just found the answer to everybody's questions," Steph said with a smile as she turned around to find a woman in her mid-thirties standing behind her in the process of shaking the extra water from her bright yellow raincoat. "Hi, you must be Iona? I'm Steph."

"Oh! Hi," Iona said surprised, then looked down, taking a step back. "And... I'm shaking water on you - sorry about that."

Steph looked down, but only saw a few drops of water on the floor in front of her. "Well, if Mother Nature doesn't get me outside, she'll find a way to make sure I get rained on inside," she answered with a smile, looking back up at Iona who had backed up another foot or two after Steph turned around. "Don't worry about it. Glad you made it through the torrential rainfall, though."

"No kidding! I got here just when the rain started

and I figured I would sit in my car and wait it out. But as you can tell," Iona continued, glancing over her left shoulder and then back to Steph again, "I don't think it's going to be stopping anytime soon."

"Yep, wouldn't be surprised to see Noah's Ark float by anytime now with the way the parking lot is flooding!" Steph laughed, turning to finish filling her coffee mug. "Why don't you get some coffee and I will join you over at that table in the back corner, by the bathrooms."

"Sounds good - I'll be right over!" Iona smiled, nudging her tote bag toward the counter along the floor with her foot, deciding on what to order.

"Thank you for getting out of your car, and coming in - if I was you, I'd probably still be sitting in my car!" Steph chuckled, watching Iona lay out her soaked coat on a nearby table to dry, equal amounts concerned and amused.

"No worries, I'm used to standing in the rain for long periods of time. I help with the crossing guard at the local elementary school," Iona answered while pulling out the chair across from Steph, and sat down. "So, much like the U.S. Postal Service I'm out in all types of weather to make sure the kids are safe, both morning and afternoon, every school day for the past six years."

"Wow! You have patience! And you're also a morning person, then, which I am not," Steph grinned, shaking her head.

"Fortunately, I don't have to look good, I just have to be there," Iona answered. "Most mornings find me falling out of bed, getting the kids out the door and standing out there with a coat over my pajamas... I've almost left the house a few times with my slippers still on!"

Steph added, "And if it were me, I would be sleeping

on the job. So, thank you for making sure all of those little ones are safe... How many kids do you have?"

"I have four, and my youngest is finishing first grade this year, but I'm not doing any more traffic patrol!"

"I bet the school will be calling you for next year if you've done it for this long," Steph said, beginning her coffee fixing ritual.

"They already have and I've turned them down; I've done my time," Iona answered, prepping her coffee with half a cream and two sugars.

"Don't give them my phone number..." Steph said jokingly. "Anyway, what sort of secret brings you to me on this stormy afternoon?"

"My father-in-law," Iona stated matter-of-factly.

Steph, having expected to hear a longer answer, looked up at Iona quickly from prepping her coffee, "You have that answer down to the shortest version possible, don't you?"

"He's a real piece of work!" Iona fumed, testing the temp of the coffee. Deciding it was too hot to drink just yet, she put the mug down.

"Oh! Before we start, let me get my disclaimer out of the way."

"The same one as on the sign-up sheet?" Iona asked, pointing behind her toward the front counter.

"Yep, the same one, but I want to make sure we're all on the same page."

"Okay."

"I'm a law-abiding citizen who would rather not hear about anything illegal done by you or anyone you know because I don't want to be put into the position of knowing something that should be reported," Steph stated without even really listening to the words, herself, since she had said it so often over the past couple of months.

"Hmmmm.... Well, it's all definitely illegal, but I'm sure the statute of limitations have already expired on these issues. Not sure, though. But even if they haven't, he would find a way to evade criminal prosecution," Iona said, wrapping her hands around her warm coffee mug. "He's a bit of a snake, that one."

"He sounds like it and you haven't even said much, yet," Steph sipped her coffee, waiting for Iona's confession.

Iona took a long drink of coffee before setting her coffee mug down. "Well, here goes. Here's the scoop on my husband's snake of a father. First off, he's a criminal. He's actually already been convicted and around fifteen years ago, spent a couple of years at Club Fed, in Hermantown, Minnesota - up by Duluth. It's a minimum security location for all the guys who've got money to get a real slick lawyer to keep them out of a medium security place; think white-collar crimes."

"So they stick them in Canada's backyard?"

"Darn close to, yeah," Iona smirked.

"Was he there for the illegal thing he did, or was there more?"

"More, but wasn't caught."

"What did he do to get himself to Hermantown?" Steph crooked a brow.

"He used to work for a big retailer based out of Minnesota and was paid well as the vice president and buyer of one of their departments. However, he decided he would start a separate company to be the go-between for this company and its suppliers. So, by making his personal company the middleman, his company bought the goods from the original suppliers, then turned around and sold the goods for a higher markup to this large retailer," Iona explained.

"He was getting income from two places on what should have been one transaction?" Steph asked, trying to follow along.

"Exactly... Instead of simply taking his already over-inflated paycheck from this large company for buying goods from their established suppliers, he positioned his own company in between them and then made a profit while selling to this large retailer by using his own company as the only supplier he purchased from."

"Ahhhh, I think I understand.... And this is illegal?"

"Yes, it's referred to as a *kickback*."

"How long had he been doing this?" Steph asked.

"A handful of years," Iona answered.

"Why wasn't he caught sooner?"

"Because he made sure his name was buried in layers of paperwork, and had his wife's first name and maiden name on it as the co-owner. He was the 'silent partner' on all of this," Iona said, tapping her fingernail on the side of her coffee mug.

"Did she get caught, too, then?"

"Yep, she did some time in a women's prison in the Twin Cities."

"Did they have kids at the time they were in prison?"

"Yep, just one... So, my father-in-law served his two years of time first, and then my step-mother-in-law served her one year of time afterwards."

"How did he get caught?" Steph asked.

"I'm sure there was an audit in that particular department, or maybe company-wide and red flags were raised with a whole lot of questions. Then someone bothered to do some research and found the primary owner of this company was, in fact, the current wife of their very own VP in one of their departments."

"I bet that went over well!"

"So well, in fact, they decided to make an example out of him to deter any other employee from trying this little stunt. So, off to prison he went for two years, even though he spent nearly $100,000 in legal fees."

"What company was it, if you don't mind me asking?" Steph took another sip of coffee.

"I won't say, specifically, but they're one of Minnesota's largest homegrown companies, based out of

Minneapolis, and I think they have a stadium named after them," Iona said, nodding her head.

"Well, the stadium hint doesn't tell me much since I'm not into sports, but okay," Steph smiled. "But did he do more illegal things he didn't get caught for?"

"Yes," Iona answered while shifting in her chair. "Part of his sentence was not only all the legal fees and prison time, but it also included paying back the money he essentially stole from his employer from being the 'middle man', plus interest, fees, and punitive damages to the company *and*... You'll love this... He didn't report that extra income, either. So, he also owed back taxes, plus interest, plus fees, plus fines, to both Minnesota's Department of Revenue and the IRS. *Except* - when things started getting shaky at work, he hid the money. When he was discovered and fired, he claimed bankruptcy to avoid paying anything at all."

"Where'd he hide it - in his mattress?" Steph asked, incredulously. "How do you hide money?"

"You hide money under someone else's name who is not associated at all with the case, or your family, etcetera; essentially, an unknown," Iona looked vindicated as she continued to tap the side of her mug with her unpolished fingers, as if she had caught him herself.

"Who would hide money with an unknown person?" Steph asked, questions forming rapidly in her mind. "And if you're hiding money in the first place, I'm guessing we're talking large sums of money!"

"Yes, we are... millions of dollars, actually."

"But it can't go in a bank - it would be tracked."

"It can go in the bank if it's under someone else's name," Iona pointed out, lifting her coffee mug for another sip.

"But whoever that other person would be would ask questions about where the money came from, wouldn't they? I mean, if someone asked me to do this, I'd certainly want to know where the mysterious millions of dollars came from and why it was being hidden under my name? Actually, I wouldn't even go there, in the first place. Sounds too..." Steph trailed off as she waved her hands in front of her, looking for the right words to say. "It sounds too complicated, from *all* sorts of angles."

"Not to mention illegal," Iona added.

"Yeah, so who did he get to hide the money from the courts, the department of revenue, *and* the federal government?"

"His girlfriend," Iona said, a sly, snake-like grin spreading on her face.

"I thought you said he was married?"

"He was. But she was living up in the Twin Cities with their son in the family home while he was *travelling for business,* and set up his own household in Des Moines, Iowa as a centrally-located hub for his business travels.

"Okay..." Steph said, continuing to follow along.

"Except... Once a cheater, *always* a cheater... He had cheated on his first wife, who is the mom of my husband, and he was cheating on his second wife, who was raising his second child in Minnesota."

"I'm starting to think I should get a piece of paper and pen to start mapping this all out," Steph suggested with a smile.

"It wouldn't be a bad idea... There's a lot more."

"Okay, I'm still listening, and I hope I can keep up."

"So, while he's living in a community of connected townhomes down in Des Moines, he notices his next conquest lives a couple of doors down and starts hitting on her. He has someone to occupy his time and sexual urges while he's in Iowa, then when he comes back to the Twin Cities, he jumps into the family-man role and into bed with his wife like business as usual."

"Good grief!"

"When questions started flying around work during the auditing, he took ninety percent of the money and put it in an account under his girlfriend's name in an offshore account. Then he went through the whole rigmarole of court and prison and claiming he was bankrupt, when in fact, he had millions sitting in an offshore account."

"How did he know his girlfriend wouldn't take the money and leave?" Steph asked, pouring herself a fresh cup.

"Because he promised to marry her when he got out and was a free man again," Iona smiled, rolling her eyes.

"Oh, she was in love with him, right?"

"Yep, she fell for it: Hook, line and sinker... The story *older than time itself* of leaving his wife to marry the girlfriend," Iona said with another smile and a roll of her eyes.

"Did he divorce his wife?"

"Yep... when this all blew up, he and his second wife did get a divorce, and both claimed bankruptcy."

"Didn't his wife ask where the money went?"

"The only way she was even tied to his business dealings was with her name, and social security number. She was one of those wealthy housewives who had no flippin' clue as to what was going on in her world except the money better be in the account when she went shopping; the title of wife came with a complimentary American Express card. She served jail time because her info was tied to the company, and she unknowingly spent money which was obtained illegally and never reported to the IRS."

"Talk about being careful about who you get married to," Steph shook her head, reminded of yet another reason why she was iffy about getting hitched.

"Oh, this marriage was never a solid built communion of two souls who truly loved each other; I don't think either one of them was, or ever will be capable of having much depth. They are both very shallow people."

"No kidding," Steph frowned.

"Okay, so where did I leave off?" Iona asked, looking up in the air.

"He got a divorce, which freed him up to marry his girlfriend..."

"Oh, yeah, girlfriend. Right..." Iona chuckled. "Okay. Well, here's the thing... While he had the money stashed under his girlfriend's name in an offshore account, he had *another* girlfriend he would take on business trips with him, and she was also the one who would drive all the way up from central Iowa to Canada's backyard to visit him while he sat in prison."

Dumbfounded, Steph stammered, "Wait! What?"

"Once a cheater, *always* a cheater..." Iona answered in a singsong voice.

"So, he had another girlfriend?" Steph asked in disbelief.

Still talking with her quick, matter-of-fact voice, Iona continued with her story, "Yep... the girlfriend who was keeping the money was closer to his age, more responsible, had a fulltime job, that sort of thing... While his other girlfriend - the one whose sole purpose was hanging off his arm, and who was younger than his oldest son, was the one who went on business trips with him because she worked temp secretarial jobs - that's actually how the two of them met - he asked her out for drinks, she giggled, and then before you knew it, they were bedroom buddies. Took only two hours, the way they both tell the story."

"Wait. So, those two got married then?" Steph asked with a perplexed look.

"No, they split up."

"I can tell I should have started mapping this out when we first started!" Steph chuckled.

"I told you that would've been a good idea!" Iona said with a light laugh.

"So, why did this younger girlfriend visit him all the way up in northern Minnesota? Why didn't she just leave when he was locked up?"

"Because he told her he would marry her."

"And..." Steph started to say with a roll of her eyes, "I'm lost."

He kept her around so he'd have someone to visit him in prison, and she could stick around weeks at a time because of her work situation," Iona clarified.

"Well, everyone has to work at some point... She must have needed money in her gas tank to get up there and money for a motel room," Steph rebutted.

"Yep, and all he had to do was call down to his older, more responsible girlfriend who was sitting on the money waiting for her one true love to get out of prison, and tell her she needed to transfer some money into a different account number without telling her anything else. If I remember correctly, the code was something like needing more cookies in different colored cookie jars in order to get funds transferred from one account to another for various purposes. She never asked questions being she was dutifully fulfilling her position of a loyal and trusting girlfriend, and he continued take care of business and be Donna's sugar daddy. The world was good."

"So, Donna is the younger one?" Steph asked, trying to keep the story straight.

"Yep," Iona leaned back in her chair and folded her arms in front of her.

"And who's the older one?"

"Cathy."

"No kidding once a cheater, always a cheater! I wouldn't be surprised if he had every STD known to the modern world!"

"He confided in me that he has herpes but has it

under control, and he's had crabs a couple of times in his life," Iona rolled her eyes. "Shocking it hasn't been anything worse!"

"He confided in you?" Steph asked - her disbelief evident.

"Yep, and I'll get there in a bit. I'll explain all of that, too," Iona waved her hand.

"And he's your father-in-law?"

With a chuckle, Iona said, "Yep - he's a work of art, isn't he?"

"Uh, yeah.... I would say so."

While Steph was sitting there doing her best to comprehend everything she'd been told, Iona continued. "Anyway, when he got out of prison, he had to spend six months in a Minneapolis halfway house which meant he lived at this residence with other recently released men, but had to go out into the world and work during the days. Of course, with him, he didn't have to work... he was sitting on millions of dollars. So, he got all dressed up every day, in a business suit to go out and *look* for a job. But in reality, he drove over to Donna's hotel room and ordered room service all day, while the two of them, as he put it, jumped on the *velvet trampoline*."

"He told you what they do, too?"

"Oh, no," Iona said, sitting up straight. "Both of them told us - myself and my husband - when we met them for lunch one day, while he was out *working*, according to the halfway house and Minnesota's Department of Justice."

"So, you had lunch with these two when you knew about Cathy?" Steph asked, her face contorting.

"Hadn't heard of Cathy, yet... As a matter of fact, Donna was sporting a decent-sized bauble on her left ring finger. She was all ready to become the missus to her sugar daddy. They were both sitting there telling us about their wedding plans as my husband and I were trying to comprehend the fact that his next 'step-mother' was three years younger than him."

Steph lightly slapped the table top with her hand and jokingly said, "Now we've moved onto a flowchart. This conversation *needs* a flowchart in order for outsiders to follow along!"

"Yeah, welcome to a corner of my dysfunctional family - both sides, really... where we take pride in putting the word *fun* into dysfunctional!"

"Good one! Do you write slogans?" Steph asked once she'd finished nearly choking to death on laughter and coffee.

"No."

"You should..." Steph urged.

"Thanks."

Continuing to do her best to track the conversation, Steph summarized the last bit of info, "Alright, so, your father-in-law didn't marry Donna... When did that end?"

"The party started to end for Donna when he got out of the halfway house and was thrust back into his version of real life; going home to Cathy."

"Ahhh, yeah, that would do it," Steph agreed.

"Mmmmm hmmmm. He told Donna that he really thought long and hard about it, and decided he was too old for her, and really didn't want any more kids. So instead, he gave her a lump sum payout so she could be off on her way and have a nice life."

"Yeah, I suppose she was looking for kids, wasn't she?"

"Yep, a whole yard full of them being she was only in her early twenties."

"So, she took the money and ran?"

"Yes. She was smart on that point," Iona said, leaning back in to warm up her coffee.

"So, he went home to Cathy and married her?" Steph asked.

"Yep, just as he promised, but of course, he left out

the juicy details," Iona traced imaginary lines on the table with her fingers.

"Yes, I suppose he did."

"Mmmm hmmmm, then give it a year or two and Cathy's daughter decides to move from Des Moines to Louisville, Kentucky for a job transfer. She's out there for a while, and Cathy gets distressed over missing her only child and her only grandchild so she convinces my loser father-in-law to pick up and move to Kentucky because there really isn't any reason for them to be in Iowa anymore. So, they do and they wind up building a huge house out there which eventually Cathy's daughter moves into with the grandchild because it is a *definite* upgrade compared to the hole-in-the-wall apartment she's been living in, in a nearby town," Iona said, starting to chuckle again.

"Oh... I'm guessing that went over too well, too?" Steph commented sarcastically, starting to laugh.

"Yep... So well in fact, my father-in-law ended up spending another one million building a nearly identical house for Cathy's daughter in the same neighborhood to get her and the grandchild out of the house."

"And, I'm lost again. How did that happen? Why did that happen?" Steph asked with confusion in her voice.

"Well, my father-in-law didn't want two additional people in the house; one being a kid who was loud and rambunctious, and the other one who didn't like him and couldn't control her kid. So, he moved them out," Iona explained.

"Yeah, you move them out of the house, but most people wouldn't go and build someone they don't like a one million dollar house."

"But he's not like everyone else. He has money... illegally obtained... and hidden... from the US government, among others..." Iona said slowly, giving Steph time to catch up.

After a moment of taking Iona's words in, Steph's

eyes widened. "Ahhhh.... Oooohhhhh! Blackmail! She blackmailed him! Oh my gawd!!! Is that it?!"

"Yep," Iona's eyes gleamed. "Cathy started figuring out that *maybe* her one true love wasn't all that true, so she put a private investigator on him for a while, and found out he's a philanderer... The same way she showed up in his life was the same way countless women were being churned through his personal turn-style on nearly a weekly basis. So, their marriage started falling apart and they started living separate lives."

"So... why didn't they get a divorce?"

"He can't divorce her because she knows too much and for protection purposes, should something ever happen to her, Cathy's daughter knows everything and holds the videotaped evidence of what all went down according to Cathy, all the transactions she made at his request – including the Donna transactions; she literally had him by the balls."

"Karma sucks for some people, doesn't it?" Steph said, a smile growing on her face.

"Yes, it does! And for all the rest of us, we just laugh and laugh and laugh..." Iona smiled, looking satisfied.

Steph took this opportunity to laugh along with Iona as she leaned back in her chair, too, thinking she had heard everything.

"But that's not where the story ends... There's more," Iona said, taking another sip of her coffee.

Steph stopped laughing and sat up straight, "What do you mean, *there's more?*"

"Mmmm hmmmm," Iona gloated, "So that's where we leave Cathy and her daughter and their disjointed family. Now we back up to when my loser father-in-law and his second wife were in court for kickbacks."

"Okay," Steph said, "Okay, I'm there."

"Do you remember when I told you he served his time first and then she served a short prison time?"

"Yeah," Steph confirmed.

"Well, while he was sitting in prison and being visited by Donna - you remember her, the second girlfriend who giggled and is younger than my husband?" Iona drawled, her voice dripping with disdain. "Yeah, that's when he started filing papers against his wife for not only a divorce, but also for one hundred percent child custody."

"What sense does that make if he was never home with his kid for all that time he was in Iowa?" Steph urged.

"Exactly... It makes absolutely no sense to normal people, but on the advice of his crooked attorney who also happened to be a close, personal friend of his, they managed to find his second wife incapable of being a good parent, and he received full custody of their kid."

"So, when he got out of prison, didn't he move back down to Des Moines? Did he move his kid out of state then?" Steph asked.

"Yes and no." Iona began to explain. "Yes, he moved back down to Des Moines after his halfway house stint and paying Donna off to go her separate way. But... and here's the fun part... He didn't take the kid with when he left for Iowa..."

Steph held up her hand and interrupted Iona, "Wait, whoa! Didn't his wife have to serve prison time? Who watched the kid if she was sitting in prison and he was in Iowa?"

"Her parents did. The grandparents watched the kid while both parents were missing in action."

"Then why in the world did he bother to get one hundred percent custody if he left the kid in Minnesota?"

"Child support - he didn't want to pay child support. So, he made it look like his second wife was an unfit parent, got full custody then left town... Which meant he was free as a bird; he didn't have to raise a child, and he didn't have to pay for one, either."

"So, he takes off to Iowa and is pretty much out of the picture. The kid sits in Minnesota with his maternal grandparents the entire time his mom serves time in prison..." Steph said, recounting all of the new information she had just been given. "Was it just because of greed that he didn't want to pay child support or was there something more to it?"

"Yes and yes. My father-in-law is definitely greedy, there's no question about that! But, if he didn't sever that tie to his now ex-wife, who was certainly going to be asking for alimony to keep up her lifestyle, along with child support, there was a very good chance the books would have been reopened to figure out where all the money had gone. And if she didn't get the money... well, whether or not she got the money, he probably would have landed back in prison for even longer."

"But didn't you say she was not the brightest wife and didn't bother to ask where the money came from? Why would she ask about where the money went?" Steph asked.

"I said she didn't *concern* herself with where the money came from so long as it was in the account when she went shopping," Iona clarified. "But she was definitely not stupid. She knows the old adage of *all good things must come to an end*... she was taking money, over time, and stashing it away in her own off-shore accounts."

"Holy shit! Your husband's family is messed up!" Steph smiled in disbelief, leaning back in her chair and throwing her hands up behind her head.

Iona pushed on, "She didn't put away as much as he had, but she knew he'd hidden the money. In retrospect, she was smart to put money away with how everything went down and where she ended up settling out at. She couldn't snitch on him and his offshore accounts to anyone because she had them, too, with illegally obtained funds. Both of them would have lost everything and they both would have landed in prison again!"

"So, what happened with their kid? How did he fare in all of this?" Steph asked.

"The parents may be smart, or at least smart enough to steal and hide a ton of cash, but I don't think their kid could. It's not that he's unintelligent, but it's because he's a spoiled, self-entitled, naïve little shit," Iona explained.

"And this kid is your brother-in-law?"

"Yep, his parents played him for his affection and for information on the other parent, and showered him with money and gifts and trips... He lives in his own lala-land with absolutely no responsibility or accountability, and will depend on his parents for the rest of their lives, and then his inheritances - if there's anything left when they die," Iona concluded.

"Wow!" Steph exclaimed, sitting there dumbfounded from everything she'd just heard. "Just wow!"

Iona watched Steph's face for a moment, then added, "Okay, now we're going to go back to all of the STDs my loser father-in-law has had and why he felt the need to tell my husband and me."

With that, Steph's mind snapped back to herpes and crabs. Without thinking about it, she blurted out, "Your father-in-law really is a loser, isn't he?"

"Yes. Yes, he is," Iona smiled. She began to count off on her fingers. "He's also a jackass, a racist, a homophobe, a sexist, and oh so many other things... It's just so hard to keep track of all the nouns!"

"So, why did he tell you guys about his STDs?" Steph asked.

"Since I've known him, which has been about seventeen years now, he has always tried to flirt with me."

"What?"

"Whenever I'm around, he will point out things like how hung he thinks he is, or how some women appreciate his big nose since it can be used for stimulation on a certain part of a female's body, or his hugs goodbye are usually longer than they need to be as well as more hands-on than they need to be, too. And then of course, there was that one time everyone was hanging out in the basement but started to go upstairs for Christmas Dinner... I was busy putting the kids' gifts away into a corner, in order to keep track of them for when we left later that evening, and as I was starting to go up the stairs, he came out from the dark laundry room and grabbed my wrist, pulled me over and kissed me."

Steph sat there with her mouth open. She wanted to say something, but nothing was coming to her except revulsion. Since Steph had been left speechless, Iona continued, "I didn't return the kiss, and I pulled away. He looked at me for some type of a response and I simply went upstairs. The rest of the evening he was quiet towards me, but still managed to get in a handsy goodbye hug when we were leaving."

"Didn't your husband catch on? Didn't you tell him?" Steph finally blurted out.

"Oh, I told him and he tells me I'm making stuff up. Or that his Dad was just being funny. Or that his Dad is a dirty old man and that's how men get when they get older. Or I was just being over-dramatic..."

"Did you tell him about the kiss?"

"Yep, and he told me that it wasn't funny to joke about such things and I was the one who was being gross," Iona answered.

Since Steph was once again without words, Iona continued with growing exasperation, "We've been together for seventeen years and married for twelve. I have been telling my husband about these happenstances over the years and he just doesn't seem to get it... or refuses to get it. Even when it happens right in front of him... His father will have his hands all over me in an inappropriate hug and my husband will be right there and not have a clue! I have to tell you, I'm quickly realizing my husband isn't the brightest bulb on the tree and it's getting old."

"So, what was said then when the herpes and crabs came up?" Steph finally asked. "What was his reasoning for telling you two that information?"

"He was talking about all of his conquests over the years - how many women he has bedded and how closely he's related to a donkey... I, of course, see him as the biggest ass on the planet, but I know he was referring to his penis size. Then my husband tells him it's good he never got any STDs, and he countered with the fact he had but has them under control. So, I asked him why in the world he would tell us any of this? He waits for his idiot son - my husband to be sidetracked with the TVs in the restaurant, then looks at me only, and says he thought I would be interested in his track record! My idiot husband is sitting at the same table and watching TV over his lecherous father's head, while he hits on me. Rather than protecting my honor, my betrothed is out to lunch, watching friggin' car commercials!"

"I have to apologize," Steph said. "I am completely without words..."

"It's okay," Iona said. "I wasn't looking for advice or anything - I just needed to say what's been building up in me over the years."

"What are you going to do? *Are* you going to do anything or just keep status quo?"

"I don't intend to stay married for much longer. I'm in the process of building up funds to leave my marriage, and with what I know about how this family operates, I need to have plans A, B, C, and D through Z lined up in order to be several steps ahead of any crooked shit they try to pull," Iona confessed.

"Was that your confession?" Steph asked as she leaned into the table.

Iona leaned in too and smiled sadly, "Yes, I suppose it was, wasn't it? The rest of this has all been the lead up, or I should say partial lead up of why I can't stand being married to that person anymore, and why it's high time for a change. I guess I just needed to hear myself say it out loud."

Steph gave a small smile, "You certainly have a lot of material to work with, and to glean intelligence from to help you on your upcoming mission of getting away from this toxic family, don't you?"

"That I do, don't I?" Iona acknowledged, exhaling deeply.

The actual confession finally out on the table, both Steph and Iona looked out the window for a couple of seconds.

"I think I see some blue sky out there," Steph pointed out the window toward the south.

Iona glanced a little further over her left shoulder to see where Steph was pointing, "It would appear the clouds are moving out, both literally and metaphorically."

They smiled at each other in understanding. Iona looked down into her still-full coffee mug and frowned, "Well, I didn't drink much coffee today, did I?"

Steph looked down into her mug, too, "Neither did I... That's probably a good thing, though, as I would love to get a good night's sleep for once."

"Me, too... I could use it, especially since I have to be up early tomorrow morning directing traffic again," Iona sighed. "I can't wait for school to be done in a couple of weeks!"

"Well, thank you for coming in this afternoon and sharing all of your scandalous stories with me," Steph said, gathering the dirty dishes and garbage on the table into one pile.

"Thank you for listening to me and being my witness. The listening is the biggest part, since no one else listens to me, and I'm often told I'm being over-dramatic."

Steph looked at Iona and firmly said, "You are definitely not being over-dramatic. You shouldn't have to live with this and if this is only part of the reason you need to leave, I can only imagine what you aren't telling me... You and the kids don't need to live with this kind of garbage in your life - an unrealistic husband and father, and a lecherous father-in-law slash grandfather..." Then Steph added, "Do you have any daughters?"

"Yeah, why?"

Steph picked up her backpack and looked at Iona with all seriousness, "Two words: Perverted grandfather."

Iona looked at Steph for a moment and then said, "Yeah, I hadn't even gotten around to thinking about that, but you're right... When they start their teen years, they certainly don't need to be visiting their grandfather, and having a father who doesn't believe them... That'll set them on the wrong path their whole lives," she shuddered.

"Yep," Steph nodded.

Iona picked up her bag and looked over to her raincoat, then back to Steph, "Thank you again for meeting with me... I have to skidaddle and get home to the kids before they eat everything in the fridge, again!"

With a smile, Steph stood up and laughed, "I can remember how much I ate as a kid - I can't imagine what it's like with four kids!"

Iona stood up too and extended her hand toward Steph for a handshake, "Thank you again, Steph, for all of your help and your listening ear... so very much appreciated."

"You're welcome," Steph said, returning the

handshake and nodding toward the dishes. "Don't worry about the dishes. I'll get all of this. You get home and take care of yourself and your kids."

Iona smiled and stepped in to give Steph a quick hug of appreciation, then turned and picked up her coat to leave. Steph watched Iona walk out to her minivan, start it up, and drive away. As she turned out onto the street, the sun peeked through the clouds and lit up the front of the coffee shop.

Weston

Steph was busy doing the daily crossword when an index finger slid over the newspaper, into her view, stopped at thirty-four across, "That word is *epitaph*."

"How in the world do you know that?" she asked, looking up from the paper, thinking she was going to see Tom. Instead, *Mr. Tall, Dark and Handsome* stood in front of her. Without another word, she followed the motion of his arm retracting back to his body, having his hand come to rest on what appeared to be finely sculpted abdominal muscles by the way the daylight, through the window, was hitting his form-fitting t-shirt. His right hand was in his pants pocket.

As Steph continued to take in the modern-day Adonis standing in front of her, he spoke again, "I did the crossword earlier this morning, and thought I'd help you out."

By the time Steph's gaze managed to move up the body of this fine male specimen who helps solve crossword puzzles, and lock with his gaze, the words "thank you" semi-coherently dribbled out of her mouth.

"You're welcome, and by the way, my name is Weston. I am your confession for the day," Weston said, pulling out the chair opposite of Steph and sitting down.

"Hi, my name is Steph. Would you like to sit down?"

Weston, enjoying his effect on her, answered Steph with, "Thank you. I would love to have a seat," flashing a megawatt smile her way.

"Thank you!"

"You're welcome," Weston replied, not sure what he was being thanked for, but thought he'd be cordial all the same.

"Yes, thank you for sitting down and the answer to number thirty-four, although I hadn't gotten there yet," Steph pointed out in a light-hearted way.

"Oh! Apologies on that - my bad... Did you just start?"

"Sort of, but that's okay," Steph said, folding her newspaper and putting it into her backpack. "So, you're Weston, huh?"

"Yes."

With a light chuckle, "Hey, I'm sorry about the way I greeted you. I thought it was Tom giving me grief and making up stuff, plus I didn't even hear you come over to the table; you surprised me."

"Oh, no worries. Who's Tom?"

"That's Tom over there, behind the counter. This is his coffee shop," Steph said while pointing to Tom fixing up one of his specialty drinks for a waiting customer.

"Ah, he's the guy who allows you to have this reserved table in the dark corner where people from all walks of life confess their sins to you?"

"They're not all sins... I don't think... Actually, I don't know. I've never thought about it that way," Steph said, tapping her fingertips on the table and looking up in the air. "Hmmmm, good question... will have to put more thought into that. But now that you're here..." Steph said then paused as she looked back toward Weston with a smile, "Do you have a sin you would like to confess?"

"Yes. I'm a cad."

"A what?"

"I have a bad little habit that makes me not a very nice person, sometimes."

"Oh!" Steph exclaimed, surprised at the idea of Mr. Tall, Dark, and Handsome ever being a not very nice person. "Before we go any further, I do need to go over my disclaimer."

"Oh, yeah… Sure. Go ahead. Do what you gotta do."

"I'm a law-abiding citizen who would rather not hear about anything illegal done by you or anyone you know because I don't want to be put into the position of knowing something that should be reported."

"Wow! That sounds official!" Weston exclaimed, a devious grin playing on his lips.

"It is," Steph said, trying to maintain her composure and not just stop and stare. "I will also add I'm not a licensed therapist. So, whatever we talk about, this should be thought of as two people chatting over coffee."

"Okay, cool… and yeah, this isn't illegal, it's just not very nice, and I know it'll catch up to me one of these days."

"Well, I'm ready to hear it if you're ready to say it," Steph said, smiling and sitting up straight in her chair, doing her best to not make Weston feel uncomfortable since she couldn't stop staring at him.

"Okay, here goes…" Weston said, exhaling and sitting up straight, himself. "I'm the *Best* Man."

"I thought you said you were a…"

"Cad. Yes, I am a cad… a Best Man who is a cad."

Steph looked at Weston with confusion and said, "I'm really not stupid, or at least I don't think I am, but what are you talking about?"

"I have a lot of friends from high school and college, and now as I work in the professional world; I'm a friendly guy. People like me…"

"Well, that's good. That's better than being hated."

"Exactly, so with my age range and having a lot of

friends, I tend to get chosen as the Best Man for a lot of my friends' weddings."

Steph couldn't pass up the opportunity to interject, *"Always the Best Man, but never the Groom!"*. But upon noticing she'd just interrupted Weston's thought process, she waved her hand and said, "Just kidding. Please continue."

"About nine years ago when I was the Best Man at my brother's wedding, and as a joke I asked my soon to be sister-in-law if I was designated as the Best Man, what was she doing marrying my brother?"

"Okay..."

"And she answered me with something along the lines of *'If you're the Best Man, you've got less than an hour to prove it,'* and that's when it all started," Weston confessed, looking down at the floor, not necessarily with shame.

Steph didn't say anything immediately which caused Weston to look back up at her. After an awkward moment of silence, Steph finally mustered, "How many women have you proved your *Best Man* status to over the years?"

"Total? Or just brides?"

"The number is so high you have to have categories?"

"Yeah," Weston said while he reached for a sugar packet and started playing with it nervously in his hands.

"What are the categories?" Steph asked.

Weston looked up in the air and started counting on his fingers, "Well, there are the brides... I can't help myself with a wedding gown! Then there are the maids and matrons of honor - I categorize them as one. Then the bridesmaids but sometimes I have to card them. I'm not robbing the cradle on those..."

Steph leaned forward and in a hushed tone asked, "Can I just interject here and agree with your opinion of being a cad?"

"Yes, you can. Do you want to hear more?"

"You have forty minutes left..." Steph confirmed, sitting up straight in her chair again.

"Then you have the mothers of either the bride or groom..."

"What?" Steph exclaimed, eyes practically bulging out of her head.

"And sometimes the grandmas want to go for a little ride... It depends on their age and agility, though."

"I'm speechless."

Flashing that devious smile at Steph again, Weston reminded her, "You have to remember it takes two to tango, though..."

Steph blurted out, rather loudly, "You sound more like a party favor than a Best Man!"

Leaning into the table and shrugging his shoulders, Weston gave a sheepish grin, "Yeah, but I enjoy it! They enjoy it! It's lots of fun! I make people happy! I'm happy!"

Steph grabbed a sugar packet herself and nervously started playing with it, too. "You do this at every wedding?"

"Oh, no. Only for the women who ask," Weston confirmed.

"They ask you about this? They're the ones who bring it up?"

"At first, it was me offering my services - actually, joking around with the designation of being the *Best Man*," Weston explained. "Now, with the way women gossip among each other, it isn't uncommon to have at least one woman at a wedding ask me about it and as soon as I confirm the rumors are true, my dance card starts filling up."

"How many women do you have on your *dance card* on any given wedding day?"

"Sometimes none..."

Steph retorted, "I find that hard to believe!"

"Well, it's true. Sometimes no one is interested, but then there are weddings where the bride wants to have one last fling... or the maid of honor, or the Bridesmaids... It can range from no one up to, I think, eight was the most for one wedding."

Steph blurted out again, "You're wearing condoms, right?"

"Definitely..."

"Okay, hold on... I have to process this..." Steph said, holding up her hand to halt the onslaught of grotesquerie.

"Take your time," Weston said, trying to be accommodating.

After collecting her thoughts, Steph leaned into the table again, "I can imagine weddings are busy days..."

"They are," Weston nodded his head.

"Where in the world do you find the time to *tango* with eight women in *one day*?"

"Well..." Weston said, shifting uncomfortably in his chair, "Depending on when the subject is brought up and what the wedding day's timeline looks like, I may start with a few the evening before at the pre-nuptial dinner. Well... after the dinner."

"Uh huh..." Steph said, leaning back in her chair with her arms folded in front of her.

"Then with the wedding day, there may be some time before getting to the ceremony location for pictures - maybe if the wedding starts at four o'clock in the afternoon, there's some time in the morning..."

"Yeah," Steph answered, mesmerized by the sordid details of his confession.

"When the pictures and the ceremony are happening, there usually isn't a lot of time," Weston continued.

"Would make sense..."

"But at the reception, that's when time frees up again!" Weston exclaimed with another devious smile.

"I would think that's a busy time, too."

"It's busy but there are always coat closets, bathrooms, elevators, golf courses, helping people carry things up to their rooms - that's when I usually get nominated as the 'errand boy', cars out in the parking lot, you name it. Wherever the two of us can get a little *wham bam thank you ma'am* in, I'm on top of it.... or underneath it... or..."

"I get the point," Steph said, waving her hand to show she had heard enough.

"Yeah..."

"And you haven't been caught yet?"

"No... but I know one of these days it will end," Weston said, leaning back but then added, "knock on wood," while he rapped on the laminate table top.

"Yeah, it'll end, and not on a good note, either," Steph chimed in with a motherly tone in her voice.

"I know."

"Well, how do you, and whoever, manage to... *do this*... and not look disheveled afterwards?"

"There are rules, of course," Weston answered with an air of professionalism surrounding him.

"Naturally," Steph smirked.

"No touching of the hair, face, etcetera as to not mess up the hair-dos and the make-up."

"Makes sense... that's a lot of time and money right there."

"Exactly," Weston agreed confidently.

"And?" Steph prodded for more rules.

"And what? I just gave you all the rules," Weston answered while he continued to stare at Steph.

"Well, from what you're telling me, it sounds like you are the one benefitting more than they are..."

Weston arched his eyebrow, "How so?"

"Rules with a couple of minutes... Sounds like you are benefitting more than they are," Steph pointed out.

"No, no," Weston answered, shaking his head and waving his hands in front of him. "This whole concept...

if you will... is to prove that I *am* the *Best Man,* and in order to do *that*... the recipient *must* be satisfied."

"That's a great plan! But as a woman, I personally know sometimes... or a lot of times... satisfaction is more than a couple of minutes in a coat closet," Steph revealed.

The devious smile reappeared on Weston's face, "True, but I give it my all!"

"So, sometimes satisfaction is not completely achieved?"

"There are all sorts of levels when it comes to *satisfaction*," Weston said wisely.

"So, then the answer is *'not always'* to the big kahuna of overall satisfaction?"

"Big kahuna... That's funny!" Weston chuckled.

But Steph continued for an affirmative response, "But you get an 'E' for 'Effort', sometimes?"

"Yes, an 'E' for 'Effort', but the point is for some, at least an effort is *made*."

"Good point," Steph confirmed while playing with her spoon on the table.

"Put it this way," Weston clarified, leaning in again, "Whether or not the end all earth-shattering orgasm is reached, the whole idea of the *secretive-what-if-we're-caught naughtiness* - along with the fun and reckless inhibition of being with someone who is not your regular partner, is still thrill enough for some. Although... I will say again, I do my best to make sure my dance partner is fully satisfied before I finish off the escapade."

Steph, accepting Weston's working theories on why he does what he does, offered up, "At least you are a giving and thoughtful lover, which is more than most men can say."

"I have a reputation to live up to... Whether it's good or bad, I must do my best."

"Well..." Steph paused, trying to formulate her next

question.

"Yeah?"

"Do you ever bring dates with you to these weddings? Steph asked. "How do you handle that?"

"Strangely enough, I don't date a lot," Weston replied.

"Wow! I didn't expect that!"

"I know... Weird, right?"

"To say the least," Steph agreed.

"Outside of this odd habit of mine, I work a lot and am very focused on my career, and just don't have the time to be looking for a life partner," Weston gave a bittersweet smile. "So, as you said earlier, *Always the Best Man and never the Groom'* seems to ring true for me."

"I'm sorry to hear that. But then again, I suppose that does make it a lot easier to sneak off to coat closets with other women if you don't have a date on your arm."

Flashing that devious grin again, Weston nodded, "That, it does!"

"Do you ever offer your services to guests?"

"No. If I did, I would never get a chance to enjoy the reception if I had too *many* people on the ol' dance card."

"Well, yeah... You wouldn't want to miss the song and dance of *'I Knew The Bride When She Used To Rock-n-Roll,'* would you?" Steph said in a bit of a snarky tone.

Weston sidestepped any sarcasm and laughed at the humor of it all, "Ha! Good one!"

"I thought so..."

"No, I keep to the bridal party... I especially like the dresses that are floor length and are not as form-fitting so I can get underneath them..." Weston started to explain, as if he were a kid reliving a story about being allowed to run wild in a candy store.

"Okay, I get it..."

"Sorry, just getting in the mood..." Weston answered looking down at the table and then back up at Steph.

"So, do you have any upcoming weddings you're invited to where you'll be a part of the bridal party?"

At that, Steph nearly laughed so hard she almost fell off her chair. "*Oh... my... gawd*, that's funny! Is that your pick-up line?"

"Well, I don't get out very often with my work schedule, but I thought I'd bring it up," Weston shared, reeling back from Steph's response, eyes averted to the floor in embarrassment.

"Ohhhh... I'm flattered! I really am... but... wow! Okay, yeah...." Steph said, trying to stifle the laughter and remember her standards as she had just been propositioned by Mr. Tall, Dark and Handsome, who likes to give free rides to women wearing big, poofy dresses, in coat closets. But on the flip side, her mind was running rampant with ideas of where she could find a bridesmaid dress on short notice!

To save face, Weston muttered, "I'm sorry. I need to work on my pick-up lines a bit more, huh?"

"Yeah, that would be a good idea," Steph smiled kindly.

"Well," Weston said sitting up straight in his chair again and starting to reach for his car keys, "If you're ever at a wedding, keep an eye out for me and please say 'hi'."

"I'll do that," Steph promised. "And if I happen to be in the bridal party, and you still have some room on your dance card, then I will consider taking one of the open spots."

"Sounds like a date!" Weston exclaimed excitedly.

"Not really," Steph answered, deadpan.

"I know, but..."

Steph stood up and filled in the awkward silence with a, "Yeah..."

"Anyway, you have a great day and good luck on your crossword puzzle," Weston wished Steph, getting up to go. "I'm off to go work out and then get back to work, myself."

"It was nice to meet you," Steph said.

"It was nice meeting you, too," Weston said, turning to leave. "Ciao!"

"Ciao!" Steph said, watching Weston glide between the tables and chairs toward the front door. He knew she'd be watching, so he turned around, flashed one last grin, and pushed the door open with his glorious backside.

Cal

While waiting in the corner for her fourteenth and final appointment, Steph was reading the local paper when she noticed a yellow carnation appear over the top of the left-hand page with a voice following. "Good afternoon, young lady. My name is Cal... would you happen to be Miss Dean?"

With a smile, Steph put down her paper and smiled, "If I say 'yes', do I get to have the flower?"

"I will take that answer as an affirmative, and have a seat," Cal chuckled, giving the flower to Steph before he set his plate of cinnamon coffee cake down on the table and pulled out his chair from underneath the table.

Once he was seated across from her, she extended her hand and confirmed, "Yes, I'm Miss Dean but you may call me Steph." Then she held the carnation up to her nose and inhaled the fresh cut flower smell, "Thank you for the lovely flower, too. Carnations are so cheerful, and yellow is my favorite color!" For fun, she broke off the majority of the stem, and stuck the flower and the remainder of the carnation stem behind her ear, anchoring it underneath the arm of her glasses. Although the stem bumped up her glasses a bit on the right side, she left it there as an additional approval of the gesture made by Cal.

"So, I hear you're the lady who's been listening to people's secrets here in town, am I correct?"

"Yep, that'd be correct."

As Cal reached for the full coffee pot and pulled a mug closer to him, he asked, "Would you mind sharing why you are listening to people's confessions?"

"I'm not doing this for any educational purposes, or for any business purposes... and I'm not here to give advice, either. Some people simply have things they want to get off their chests and I am making myself available to them, for that purpose."

"Can I ask what you do for a living?" Cal asked, putting the coffee pot back down on the table top and reaching for both the creamer and sugar.

"I'm in sales, actually, and over the years I've met thousands of people and I know every one of them had at least one story; a story that made them tick. That's the other reason I've been doing this little experiment... To find out what makes people tick. Find out their stories... their backgrounds. Again, only for personal interest, though."

"I used to be in sales, too."

"What kind of sales?" Steph asked, reaching for the coffee pot to warm up her mug, too.

"Home interiors, mainly, but I have since retired."

With Cal's answer, it finally clicked where Steph knew him from, "Oh! You're... You're...." Steph stammered as she snapped her fingers, concentrating on Cal's face, and remembering the commercial jingle. Once she remembered, she clapped her hands together and blurted out, "You're Cal from Cal's Carpet Showroom! Right?"

"Yes, I am. Well, I was. Now my kids run the place while I sit around being retired."

"You don't seem too thrilled about being retired. *I'd be thrilled!* I am so sick of working, day in and day out..." Steph complained, waving her arms around.

"Be careful with what you ask for," Cal cautioned.

"Ever since retiring a few years ago, I feel as if I've been put out to pasture. I'm really not used to sitting around. I've worked so much in my life, from an early age, sun up to sun down. Now I get up and wonder what to do? I have to get... *creative*."

"Creative is good. What do you do?" Steph asked, sipping her perfectly concocted coffee.

"Well, this is my secret. Here goes -"

"Oh, wait. Before you go any further, I have to state my verbal disclaimer. Are you ready?"

"Fire away! I'm listening," Cal said with a smile.

"I'm a law-abiding citizen and would rather not hear anything illegal done by you or anyone you know because I don't want to be put into the position of knowing something that should be reported."

"Well, nothing illegal here."

"And I'm not a therapist, either," Steph added.

"Neither am I, so we're even!" Cal laughed.

"Okay, good. So, let's hear it!"

Cal leaned forward and whispered in a conspiratorial way, "I consider myself to be a superhero!"

"Okay..."

"It's okay if you want to laugh. Most people do."

"I'm not going to laugh, but you certainly caught me off guard. I didn't expect to hear that today. But then again, I really shouldn't be too surprised anymore with what people tell me," Steph said, leaning forward too. "What type of superhero are you? Are you a good superhero, or a bad one?"

"I make people happy."

"A good superhero, then... Well, that's good. Why do you call yourself a superhero in order to make people happy?"

"When I retired and became unbelievably bored of golf by the third week in... I thought back to what made me happy throughout my life. From as far back as I could remember, I have always been a fan of super heroes, starting with Captain Marvel. He was my all-time favorite."

"So, you run around with a cape and tights on?" Steph interjected with a little laugh.

"No, that would look ridiculous!" Cal dismissed the idea with a wave of his hand. "If I did that, I couldn't be invisible. Plus, I would be locked up in the funny farm, for sure!"

"Invisible?"

"Yes, invisible. How can anyone be invisible if they're running around in tights and a cape? They would stand out like a sore thumb!"

"But you claim to be invisible?" Steph asked again, making sure she'd heard him correctly.

"I hide in plain sight. I look like everyone else. In the past, if I wanted to be really sneaky, I would put on a ball cap and sunglasses, but my wife told me I looked suspicious, so I stopped doing that. I don't want to be looking suspicious when I'm out on a mission."

Amused to have Cal be her last confession of her experiment, Steph smiled and asked, "What type of mission?"

"Well, missions to make people happy, of course!" Cal answered, leaning back and folding his arms in front of him.

"And those would be?"

"My biggest mission is the anonymous flower giving. I send out a hundred carnations per month, whether they go to an assisted living home, a hospital floor, or a random business of people who are sitting in cubicles in the center of the building unable to see out a window, non-profits, that kind of thing..." Cal revealed with a wave of his hand.

Steph sat straight up and exclaimed in a hushed but surprised voice, "That's you? *You're Shazam*? The newspaper and every newscast have done stories on these anonymous flowers, and no one knows who it is! Why are you telling me?"

"Because you opened yourself up to knowing deep, dark secrets about people, and I thought I would share a light-hearted, deep secret with you," Cal said, but then held his finger up to his mouth. "But, you must keep this a secret! If anything ever gets out and I'm approached, I will deny everything and go back to playing way too much golf, and the flowers and my other secret missions will stop."

"Well, yeah... Of course I won't tell anyone! Those flowers make a lot of people very happy – me included!" Steph exclaimed, pointing to the flower behind her ear. "But, how'd you come up with this idea in the first place?"

"When I was little, I would always pick flowers for my mom. One day, though, I picked goldenrod out of the fields and my mom refused to go into the house until the flowers were removed," Cal explained, leaning forward. "That's the day I learned what allergies were!"

"Uh oh!" Steph smiled.

"Yep, my Mom was allergic to goldenrod!" Cal said, pulling his plate of coffee cake towards him. "But anyway, I used to pick all sorts of flowers for my mom when I was a kid. One day in second grade, sixty years ago mind you, I became rather enamored with this one little girl. For fun, my mom suggested I pick her some flowers, so that's just what I did. But I was too chicken to give them to her outright, so I picked them and then left them on top of her desk during recess. After recess, when she came into the classroom and saw the flowers, she was very happy, but I never told her who they were from…"

"Why not?" Steph asked, leaning back in her chair, cradling her warm coffee mug with her hands.

"Because I was seven years old, shy, and girls were

terrifying to me!"

"So, that's how you started doing this in your retirement?"

"No, that was the start of a lifelong... hobby," Cal mused, "similar to your experiment, actually. After giving this particular girl some flowers, I told myself I'd either tell her it was me, or I'd remain anonymous and give other girls flowers, including teachers. You know, to make it seem like it could be anyone."

"What option did you pick?"

"I naturally chose the latter option and began giving *every* girl flowers. However, the teacher did catch me, eventually."

"Did you get in trouble?" Steph asked, setting her coffee mug back down on the table.

"No, but my jig was up! I'd been discovered... She'd told me she wouldn't tell anyone, but I always thought the other teachers in the school were looking at me funny, so I think she probably told them."

"But how does that connect to the here and now?"

Cal held up his hand to signal there was still more of a backstory. "Fast forward seven years to when my family moved to a different city. At the ripe age of fourteen, I became fond of another girl in my new school and remembered my mom's advice of giving flowers..."

"Did you give them to her, personally?" Steph asked with another smile.

"Well, that was the plan, initially. But as soon as I picked the flowers on the way to school, my nerves got the best of me and I set them on her family's front steps instead, rather than carrying them all the way to school... I chickened out," Cal confessed. "Girls were *genuinely* terrifying at age fourteen! Plus I probably would have been made fun of, big time - the new boy in school giving out flowers... Nope, that wouldn't have been good."

"Yeah, that was probably a good idea," Steph agreed.

She shifted in her chair and asked, "Well, who found the flowers?"

"Through the neighborhood grapevine, my Mom found out the lady down the street had received a bouquet of fresh-picked flowers on her front doorstep."

"Did she see you drop them off?"

"No, but she told all the ladies on the block she married the sweetest man!"

"Ah. So, the flowers went to the wrong person *and* the wrong person got the credit? Bummer!"

"At the time, yes, I'd let myself down again. But my dad had told me the guy who supposedly had given his wife flowers had become a bit nicer to hang out with, and the girl they were intended for was never very nice to me, so I justified the whole mishap as being okay. However, the next year, my future wife moved into the neighborhood and she stole my heart and my nerves, and, oh..." Cal said with another smile as he widened his eyes and shook his head again.

"Did you give her flowers?"

Cal blushed and leaned into the table. "Yes, and she caught me! I was going to chicken out and leave them on the doorstep again, but then she opened the door and caught me red-handed, red-faced, about to flee..."

"What'd she say? What'd you say?" Steph asked, forgetting about needing more coffee in the middle of reaching for the pot.

"She told me to stop right there and explain what I was doing?"

"And? What'd you say?"

"She told me I sort of stood there and stared at her while my mouth was moving, but nothing came out. She'd caught me! No one had ever caught me... She said she'd just been going out to sit on the front porch to enjoy the weather... She said my timing was off if I was trying to be sneaky."

"Yep, it sounds like you lost your sneakiness that

day!"

"Yes, I did. But in retrospect, it was good that I was caught, and I'm even happier she was the one who caught me! Eight years later, she became my wife," Cal beamed.

"Did you continue to give her flowers throughout your courtship?"

"Yes, but I no longer had to be sneaky," Cal laughed.

"So, you just got back into it in retirement, then?"

"I extended it. Throughout our marriage, and still to this day, I have given my wife a carnation every Monday of every week since our wedding day."

"How long have you two been married?"

"Our forty-fifth anniversary is coming up in a couple of months!"

"Congratulations! That's very cool!"

"Thank you! A couple of days ago, she received her 2,330th carnation!"

"Oh, my gosh! That's a lot of flowers! Wow! And this all started from giving your mom flowers?!?"

"I may have been a shy kid, but I knew what got me out of trouble or at least lessened the degree of trouble I managed to get into..." Cal admitted, leaning back in his chair with an air of superiority, and a coy smile.

"So, you again hadn't lost your sneakiness! How much trouble did you get into in your marriage?"

"None... I was only interested in getting out of trouble with my mom... plus I enjoyed seeing my mom happy with the flowers on the kitchen table all the time. For everyone else," Cal shrugged, "I simply enjoyed the happiness, and up until the fateful day I was caught red-handed, I enjoyed the surprise and the anonymity, too."

"That all makes sense, then... You took your comic book hero from a young age, and combined it with your flower giving talents and sneakiness to make people happy."

"Exactly!"

"That's awesome! And no, I won't ever tell. I want to make sure people continue to be surprised and be happy... definitely!"

"Thank you for keeping that secret for me. It really means a lot to me to be able to do this for random people, *and* to remain anonymous. Invisible, if you will..." Cal said, taking a sip of his coffee only to find it had grown cold while he told his story.

"Yeah, you threw me for a loop when you told me your super power was invisibility," Steph admitted.

Cal reached for the coffee pot again and carefully topped himself off with still-warm brew. "You were going to call the loony farm right there and then, weren't you?"

"Yep. It's on speed dial; all of my relatives live there!"

"My family probably lives right down the hallway from yours then," Cal grinned.

"Why do you sign all of the flower deliveries from Shazam if Captain Marvel is your favorite superhero?"

"Captain Marvel would call out 'Shazam' when he wanted to pull up his superhero powers from his ordinary, everyday self," Cal began to explain, mixing more sugar and cream into his cup. "Shazam was a wizard who provided all of those powers. So, when I'm in *superhero mode* and on my *special missions*, I refer to myself as 'Shazam'."

"Why don't you refer to yourself as Captain Marvel?"

"Because I want to be the guy who makes things happen - the guy who has the magic all the time rather than the one who has to depend on another for their super power. Plus, it's catchy... Don't you think?"

"It *is* catchy!" Steph agreed. "Do you have other missions?"

"Yes, I do. But I will keep those a secret... can't tell everything!" Cal said, holding his finger up to his pursed lips again.

"Please?"

"Nope, nope, nope... But if you ever hear of a random act of kindness in the news, it's either me or a copycat. I do things to help people out. I'm all for the theory of paying it forward."

"I've done that, a couple of times as a matter of fact..." Steph began, watching Cal finally start eating the coffee cake he'd brought over to the table when he first arrived. "Just last month, a young couple with their small kids were in a restaurant the same time I was, and I overheard them tell our waiter they were on their monthly *date night* but couldn't find a babysitter for the kids. Although somewhat well-behaved, their kids were still underneath the table part of the time - like all kids do... I even remember sitting under the table if I could - it was like a fort. Anyway, they looked tired and overwhelmed but were still trying to make a go of hanging out together. So, I had the waiter bring their check to me and I paid it along with their tip, before I left."

"It feels good, doesn't it? Helping other people out, surprising them... making them happy... It makes you happy, doesn't it?" Cal asked between forkfuls of the coffee cake. "By the way, this is delicious cake!"

"It is!" Steph agreed. "The owner of the shop bakes it himself... The cinnamon coffee cake is my favorite!"

"I'm sorry, I cut you off," Cal said after his next bite, rolling his fork in mid-air and urging Steph to keep going, "Please... Continue."

"Where was I again?" Steph asked.

"Paying it forward," Cal mumbled with a mouth full of crumbs.

"Oh! That's right! Yeah, it does make me feel good to do that and to volunteer - help people out..." Steph agreed, taking a sip of her now-cold coffee. "Another question for you: How did you come up with carnations?"

Cal was finishing his last bite of the coffee cake, and held up his hand to have Steph hold her thought. After a short pause to finish eating, Cal began, "That would be my wife's doing. For the first four years we were together, I followed her around like a love sick puppy dog. She'd always receive random wildflowers, or a rose here and there around birthdays and Valentine's Day, and such. But when she was seventeen, she had seen a variety of carnations in a flower shop. She loved all the colors and the fresh floral smell, and that was it. Roses were nice, daisies were nice, but carnations were the best according to her. So, from that point on, roses were replaced with carnations although wildflowers were still welcomed on a near-daily basis."

"Economical, too; two thousand some odd carnations versus two thousand or so roses... It sounds like you got lucky she liked carnations more!" Steph pointed out.

"I'm lucky she liked me, and even luckier she married me and continues to put up with my quirks!" Cal exclaimed loudly.

"She sounds like she's the lucky one... Actually, you're both lucky to be quirky and sneaky, together!"

"That we are!" Cal said, placing his coffee cup down and then setting both hands on his knees, getting ready to stand up. "Well, young lady, I am off to go play a game of golf."

"I thought you couldn't stand golf?"

"There's always time for golf, just not three weeks solid of it. Plus, I have to keep up the retirement ruse - we don't want anyone knowing I am a superhero now, do we?" Cal said with a sneaky smile.

"No, we don't."

Cal stood up and extended his hand toward Steph, "I need the super-duper, secret handshake from you guaranteeing you won't divulge any of the top secret information you've learned here today about the top priority missions of Shazam."

Steph stood up and met his hand for the super-duper secret handshake and smiled, "I promise I will never divulge any of yours or Shazam's top priority missions to any other souls, living or non-living, for the rest of my days. Cross my heart, but not really hoping I die anytime soon."

"Agreed and thank you," Cal said while he finished shaking her hand. "Well, I'm off to go play golf and then later, tell far-fetched stories about my golf game. Take care, Miss Dean. Keep up the good job of being selfless and doing good deeds for others!" And with that, Cal spun around and in a flash, was out of the building with a spring in his step.

Steph & Tom

"So, you're all done with these confessions, huh?" Tom asked, walking over to the corner and setting down his coffee mug and bran muffin before taking a seat.

"Yes," Steph answered, looking up at Tom. "And it's been quite the interesting earful, too!"

"And you're still not going to tell anyone, including me... the shop owner, what you heard?"

"No," Steph laughed. "But maybe I'll write a book..."

"Do you think you have enough material for a book?" Tom asked, cutting into his muffin.

"Definitely!" Steph sipped her coffee with an air of accomplishment.

"Oh, that reminds me!" Tom snapped his fingers. "A couple of days ago, a reporter from the local newspaper came in and wanted to know if you or I or both of us wanted to sit down for an interview about the confessions."

"Well, they're sort of late, don't you think?" Steph asked.

"I told them that, too, but they're interested in writing about it anyway. Are you interested?"

"Yeah, sure... But I'm not going to talk about any specifics," Steph winked.

"What was the wink for?" Tom asked.

"Just in case you were thinking I would divulge any information through a newspaper article, too... Not going to happen!"

Tom looked up in the air with a smile, "Oh, that idea had never crossed my mind! I'm insulted that you would think I'd be that underhanded!"

"Well, just in case that thought *had* crossed your mind..." Steph said, smiling and rolling her eyes.

"Actually, do you want to keep up with these confessions?"

"Sure, I wouldn't mind. But I'm going to take a few months off first. My busier time at work is just around the corner, and that's going to be running me ragged for a few months," Steph frowned.

With a worried look, Tom asked, "We're still on for our Tuesday mornings, right?"

"Oh, yeah... But to take any more time off throughout the week is not going to happen for a while. Too much going on..."

"Speaking of too much going on, Erin told me you got yourself a date out of these confessions... What's that all about?"

"Oh, yeah. That was Pete a few weeks ago. We met for coffee the following Saturday, after his confession," Steph said.

"And... how'd it go?" Tom asked, prodding for more information.

"It was nice," Steph said innocently, knowing she was going to get under Tom's skin for not telling him more information.

"Nice? That's it?" Tom asked with frustration in his voice. "I take it it didn't go so well, and that's the end of that?"

"No, it went well, I thought. We are meeting up again here, in a couple of weeks."

"Why so long between getting together?" Tom

questioned, looking perplexed.

"He's been travelling around for business and when he gets back, we're going out for dinner," Steph answered.

"Coffee to dinner, huh?" Tom grinned. "Any promise of a future in these little get-togethers?"

"We'll see..." Steph teased.

"Okay, I'll bug you about it again after your dinner, you can count on that!"

"Yep, already counting on that... I would be surprised if you *didn't* grill me on my dinner date!"

"So, you're thinking of starting the appointments back up in August or September?"

"After Labor Day, for sure... And maybe up through Halloween? I don't want to get too close to the winter holidays. Everyone gets so busy," Steph suggested.

"Good point," Tom agreed.

"I'll have to get a 'Reserved' sign back here, too. I think that would be great!" Steph laughed.

"I could probably find one of those for you, especially if we put this in the newspaper - it'll look more official!"

"I wonder what sorts of secrets I'll hear in the future?" Steph pondered out loud. "Lord knows I've already heard quite a bit, so far!"

Tom, knowing he wasn't going to get much out of her, still asked, "Did you get any of the same secrets, or were they all different secrets?"

Steph looked back at Tom and mulled over the different confessions she'd heard. "I think they were all unique... I'm surprised I didn't hear duplicates, quite frankly."

"I would imagine if you keep this up, you'll start hearing some of the same stuff."

"I would imagine," Steph agreed and then added, "But everyone's secret, even if it's the same as someone else's, is still unique to them."

"True. So, do you think you'll write a book?" Tom

asked.

Steph laughed at Tom, "You just can't let this go, can you?"

"Apparently not," Tom pursed his lips.

"If I get the time... and that's a joke right there... But if I get the time and the energy to sit down and write a book, I'll be sure to let you read the first book, hot off the press, okay?"

"Okay," Tom said, gathering his dirty dishes and napkins. "Promise?"

"Promise," Steph grinned.

Everyone has a secret.
What's yours?

September 2017
Corner Confessions Two
Everyone has a secret. What's yours?

 Meet…

Yvette

Greg

Martin

Rose

Frank

Vicki

Ed

Nathan

Lydia

Kelli

Hope

Scott

Mara

Alex

Beth

Crystal

Books by Kiersten Hall

Memoir:

"I Do" ~ 15 Years of True Stories
    from a Wedding Videographer

*'It's just an awesome page-turner. If you're getting
married, you definitely need to buy it. If you're not
getting married/already have gotten married and you're
looking for some good laughs, it's totally worth it.
Kiersten's style of writing is also just really refreshing
and makes funny stories even funnier - crisp, satirical
prose elegantly put together. She takes years of great
stories and boils them down to the best ones for the
reader to enjoy.'*
~ Amazon Customer Review

Fiction:

Corner Confessions
    Everyone has a secret. What's yours?

*A story about stories, Corner Confessions is an
intriguing tale of secrets and the humans who keep
them....and of the sheer and utter relief one feels once
unburdened by them. The confessions are riveting and
the characters relaying them are fascinating, from the
self-proclaimed town liar, to the middle-aged
unobtrusive super hero. Ms. Hall has the ability and
talent of being completely conversational and engaging
so that her readers feel as if they are hearing these
confessions in person over tea and crumpets rather than
simply reading words on a page. One is quite easily
drawn into the web of the stories she weaves.
Melissa R. ~ Leavenworth, KS*

K Hall Books

www.idovideostories.com
www.cornerconfessions.com
www.khallbooks.com